"Have You Any Questions?"

"My lord," Lilith paused for a breath and asked archly, "am I required to remain celibate as well?"

She saw Dunraven straighten. In a cool, composed voice he answered, "Under English law you are my wife. I expect no less, madam."

"You wish me to be a wife who is no wife, sir?"

"Correct. For I am to be a husband who is no husband."

" 'Tis unnatural—unless you yourself are so."

Her implication goaded him, and it took him but a second to shoot back a retort. "Madam, take care before you cast a stone. To bide one's days secreted behind a veil is equally unnatural."

He saw the braid in her fingers tighten. "I do not veil myself by choice."

"Then, pray cast off your veil."

"Pray, in turn cast aside your celibacy."

Books by Betina Lindsey

The Serpent Beguiled
Swan Bride
Waltz with the Lady

Published by POCKET BOOKS

The SERPENT BEGUILED

BETINA LINDSEY

POCKET BOOKS

New York   London   Toronto   Sydney   Tokyo   Singapore

An *Original* Publication of POCKET BOOKS

POCKET BOOKS, a division of Simon & Schuster Inc.
1230 Avenue of the Americas, New York, NY 10020

ISBN: 978-1-5011-3381-7

First Pocket Books printing December 1992

10 9 8 7 6 5 4 3 2 1

POCKET and colophon are registered trademarks of Simon & Schuster Inc.

Cover art by Lina Levy

Printed in the U.S.A.

To dreams, soul mates, and karmic promises . . .

Lovers don't finally meet somewhere;
they are in each other all along.

—Rumi

Chapter

1

England, 1885

Lilith Cardew waited.

She lay in a strange bed, in a strange house—waiting for a stranger.

Her ears strained to catch each unfamiliar sound: the footfalls along the terra-cotta tile beyond her latticed screen door, the gentle rain of water from the marble fountain in the solarium court, a tropical bird's lively caws and the flurry of its wings stirring the palm fronds as it flew through hothouse foliage.

She shifted, smoothing the neck-to-toe lawn nightgown knotted about her legs. Incense swirled into her nostrils and she neared the point of sneezing. Perfume, tobacco, and springtime always made her sneeze—now incense. She felt misplaced, nervous, and wildly curious.

She had never quite experienced a room or a house such as this. Though she knew she was in London, the moment she and her mother had stepped across the threshold of Eden Court she'd felt as if she'd stepped into the Forbidden City. All that was rare, exotic, and bizarre from every corner of the world was reflected in this household. Her gaze circled her bedchamber from the fierce-eyed stone cobras coiled on the blazing hearth to the demon ceremonial masks glaring against the walls of ebony lattice. There was no true privacy here; the rooms opened to the garden court. One could easily hear and see the muted shadows of passing servants through the screen walls.

It all seemed fantastic to Lilith. This November night, the circumstance of being in this house, the chiming strikes of midnight which echoed through the garden court colonnade like a litany in a sacred temple. She doubted she could ever fall asleep in such strange surroundings.

In the candlelight the scarlet brocade drapes of the Mandarin canopy bed shadowed and shimmered scenes of gardens, firebirds, and dragons. On closer look she discovered the headboard was carved with high-born men and women in various diversions— no, they were more than diverting, they were . . .

Lilith's eyes widened and she swallowed back her nervousness. Slipping from under the red silk sheets, she sat up and reached for the candle and pulled the drapes closed, encircling herself beneath the canopy. By candle flame, she slowly studied the intricately carved columns, seeing men and women embracing and kissing—nude. At that moment Lilith's conscience urged her to shut her eyes to such lewdness and blow out the candle. But she could not muster the breath to do so. Her eyes riveted to still another more explicit portrayal. A maid lay supine as a man kneeled between her open legs. Lilith swallowed again. Her insides felt like melting butter and a cloying warmth spread between her thighs. Her curious eyes moved on. . . .

She could not decide whether this was art or depravity. Could such actions be welcomed? Her prior—and only—governess, Annie Tuft, would declare she was sinning just to look. Yet, tonight was her wedding night, and she had only a vague knowledge of what might be expected of her.

The scenes were fast becoming an erotic spiral until Lilith heard a pounding which she at first mistook for her guilty heart, but soon she realized someone had knocked at her door.

He had come.

In the shock of the moment she blew out the candle as if to hide the evidence of her virginal wantonness—the flowing juices between her thighs and the piquant nubs of her breasts.

"Come in," she managed softly, not daring to peek from behind the bed draperies. She heard the lift of the latch, a latch which had no lock. Her heart pounded and her hands perspired.

"Mistress?" came a woman's voice.

Slightly disappointed, Lilith slit the drapery and peered out. Lantern in hand, Rupee, the sari-wrapped Bengali maid of the household, stood patiently. "Mistress, your mother has no more medicine. She is greatly agitated. I cannot calm her."

Keeping herself from view of the maid, Lilith questioned, "How can it be? This very morning the chemist assured me I'd enough to see her through a fortnight."

"She believes he gave you the wrong mixture." Rupee's dark face looked tired and her voice sounded weary. "She is greatly agitated," she repeated. "I discovered her dressing to go out herself."

Lilith's stomach tightened with apprehension. "We are strangers to London, but even I know no one does trade this time of night." She climbed through the bed drapes and reached for her silk wrapper and black veil which would conceal her fire-scarred face.

Wear the veil, child, was always her mother's caution. *People will run at the sight of you thinking you have the pox or worse. . . .*

Let them run! Lilith had wanted to shout. She had been ten years old when the oil lamp had fallen from the bed stand and ignited her blanket and pillow. In the subsequent months, then years, nothing could have been worse than the continual visits from one gawking physician to the next. She had been soaped, tarred, and greased with every miracle elixir known to man, but the scarring across her face remained.

She and her mother were an ill-conceived pair who now had only one another. Since early childhood, while her father explored the world, she'd given herself over to nursing and caring for her mother, whose health never seemed to improve. Her mother lived in a world apart. Rarely lucid, time held no meaning for her, as she spent her days confined to drape-drawn rooms.

Despair settled upon Lilith as she lowered the veil over her head and shoulders and reached for silk slippers. She spoke to Rupee, whose dark eyes were leveled on the floor—people always lowered their eyes when they saw her without her veil.

"Is Dunraven about?"

"Aye, he and his companion still converse in the library."

4

Lilith stepped onto the dhurrie carpet and crossed the room to the bamboo writing desk. Carefully she wrote a request that he send a servant to the chemist for her mother's medicine as soon as possible, then she folded the parchment note and put it into Rupee's waiting fingers. "Give this to him. I will go to my mother."

Rupee bowed and backed out of the room. Lilith listened to her soft footsteps pad through the tiled court, but above that was another sound—her mother's weeping.

Emotion gripped her. The fires of maidenly desire fully doused by reality, she cast a parting glance to the Mandarin canopy bed and hurried from the bedchamber. Without her medicine, her mother would begin ranting soon. And then what would Dunraven imagine he had gotten himself into?

And what about herself?

Marriage to a stranger. A stranger she had idolized for years. Even from the first when her father wrote to her of meeting Dunraven in the jungles of Borneo, she had admired him. The lines of that letter burned in her memory. *I had not expected to meet another white man, let alone an Englishman, in Borneo. But there he was, a young Adonis, his golden head above the small black haired Iban tribesmen. He wore only a breechcloth, bush knife, and native paint. Cascades of earrings spangled to his broad shoulders and a serpent tattoo coiled his left cheek. Son of a Lord, a fellow of Eton, he has turned native during the time he's been researching. Not my methods, mind you, for I'm of the old school and must have my tea. But Dunraven is of another ilk. He is a scholar of the first degree.*

At seventeen, when every other blossoming female

of Devonshire was coming out, Lilith had remained in her customary seclusion scouring map and atlas, pinpointing her father's and Adam Dunraven's whereabouts. In the past years, she had ferreted out and read his correspondence with her father, descriptions of his celebrated exploits, and his every anthropological treatise. Until this very day, when she stood beside Dunraven at Saint John's Kirk vowing love, honor, and obedience, she'd never laid eyes on him. But he was all her father had described and more. He'd worn a sleek black frock coat and silk cravat and queued, shoulder-length golden hair, looking alternately civilized and savage. Even without the serpent tattoo on his left cheek, she'd have known him anywhere.

Today when she had written her signature in the marriage register beside the hasty, bold scrawl of his own, she'd closed her eyes and swallowed back her disbelief. It was too much like a fairy tale. She was the isolated Rapunzel, separated from the world by her veil and he, the dashing prince come to take her in his arms. No, he never took her in his arms, even when the cleric paused to say, "You may now kiss the bride." Instead, he had taken a step back, left her veil lowered, and politely bowed.

As she turned down the court colonnade, the breeze of her passing caused an azure feathered parrot to flutter high into the potted palms and the candle flames to flicker in their sconces. Her breast rose with a futile sigh as she shelved her maidenly dream of a love-filled wedding night.

Adam Dunraven was a man who smiled with resistance. Yet, this moment as he opened the note handed to him by Rupee, he laughed aloud. He laughed a wry, skeptical laughter which settled on the myriad volumes of his library like dust.

"What is it?" asked his longtime friend Charles Vivian, who looked up from his perusal of the most recent Royal Geographic map charting the islands of the South Pacific.

"I must leave on an errand. Indeed, life does take its turns."

"It is not surprising for one such as yourself," smirked Charles. "The news is out 'The Daring Dunraven' has returned from his most recent exploit. Have you announced to your father he now has a Tibetan monk in the family?"

"Do not fault me, Charles," he said forthrightly. "Unlike your directionless self, my past three years have been spent in solitude, celibacy, and the ascetic life. It is a rare existence quite unencumbered by troublesome people like yourself."

A crooked smile warmed Charles' clean-shaven, almost boyish face. "And now I suppose you are reborn in Buddha."

He quirked the corners of his mouth with tolerance, thinking how much he'd missed Charles' dry wit. "I remain a gentle agnostic. But you, Charles, are a cynic of the first degree."

"We Darwinists always are. So why did you return to the illusion?"

"Honor."

"Honor?"

"You remember my longtime friend and mentor, Andrew Cardew—he died during his last expedition to the Himalayas."

"Yes, I had heard." Charles turned his full attention to Dunraven.

"When he became seriously ill, his bearers brought

him to me at the monastery in Lhasa." He paused, ever so briefly, and then said, "He died in my arms."

Charles straightened and placed a consoling hand on his shoulder. "I did not know."

Dunraven frowned. "He made a deathbed request —as of noon today, I am husband to Andrew's disfigured daughter and supporter to Andrew's opium-addicted widow."

Charles' mouth dropped open and he stepped back with shock. "Good God, man! You never cease to amaze. I have been in your company all evening and you just reveal to me you have, this very day, married a woman—married her without courtship or betrothal."

He looked over. His gray eyes leveled a hard, intent gaze on Charles. "I am not like you, Charles. I may be a peer of the realm, but since that night I climbed from our dormitory window at Eton and ran off to sea and adventure, you should not expect me to live as one."

An injured expression on his face, Charles perched himself on the edge of an overstuffed armchair. "Believe me, I have never underestimated you. I have always admired you and ever stood beside you. Perhaps I am a little offended you did not ask me to stand up with you on your wedding day."

"You have my apologies." He turned away, crumpled the note in his hand and tossed it into the hearth. For a moment he stared into the fire and watched the parchment curl up into the flames. Then he explained, "The marriage is in name only. There will be no joining and it would be a sham to celebrate it as such. Andrew died a near pauper. I give his women financial security and my protection."

"Why did you not just give them a stipend and save yourself from a loveless marriage?"

He turned from the hearth to face Charles. "Believe me, that would have been my first choice. However, Andrew specifically requested me to marry his daughter. One does not easily sidestep a dying friend's direct request. And of course there is my father, the Lord. Lord, what a lord he is! I had just received a letter from him commanding me to give up my foolish philosophy of celibacy and return to England, marry, and concentrate on producing an heir."

Charles chuckled. "Yes, I see his concern. It is impossibly difficult for a celibate man to produce an heir."

Dunraven did not share his friend's mirth. "My father will have to find another heir, for I intend to remain celibate." His jaw clamped firm.

Charles straightened with shock. *"You?* The same Adam Dunraven, a one-time devotee of the Tantra and, I might add, participant in every primitive mating rite from Siam to Timbuktu! I do not believe it! *You* give up women? Hah!"

"Scoff if you must. The man who left England many years ago has become a nomad of the world. My tribe is mankind, Charles. My God, the universe. I am primate, I am seeker, I am celibate!"

"And you are off the deep end!" Charles threw up his hand, somewhat exasperated. "I knew it would happen someday—your drinking all those native concoctions and chewing all those hallucinatory herbs. It was inevitable."

With a tilt of the head, Dunraven admitted thoughtfully and aloud, "In honesty I must say things have happened to me which defy description or explana-

9

tion." He looked down his hawklike nose to hold Charles' wondering eyes. "I walk between earth and heaven."

Not breaking his gaze, Charles asked, "And is not that place called hell?"

After a long moment he said, "It can be." Then his features lightened, his smokey eyes gleamed wickedly, and he shrugged. "But he who knows how to go about it can live comfortably even in hell."

Charles began laughing. "You are the serpent himself, Dunraven. To you, nothing is sacred."

"You are wrong, Charles. To me, all is sacred. Whether it be a savage's burlesque war dance or a gentleman's *pas de deux*. It is one and the same to me." He crossed the room. "And now I must be on my way to Upper Swandam-Lane."

"What business have you in that part of London this time of night?"

"As I have said, Cardew's widow has a fondness for pure poppy. Chandoo in Swandam is the only trader I know and trust."

"But Adam—," Charles opened his mouth to speak, but he cut his words off.

"Do not question my ethics, Charles. I have none." He sat down and began slipping off his shoes and shrugged from his shirt.

"What are you doing, man? It is usual to dress, not undress, when one goes out."

"I am about to demonstrate a point to you. Under the collective term of *lung-gom*, Tibetans include a large number of practices which combine mental concentration with various breathing gymnastics, and aim at different results either spiritual or physical. The term *lung-gom* is especially used for a kind of training I have undertaken which develops uncommon nimbleness and especially enables its adepts to take extraordinarily long tramps with amazing rapidity. With the fleetness of a panther, I intend to run to Swandam and return within the quarter hour."

"I wager that is impossible for a single-harnessed phaeton let alone a man on foot."

"Then wager and ready your timepiece."

Charles watched him strip off his shirt and wing his lean-muscled arms in preparation. Without another word, he strode toward the outside door wearing only his black striped trousers.

Charles followed at his heels, scrambling for his frock coat, cane, and narrow brim hat. "I intend to follow you."

Dunraven's eyes flashed with the challenge. "You are welcome to try." Charles near-tripped over Dunraven as he momentarily paused on the outside steps. Preparing himself, he shut his eyes, palmed his hands before his broad chest in an attitude of prayer, and breathed deeply, fully, and expansively.

Anxious not to let him out of his sight, Charles took the interlude to hail a passing hansom and leaped up beside the cabman just as Dunraven's bare feet hit the cold cobblestones of the November night.

Charles pointed his cane toward the tall spare figure of Dunraven sprinting down the lane, and to the whiskey-redolent cabby he directed, "Keep pace with him." The cabby flicked his whip and the pair trotted forward. After the initial lurch, Charles situated himself and asked, "How far to Upper Swandam-Lane?"

The cabby coughed and spat to the side. "'Bout four miles, governor. A half wink of old Ben there and back again."

Charles did a hasty calculation in his head and realized Dunraven would be sustaining the pace of a

11

mile per four minutes which was indeed remarkable. Charles turned his timepiece to the gleam of the cab lantern and marked a quarter past one. When he looked up again, Dunraven had turned a corner and disappeared into the misty London night.

"Faster man," he urged the cabby, who with a reluctant grunt, whipped his horses into a gallop.

The brisk clack-clop of the horses' hooves on the cobblestones echoed through the quiet lamplit neighborhood. Dunraven again came into his view, though the hansom could not keep up with him.

"Faster, man!" cried Charles, "We'll lose him." He held onto his hat and gripped the sideboard.

"I'll have a half sovereign for my efforts," bargained the cabby, his side-whiskers twitching.

"Yes, yes! You'll have it. Now get your nags moving!"

The hansom hurtled past the high wharves which lined the north side of the river to the east of London Bridge. The lamplight became sparser and the streets more animated. A group of shabbily dressed men smoking and laughing outside a gin shop parted ranks with surprise as Dunraven sprinted between them. When the hansom clattered by, the loungers hooted good-natured jests alluding to insanity. One coarsely asked if Dunraven might be an escapee from Bedlam.

Charles almost called back that he had on occasion wondered this himself about his lifelong friend who defied English society with every breath of his unorthodox soul. Since their boyhood days, it had always been so. Charles speculated that had Dunraven's mother not died at his birth, his escapades would have driven her to an early grave. He'd first met Dunraven when both entered Eton at the early age of six. "The Raven," as he'd called him then, had been an adventure-prone, wild hellion who stole sausages for beggars and, endowed with a good ear for languages, outsmarted his tutors. He was claustrophobic indoors and became habitually truant during good weather. Then one spring night, at the age of fifteen, the Raven climbed out the dormitory window vowing to run away to sea. "Come with me, mate," the Raven had enticed him. "Leave the books and discover the real truth of it."

Charles still felt sadness looking back, remembering the boldness of his friend and how much he himself had been tempted to run off to adventure. But it was against his cautious, predictable nature to do so. Unlike Dunraven, he preferred the comforts of civilization and chose to experience his adventures second-hand, in books. Fortunately, to his joy, six years later in London, he met Raven again. After who knows what adventures, Dunraven had become more man than most. At that time, he'd the audacity to present a lecture recounting the mating rites of T'boli tribesmen in Mindanao to the Royal Geographic Society.

Charles glanced at his timepiece. Above the rumble of wheels he shouted out to Dunraven, "I mark two minutes and your time is half gone." Dunraven was three carriage lengths ahead, but notably his stride lengthened as he turned and disappeared into the swarthy alley of Upper Swandam-Lane.

Here the cabby slowed up his horses. "I'll not go farther, governor. Hell be a safer place than Swandam-Lane aft' midnight."

"No need. Turn the carriage about." Charles squinted down the cavernous alley seeing ominous shadows lurking around the glow of street braziers and announced, "Here he comes."

Dunraven reemerged from the gloom. When he

easily passed the turning hansom, Charles shouted, "You'll have to get down on all fours to keep this wager."

Right about, the cabby flicked the horses with his whip. The hansom dashed away at the heels of Dunraven as he sprinted through the wind of deserted streets with remarkable speed. His muscled back and shoulders glistened with perspiration before the two tunnels of golden light cast by side lanterns of the hansom, then his silhouette muted into the swirls of patchy fog.

Suddenly, ahead, Charles heard a feral yowl cut the London night. He glimpsed the long tail and hind legs of a spotted jungle cat flash at the edge and leap beyond the lantern ray. The horses snorted and shied. Charles blinked. His and the cabby's eyes met and parted in the second as a chill of enigma tracked down Charles' spine.

"The devil's spit! What be that?" The cabby swore, attempting to rein in his nervous horses.

"Nothing but a trick of light," assured Charles, not completely assured himself. "Damn! What's he up to? We'll lose him. A whole sovereign if you can keep him in view."

"Nay," announced the cabby as the hansom rattled to a halt. "I've enough of yer sport. Me horses are spooked." He pulled a flask from inside his coat and took a long pull. Wiping his mouth he said, "Ye can walk from here."

Charles looked at the lathered and steaming horses, back to the rum-eyed cabby, and nodded his head. "All right. He's home by now." He fished in his pocket, gave the surprised cabby a sovereign and climbed down off the hansom.

Somewhat later, when Charles stepped inside Eden Court, he heard the house clock strike two. Fully dressed, Dunraven lounged beside the stone fountain of the garden court tapping a light cadence on a North African double cone drum. Charles realized he'd taken the time to bathe for his unfashionably long tawny hair was tied back in a slick queue.

"What kept you?" he asked, an arrogant twinkle in his gray eyes.

"It seems a jungle cat spooked the cabby's horses and he refused to take me farther. I suppose you have no clue as to how a jungle cat found its way to London."

Dunraven held his eye with maddening composure and leaned more fully into the rhythm of the drum. "None. Unless one escaped from the circus act at Covent Gardens."

"Hardly this time of year." His feet throbbing in his gentleman's boots, Charles seated himself across from Dunraven in a wicker chair and demanded, "Now, I'll have the truth from you. You've not taken up shapeshifting? I've read of such magics, but really thought it just illusion."

"It is illusion, Charles. I will explain it to you," he offered, realizing the explanation might require the rest of the night.

But at that moment a black robed, black veiled figure passed along the colonnade and caught Charles' eye. Dunraven shifted his attention as well.

"My wife." He answered the unspoken question in Charles' eyes.

"Might I meet her?"

Dunraven shrugged accommodatingly. Rising, he set aside the drum and stepped quickly to intercept her. "Madam," he bowed lightly. The muted figure came to a standstill. "Madam, my longtime friend, Charles Vivian, wishes an introduction."

The black veiled head turned toward Charles. He quickly stood and stepped forward with an affable bow. She said nothing, but offered a slim, black satin-gloved hand, which he took in his own.

"Lady Dunraven," he said, "my condolences to you on the death of your father. Indeed, he was a great and learned man. Many shall miss him."

She acknowledged his words with a regal nod, withdrew her hand, and made to continue on her way, but Dunraven inquired, "Is your mother satisfactory?" She nodded a silent affirmation and quickly made her retreat.

Charles was mesmerized. With a virile eye, he observed her rare feminine grace as she moved down the colonnade. He took her measure of form and figure, estimating her to be just over five foot, narrow waisted, slim hipped, and fleshy breasted. After the in-depth perusal, he concluded that her genteel carriage belied any disfigurement of limb. Finally, he turned back to Dunraven. "Does she ever speak?"

"Not to me."

"Have you given her the opportunity?"

"I have encountered her but twice in my life." His voice was tight. "The first at the church this noonday and the second—this very moment. Like most women, she is very secretive, more so because of her disfigurement."

"How do you know?"

"How do I know what?"

"That she is disfigured."

"Her father spoke of it."

"Any particulars?"

"A fire."

"And you have no intention of bedding her?"

His icier side surfaced. "No! Nor should you."

Charles ignored the hard glare that accompanied this admonition. "It is your right. She is your lawful wife."

"No."

The late-night escapade showed up in the rings under his slate gray eyes, but Charles knew more than fatigue kept his friend barely conversant and aloof. Dunraven was unusually tense. But then who would not be on his wedding day?

"I have heard her mother was a great beauty," he baited. "So beautiful that Cardew risked his life by snatching her off the auction block of a Turkish slave market while fleeing across the border with the Pasha's soldiers at his heels. How can the heritage of that veiled creature not tempt you?"

"She does not tempt me. I have transcended the flesh and you have witnessed the reward of that transcendence tonight. In any case, I do not choose to make love to 'civilized' women, particularly Englishwomen. On threats of fire and brimstone, they are unsexed from infancy by clergy and governesses and have no notion of their sensuality. One might as well bed a mannequin as an Englishwoman."

Charles smiled. "Now who is the cynic of the first degree?"

"Even you cannot argue that in matters of the heart it is survival of the fittest."

"I daresay you've never been in love."

"In truth, I never have or intend to be. Romantic love is one insanity I will not number among my exploits." This he confessed with inborn arrogance, and with a short bow he said, "Good night, Charles," and he walked away.

Charles stood confounded for he had never known Adam to be so touchy. Suddenly, he suspected a celibate Dunraven was as unnatural as a trout taking tea. He smiled thoughtfully to himself and took his leave as well.

Lilith turned from her eavesdropping, content to blame the openness of the lattice screen walls, not her own weakness.

So, love is the sole territory he will not explore, she thought with such deflation that she collapsed backward on the canopy bed and stared listlessly upward. *Oh, I am not so naive as to not realize some men prefer men, perhaps he is one of those. Motherless, he has lived a good portion of his life at boys' schools—and now a monastery. And how could anyone learn to love women in the sole company of men?* She nibbled her lower lip, consideringly. *Even so, much of his work focuses on marriage and mating rites. At least he is curious about men and women—together.*

She rolled to her stomach and punched the pillow. *Damn and double damn! One can never be sure. I am foolish to dwell on it, or even to have hopes he might grow to admire me as I admire—and love—him.* She sat up and clutched the pillow to her breast. *Yes! God help me. I do love him. How could I not love a man who lives his life in the way I yearn to. I have followed his explorations for years, idolizing his courage and daring. His very essence is the mirror of what I wish to do and be. Whether he realizes it or not, we are kindred spirits, he and I. With him I am not who I am, but who I should be! Meeting him face to face only confirms it, exacerbates it, inflames it. When I look into his eyes, I see the reflection of my own soul calling me to awaken to love, life, and adventure.*

But what was she to do?

Rocking to and fro, she avoided looking at the lewd carvings. Perhaps she could seduce him. Unfortunately, she knew nothing about seduction, and by his own avowal, he wanted nothing to do with a civilized woman.

How did one become uncivilized in the matters of love? She stole a sidelong glance at the bedposts. If she so chose, her tutorial was close at hand.

"The devil," she muttered and punched the pillow once again. Even if she knew the wiles of a bush king's consort it would do her no good. She wanted him to love her for who and what she was, not because she was expert in hedonistic pleasures.

What a ninny! Of course, I am wasting my time thinking about it. By his own words he is transcending —to what, I am not really sure. And I—I shall remain as chaste as clotted cream until Ascension Day.

The drumming began like footfalls in a mausoleum. It stole through the still, late-night household as coy as a Nubian seductress. Her ears keen, Lilith half relaxed back onto the silken pillows. The drum vibration was a warm wave through her body. It teased her mind with exotic images of feral beasts stalking through sultry jungles or sheen-bodied harem girls swaying loose hipped before lusty-eyed sultans.

Her eyes slipped closed and her senses melted into the gentle flowing and rhythmic lulling. . . .

Hours passed, or perhaps only moments. Magically, the air fairly shouted with the sweet redolence of flowers. Lilith crawled through a haze of dreaming. Delicate orchids, white lilies, scarlet roses—

smothered her breast. Amazingly, she didn't even sneeze.

"Had you thought I'd forgotten you, my bride?"

Lilith's eyes riveted to the shadow looming between the parted curtains of the bed. Dunraven's eyes shone like eerie bright flames. The coiled serpent on his cheek seemed to dance to the pulsing drum which still throbbed distantly. Flickering candlelight illuminated rugged cheekbones and the firm-lined mouth of his arresting face. A loose muslin shirt gaped open to tapered hips, baring his hard-muscled chest.

She felt her lips part. "I knew you would come to me eventually. I have waited." She stretched lithe arms and slim legs with soft sensuality.

Who was this woman? It seemed to Lilith as if someone else was speaking through her mouth— using her body. She ran her hands over her face in exploration and her skin felt smooth and flawless. No, it wasn't her, for her face wasn't scarred.

She gathered the blooms in her arms and laid them aside. "Come to me," she purred.

Lusty desire intensified his features.

Languorously, she drew up to her knees, her crimson silk wrapper slipping off one shoulder to reveal the swell of her breast to his smoldering gaze.

In a breathy voice she said, "I am done with waiting. Take me."

A deep rakish laugh rumbled his chest.

Reactively, his large hands reached out and grasped her throat tightly. The heat of his grip fired Lilith's blood, leaving her helpless and wanton. Wanton for what, she was not exactly sure.

His eyes glittered in a strange way and his thumb tips ruthlessly pressed on the rapidly pulsing artery of her neck.

"Swear you are not too civilized for me," he murmured in a merciless voice.

"I swear," she vowed. Then, not to be outdone, uttering a cattish hiss, she leaned forward and nipped his flesh. He chuckled wickedly. His hands released her neck and caught her face, turning it up to his own.

In mock self-defense, her long nails lightly raked his chest.

Withholding his lips, his mouth hovered just above hers. "Am I to wear your claw marks in morning light?"

"Yes, and nothing more," she breathed as her teeth seized his lower lip.

Lilith did not like this woman she'd become. Groveling for love was one thing, playing the bitch in heat was quite another.

His strong hand caught the loop of her long hair so tightly her eyes moistened. Her teeth released his lip. He proceeded to outmaneuver her, thrusting her back onto the down-filled mattress and pinioning her arms above her head. She did not enjoy this treatment. The muscular sinewy hardness of his arms crushed her. He was too powerful.

Uttering a growl, he clamped his teeth onto the careful knot of her wrapper and tore free the loop. Her wrapper fell open exposing all to his branding gaze. His nostrils flared with lust and undisguised carnality.

Her bosom heaving, she sought his lips. Hopefully, he would gentle with a kiss. But he did not condescend.

"Kiss me, please," she asked softly. Her gaze burned upward into his.

His brilliant eyes hardened. "Kiss you?"

She felt his strong fingers slowly relinquish their hold on her flesh.

"Kissing is civilized!" He drew back, his handsome face perplexed.

A mixture of relief and apology flooded through her.

"Forgive me, I—I won't ask for a kiss again."

"You swore you were uncivilized!"

"I—I am just recently uncivilized." She shriveled back and clutched her wrapper in a nervous attempt to cover herself.

"Hah! Look, you are hiding behind your robe. Have you no immodesty?"

Lilith felt a rush of humiliation. "I am adjusting. You see, because of my scars, I've hidden myself from view."

"Hidden yourself? I see no scars. Only a paradigm of virtue would do this. What duplicity!" He stood, his face awash with disappointment.

"Please come back—"

"No. I am a man of honor. I cannot ravish a civilized woman!" Stepping away, he bowed politely, "My dear civilized lady, my regrets and my farewell."

"No, wait—I didn't mean to be so civilized—I—" But he had disappeared into the shadows of the night.

Lilith's eyes opened.

Morning light cracked between the curtains of the canopy bed. The drumming had stopped. She sighed relief. Thank heaven! It had been just a dream. . . .

Or had it?

On the pillow beside her lay a scattering of wilted petals.

Chapter

2

The rain poured down and not a cabby was in sight. Lilith ducked through the doorway of the jumble shop. A brass bell tinkled her arrival and a stooped-shouldered clerk peered over his spectacles with a polite greeting upon his beard-framed lips.

"Good day," he said, clearing a space upon his counter. "Can I be of assistance?"

"You wouldn't have an umbrella about? I've gone off and left mine."

He coughed—a little consumptive—and looked searchingly around the cluttered shop. Tall shelves were stacked with a myriad of clocks, porcelains, and vases. Bolts of imported fabrics and bric-a-brac along with antique estate furniture blocked the narrow aisle. He reached to a crystal chandelier hanging crookedly from a ceiling hook. "I have this paper parasol from Peking. I'm afraid it is for sun, not rain."

"Well, the rain will soon stop. Might I wait?"

"Yes, of course. Let me offer you a chair." He

rushed around from behind the counter, toppling a pile of dusty books. He removed some brocade hatboxes from a stalwart-looking chair. "Please, sit here. Cromwell himself was said to have sat in this very chair."

"Really! Are you sure it's quite all right for me—" Lilith peered through her veil.

"Yes, yes!" He chuckled. "The man was so long-lived, I believe he must have sat in nearly every chair in England by his end."

Lilith eased herself into the chair. The clerk looked at her. She knew he was waiting for her to lift her veil now that she was settled in. She felt awkward. Clearing her throat she asked, "Might I see something— there," she pointed to the glass case directly in front of her.

"I have a choice selection of lockets and timepieces. Most in good order."

"Yes, please show me."

He hurried again around the counter and again bumped the stack of books, which again tumbled to the floor. He did not bother to pick them up the second time. Efficiently, he returned with a brown velvet-lined tray containing brooches, stickpins, and fobs. Lilith was not fond of jewelry, but she did feel somewhat obligated to purchase something. Amid the bangles, an odd brooch caught her eye.

"It is scrimshaw from the South Pacific—very old."

Scrimshaw on pearl shell, the portrait was of a dark-eyed, black-haired, native beauty. Lilith studied it closely, then turned it over. On the back was etched, *Lily, Reva Ra 1787.* Nearly a hundred years old! *Some heart-struck sailor must have etched it from memory during long days at sea,* reasoned Lilith.

"Do you like it?" he asked.

"Yes, I do. You see on the back, the name is very close to my own. I am named Lilith."

"Then it was meant for you," he replied, with a gleam in his merchant's eye. "I will give you a bargain. Five quid."

"Only that? I will have it!"

Lilith stepped down from the hansom cab and climbed the steps to Eden Court. It still rained a gray drizzle. Her mother's health was always made worse by the winter damp.

The Tibetan manservant, Narota, a short swarthy-skinned soul clad in an orange brocade robe, bowed and assisted her in taking off her cloak when she entered. Smoothing her veil, she stepped from the entry alcove into the garden court where she saw her mother reclining on a wicker lounge, sipping tea.

"Mother," she greeted, "I am so glad to see you out here." She leaned down to give her mother an affectionate caress. Samara was petite, slender, raven haired, and still exotically beautiful despite her vaporous health. Lilith remembered dressing up in her clothes as a child, pretending to be as beautiful, as gracious, and as beloved by her father. Her governess, Annie Tuft, had once mentioned she greatly resembled her mother, but then had hastily added, "Yet, it is difficult to be sure with your—your disfigurement."

Lilith was not vain, but there was one vanity which on darker days obsessed her. She longed, dreamed, even prayed for flawlessly smooth skin like the golden-skinned native woman on the scrimshaw brooch.

"Mother, are you feeling better?" she asked with genuine concern.

Samara's clouded black eyes slowly focused on Lilith. "Yes, my dear. I am very content.

"This is not the usual English home. It reminds me a little of the Pasha's harem. But in Kozan there is no need for a glass roof and a ceramic stove to maintain such a garden. Since your father brought me to England I have always been cold." She snuggled deeper beneath the cashmere throw and fell silent.

"More tea, mother?" Lilith sat down beside the tea tray.

"No. I've had enough. Did you bring your father's things?"

Lilith knew her mother deeply mourned her father. She hated to disappoint her by not returning with his personal possessions left at the Royal Geographic Society. She folded up the edge of her veil so she might take tea. "I am sorry mother, but no, I did not. As you know the Royal Geographic Society does not allow women within its interior quarters or into its membership. I was turned away with the promise that they would deliver his things within the week."

"I can wait," she sighed. "I am unlike you, Lilith. You could never accept that you are a woman in a man's world."

Lilith could not help but smile and reached into her reticule. "Do not forget, mother I am also a man in a man's world."

"So you tell me. But writing under a man's name does not make you a man."

Lilith held up the *Gazette.* "They have reviewed my—or should I say Lyman Brazen's—*An Explorer's Handbook Out* in this morning's book chat. Listen mother, it is all good.

" 'Traveling in the wild can be a tremendous adventure. Lyman Brazen's first-rate guide, *An Explorer's Handbook Out,* is for both the seasoned explorer and the armchair adventurer. All will benefit from tales of this intrepid author's travels through the remote areas of the world. The book provides a wealth of information from the practical to the daring. Learn how to find drinking water in a desert. Find what food is safe to eat in the tropics. Discover what you must do if authorities take you for a spy while you are attempting to cross a border frontier. *An Explorer's Handbook Out* is unlike any other book you've read and is bound to be an essential for the adventurer-traveler.'" She put aside the paper and declared confidently, "I do believe my book will become a success!"

"I am happy for you. Though I will never understand how you were able to write such a book when you yourself have never left England."

"You've always said I had an overactive imagination."

"Yes, that is true. I suppose it can only be expected from a child who had no playmates. In the Pasha's harem, you would have had many."

Lilith took her mother's hand in her own. "I would rather have none, than grow up in a harem."

"Mistress," came the soft voice of the Tibetan manservant who had noiselessly come up from behind. Lilith turned to him. "The master requests you meet with him in the library."

"Now?"

"Yes, mistress."

Lilith released Samara's hand. "I'll be back soon," she assured her. But already Samara's eyes had glazed and again she seemed to have retreated into that other world where she so often lived.

"Show me the way. I am yet unfamiliar with the household," Lilith said, smoothing her veil. She came to her feet and followed the odd little man through the lush greenery and down the colonnade to an ornate door. He bowed and left.

Lilith took a moment to breathe and still her beating heart. She was discovering that facing Dunraven was a mixture of pleasure, pain, and anticipation. She prayed she would not be as tongue-tied as she had been late last night when he'd stopped her in the court and introduced her to Charles Vivian.

In the past, she'd dared to daydream of meeting Dunraven. When they met, she'd imagined, there would be an instant rapport between them. Impressed by her knowledge and intellect, he would love her despite her disfigurement. In her imaginative world, he had always been familiar, settled, predictable. But now, in reality, Dunraven and his household were none of these. For a brief second, she wanted to turn and run rather than face the flesh and bone of her longing.

Without her touching it, the door yawned open.

"Do not stand without; do come in." The voice was unmistakably his and the tone softly condescending.

A hand on the latch, Dunraven stood tall, austere, and vividly virile. Even without the clarity of view that her veil prevented, his presence struck Lilith like an awakening shake. His magnetism was equal to the pull of the tides and his sculpted golden visage a witness of his noble ancestry. Yet, a tinge of the savage sharpened his cheekbones and a hint of the aboriginal deepened his gaze. Confronting him face-to-face in this unexpected manner further paralyzed her inner child—the errant part of her which dared to want the very thing forbidden. He seemed all things mysterious —sorcerer, shaman, holy man.

Suddenly, her breast lurched like a grasshopper in spring. Hiccups! Not now! She was often plagued by hiccups when she was nervous. It did not help when her eyes settled on the V of his chest exposed by the gape of his loosely fitting shirt. No gentleman would receive a lady in such a state, but then again she was no stranger, but his lawful wife.

"I fear I have wed a shadow," he said smoothly. "You do not knock, you do not enter, you do not speak—" His lips quirked at the corners, "but you do hiccup."

Lilith contracted her throat in a wild effort to halt this humiliating seizure.

"Pray, come in." He bowed lightly and stepped aside.

More than anything in the world, Lilith wished she were indeed a shadow. Her wordless entry was accented by a hiccup. In an attempt at normalcy, she reconnoitered the great room lined with floor-to-ceiling bookcases. Her hand on her leaping breast, she chose a leather chair near a gigantic African drum and quickly sat before her knees buckled.

"Allow me to offer you something to drink." He reached for a long-necked bottle of Burgundy and poured her a dose in a small porcelain cup. "Take a sip of this to take the edge off."

Her hand reached out and the cup disappeared beneath her veil. The Burgundy warmed her throat.

He in turn sat cross-legged upon the cushion of a Tibetan meditation seat. Lilith found it an interesting square-box affair, the higher side forming a backrest with a woolen sash to pass under the knees and behind the neck to keep the meditator awake and upright.

He watched her in an expectant way.

Twice more she hiccuped, and then the attack abruptly ceased.

"Indeed, it has worked." He seemed pleased.

"Yes," Lilith began weakly, "I believe it has."

"Splendid!" he proclaimed, his features lightening.

Another awkward gap of silence undulated the air.

Finally, he announced with gravity, "I have been reading." He lifted the volume which he held in one hand. "Forgive my appearance, but I became so immersed in *An Explorer's Handbook Out* that I lost track of the time. Being an explorer's daughter, you might enjoy the volume yourself. I highly recommend it. In truth, I wished I'd written it myself. Unfortunately, I am not personally acquainted with Lyman Brazen. Hopefully I will have that honor one day." He set the book aside.

The shock of his disclosure stunned Lilith. On the one hand, she wanted to leap to her feet and proclaim herself Lyman Brazen; on the other, she knew to make such a confession would be tantamount to announcing she wished to be committed to an asylum. She set the cup on an ornately carved tea table beside her, knotted her hands, and remained silently passive.

He rested a hand on one thigh and began guardedly, "I have decided to speak with you at the outset, so as to avoid any misunderstanding. Might it be clarified that the marriage between us is one of duty. I married you because of my allegiance to your father, and I assume you accepted under the same circumstance."

Lilith knew this already. Despite this, she was in love with him and his confession was no less painful. It was not easy to face the man she loved and hear from his own lips that he married her out of duty.

"The night your father died in Lhasa, I vowed to

marry you as well as give protection and security to you and your mother for the duration of my life. I am a man of my word. I give you my name and my protection. However"—here he cleared his throat, his features clouded with seriousness—"however, you must not conclude our lives will be shared as man and wife. I have no desire to offend your gentle sensibilities, but I feel I must speak honestly to you so my motives will not be misconstrued. It is not because of your disfigurement—" He paused again, as if not sure how to continue. Lilith shifted with self-consciousness. Then, suddenly he came to the point. "I have chosen celibacy and the ascetic life which clearly does not entail traditional familial intercourse."

For a long moment, he did not speak as if to allow her to ruminate, chew, and digest this anomaly of his character. She bit her lower lip because more than anything she wanted to giggle. It must be the Burgundy. She felt like a silly schoolgirl who'd just heard someone say the word "naked," or worse. It was the first time in her life she was grateful a veil covered her features for, at the same time that she bit back her laughter, her eyes glistened with the beginnings of heartfelt tears. By God, life could be so unfair!

He put his hands together thoughtfully and spoke once more. "I am leaving soon to begin research in the South Pacific. I have no timetable to return. Expect no correspondence from me. You are free to return to your home in Devonshire which is now numbered among my properties. However, Eden Court is at your disposal if you choose to reside in London. I have instructed my solicitors to provide you and your mother with a generous monthly allowance. More importantly, Narota will faithfully obtain your mother's, ah, medicine. Have you any questions?"

Since people could not make eye contact with her, ofttimes they treated her as if she were deaf and dumb. The opening surprised her. Her throat ached with questions, but the most emboldened one jumped to her unbridled lips.

"My lord," she paused for a breath and asked archly, "am I required to remain celibate as well?"

She saw him straighten. He was not the sort to give much away in his expression but she saw it—the look as if he'd not heard quite right—upon his otherwise collected demeanor. His jaw firmed, the muscle of his cheek ticked, and the snake tattoo rippled with his quandary.

Behind her veil, Lilith smiled with a touch of satisfaction and mountains of genuine relief. She read clearly that this male, even if he had no intention of taking her to his bed, considered her his possession. A hint of the territorial pulsed within his features; no matter how ascetic he might profess to be, he had not yet transcended possessiveness. Intuitively, she knew under normal circumstances he most likely desired women and more than anything she wanted to be the woman he desired. But how? How did a woman who had no beauty win a man who had no intention of giving his heart—or his body?

Dunraven came to his feet and clasped his hands behind his back in a tutorial stance. The woman's question left him surprised, speechless, and unabashedly intrigued. He stared at her, seeing the faint hint of refined cheekbone behind that damnable veil.

After passing three years in a Tibetan monastery, he was unused to being in the company of a woman, particularly a woman who had been as mute as a meadow mouse but chose now to speak forthrightly. In truth, he was unused to women speaking at all. In his travels, the tribal women he'd been intimate with rarely spoke, always deferred, and never challenged his supremacy.

In a cool, composed voice he answered, "Under English law, you are my wife. I expect no less, madam."

"You wish me to be a wife who is no wife, sir?"

"Correct. For I am to be a husband who is no husband."

"'Tis unnatural—unless you yourself are so."

Her implication goaded him, and it took him but a second to shoot back a retort. "Madam, take care before you cast a stone. To bide one's days secreted behind a veil is equally unnatural."

He saw the braid of her fingers tighten. "I do not veil myself by choice."

"Then, pray cast off your veil."

"Pray in turn cast aside your celibacy," she parried.

Her audacity chafed him, but he bit back his irritation and continued to school his face circumspectly. "You would have me bargain my abstinence for your maidenhead. A tempting notion for one like myself who has just come down off the mountain. If your name were Eve, I being named Adam might subject me to the temptation."

"I am named for Lilith, Adam's first consort."

"Indeed? I vaguely recall that legend. I believe it is from the Hebrew tradition. Wasn't it written when the Holy One created the first human being, Adam, He created a woman also from the earth and called her Lilith?"

"Yes, you have it right."

"Wasn't there some misunderstanding between them?"

"I think the legend recounts the first divorce," said Lilith adeptly.

Her postulation made him smile. "And why do you think this?"

"It started out roughly for Adam, who with innate male arrogance, I might add, said to Lilith, 'You are fit to be below me and I above you.' Lilith returned, 'We are both equal because we both come from the earth.'"

"Ah, yes," he now remembered. "Lilith refused to make love in the missionary position and so Adam cast her off. And *I* might add, it was to his detriment for in my experience there is more to making love than having the woman lie flat on her back."

"I would not know," she confessed, "but it has been my hope that it was so."

The air became pregnant with silence.

Had he heard her correctly? He'd assumed that, like all Englishwomen, she was prepared to martyr herself on the marriage bed. However, her words belied this. He looked at her hard and long as if seeing her for the first time. In his mind's eye, a vision of her in his bed flashed vividly. He'd not shackled himself to a shadow after all. Only a flesh-and-blood woman could provoke such thought. And only a flesh-and-blood man would physically react as he felt himself reacting. Like a buck at the outset of rutting, his senses leaped with acute arousal. He felt the rush of sensation, the thirst of desire, and the pulse of engorgement. For three years he'd been chaste, and now suddenly he'd landed feet first under the spell of the feminine mystique. Her woman's scent embraced his nostrils and her woman's form arrested his gaze.

It had been difficult enough returning from the austerity of a Tibetan monastery to the excess of English society, without in turn facing the rekindling of his own masculine urges. He'd passed years attuning his senses to the ascetic. Now, a mere two minutes within the company of this veiled mystery, and his higher mind plummeted to his groin.

He broke the silence and said briskly, "I fear I have taken too much of your time. I myself have many preparations to see to before I leave at the end of the week." Thus, ending the interview, he bowed. "Good afternoon to you, madam."

She stood. Then with a step forward, apparently undaunted by his curt dismissal, she offered him her small, satin-gloved hand.

He was hesitant to take it in his own—and for good reason. The moment his fingers touched hers, his desire smoldered.

"I request you call me Lilith. If we are not to be man and wife, I would have us friends." Her slim fingers caressed his own gently and then released them. "Safe journey to you, Adam Dunraven."

She left him. Dunraven's eyes held on the sway of her retreating hips while his body wrestled with the potency of the human touch.

The morning after Dunraven's departure for the South Pacific, Lilith rose early and made her way to the library. She paused in the doorway with anticipation and took a slow visual inventory of the vast holdings upon the shelves. Her father had told her Dunraven's book collection entailed the rare, the bizarre, and the banned. *If I were to be imprisoned in a single room for the remainder of my life, I would request it be Dunraven's library,* her father had once declared.

As she'd requested, a fire had been lit in the hearth. The atmosphere radiated warmth, adventure and the essence of Adam Dunraven. The room housed not only books, but an assortment of artifacts and native drums he'd collected on his travels. He'd a penchant for drumming. Now that he was gone, she missed the mesmerizing beats echoing through the household. She hugged herself and let loose a deep breath of expectancy. Where would she begin? Her eyes rested on a Zulu basket constructed for catching human souls, then moved to a gazetteer of West Africa. She stepped forward, spying a thick, leather-strapped diary shoved crookedly on a lower shelf. She pulled it out, unfastened the leather ties and opened to the first page. *My Journey to Lhasa: An Account by Adam Dunraven, 1880.*

With glimmering expectancy, she turned the page, backed into the overstuffed chair, and sat down before the hearth. She began reading the words penned in Dunraven's own hand.

For westerners, Tibet is wrapped in an atmosphere of mystery. This Land of Snows is for us the country of the unknown, the fantastic, and the impossible. What superhuman powers have not been ascribed to the various kinds of lamas, magicians, sorcerers, and practitioners of the occult who inhabit these high tablelands, and whom both nature and their own deliberate purpose have so splendidly isolated from the rest of the world?

It was therefore quite natural that a scholar like

myself, accustomed to the strict discipline of experimental methods, should pay to these traditions merely the condescending and amused attention that is usually given to fairy tales. Such was my own state of mind up to the day when I had the good fortune to cross the high mountain passes and firsthand discover the magic and mystery of Tibet. . . .

The hours passed, and wholly immersed, Lilith could not put down the fascinating account of Dunraven's early experiences with erudite lamas, hermits, and peoples of that faraway place. She took lunch and tea in the library. In the late afternoon, nearing the end of the account, she was preparing to ring for supper when the Tibetan manservant knocked on the door and announced a caller.

"Madam," he said softly, "Charles Vivian is without."

"Charles Vivian?" she echoed, hastily lowering her veil. "By all means, invite him in," she said, coming to her feet.

A moment later, Charles stepped through the doorway and smiled politely. "I hope I am not intruding, but I came to fetch two books Dunraven left for me."

Lilith looked about on the desk. "Yes, the pair tied with string. There is a note as well."

"Thank you," he said, as she placed them in his hands. "I was passing and did not mean to interrupt."

"It is no interruption."

"Yes, well," he stepped to leave.

"Do not leave—," she paused. "Could you stay—that is, if you have no other plans."

He smiled broadly. "In truth, I do not. My evening is quite free."

"Well, then," she clasped her hands nervously, "why not take supper with me."

"Why not indeed!" he returned agreeably.

"I hope you like curry."

"I confess my constitution does not abide spicy food. But I am content to sup on bread and milk."

"There is no need," she declared. "I am sure the cook can prepare something which will delight your conservative palate." She walked to the doorway and asked the Tibetan to see to it.

Five hours later, at nearly a quarter past eleven, after lengthy discussions on a myriad of topics from her father's expeditions to goddess fertility cults, Charles reluctantly stood to take his leave.

"I have stayed over long. With Dunraven off to the South Pacific, I realize I must observe the boundaries of propriety. However, I cannot remember experiencing such an invigorating evening. You are delightful company."

"I am afraid I have held you hostage with my prattle."

"Never! We are both armchair adventurers and like-minded." He stepped toward the door.

"Do not forget your volumes," Lilith snatched up the books and followed him.

"Ah, yes. I almost forgot why I came." He took the volumes in hand, then paused. "These volumes might interest you as well. Dunraven intends to base his research in the South Pacific on their contents. There is a particular tribe of natives purported to fire walk."

"Indeed! I am intrigued."

"My own and Dunraven's research have turned up no fewer than twenty-five places around the world where the fire walk has been practiced. In these places, the ability to walk or dance upon fire tends to be viewed as a special trait or power of the individual, a sign that he or she is uniquely possessed."

"Are you sure it is not a sham by misguided village elders, or a circus stunt?"

"I am not sure of anything. There remain enough reports from reliable witnesses. Do you read your Bible?"

"I must confess not so devotedly as Vicar Heathcote Holmes might like."

"The fire walk seems to have had a place in early Judeo-Christian culture. I recount the biblical story of Shadrach, Meshach, and Abed-nego, who proved that they were divinely connected when they were tossed into the fiery furnace by Nebuchadnezzar. Isaiah states, 'When thou walkest through fire, thou shalt not be burned.'"

"That is all well and good for religious fanatics, but you would not find me anywhere near such a pyre. I have a fear of such things. Though I do admit it is quite fascinating."

Charles' face lit with the academic's enthusiasm. "Setting aside what is actually happening at a fire walk and what is actually proven or not proven, we can quite safely say that fire walking is one of Earth's oldest and most widely spread rituals. The practice shows up in a wide range of cultures. In addition, there are many varying styles and manners of fire walking. During his sojourn in the South Pacific, Dunraven intends to track down a particular island where it is purported the natives walk upon molten lava."

"Goodness, that gives me the shivers just imagining it!"

"For right reason. Everywhere we have encountered people walking on fire, we have also heard warnings of the danger involved, and very explicit tales of the worst that can happen from minor blisters to death."

"Stop. I cannot bear to hear," she declared, holding up her hand. Flashes of the past—the fear, the suffocating flames, the pain—collapsed in on her. Even at her adult age, the memory of that night still haunted her thoughts. Sometimes the mere sight of a lit lamp could bring it all back again.

"I'm sorry," Charles said, abruptly aware he'd crossed into sensitive territory.

She swallowed back her discomfort and composed herself. "Tell me, where exactly will Dunraven find this tribe?"

"There was some doubt he would find them at all. His sole information was based on rumor and a few lines in these volumes."

He walked over and pulled out a map from the map case. Unrolling it, he weighted one side down with the books in his hand. "His destination is the Society Islands. I believe he intends to begin in Raiatea or Tahiti, and end up in the Cook or Tubuai Islands. These islands are partly uncharted, but approximately here." His finger touched a smattering of fly specks on the parchment. "I realize that neither of us will ever set foot there, but somehow I believe it is important to know."

"Yes, I agree," said Lilith.

"Well, now I must really be going." He picked up the books and strode out the door. The Tibetan handed him his hat, cloak, and cane. "Thank you, Narota," he said kindly.

Lilith watched the small, orange robed servant open the door for Charles' departure.

"Good night, madam." Charles touched his hat and stepped out into the night.

"Good night, Charles," she bid, and turned back into the library.

"Do you wish me to add coal to the fire, mistress?" asked Narota.

The ebbing dance of flames caught Lilith's eye and momentarily mesmerized her. "No—," she finally said. "No, I plan to retire."

He bowed deeply and withdrew.

"Narota."

"Yes, mistress?" He turned back.

"You are from Tibet?"

"Yes, mistress."

"I have been reading Dunraven's account and find it riveting. Have you ever wished to return to your homeland?"

"Yes, mistress, but I cannot."

"And why not?"

"I am in exile. I was imprisoned and destined to be executed when Dunraven assisted me in escape. If I returned, I would surely meet my end."

She realized his high regard for Dunraven was more than a servant's loyalty. "I see," she said thoughtfully, fingering the scrimshaw brooch at her throat as if it were a tool of divination.

He stood patiently before her, and she realized he was waiting for her to dismiss him. However, she was not finished. "Could I safely entrust myself into your hands?"

"I would guard your life with my own."

"And what of my mother?"

"The same, mistress."

"If I were to leave for an extended time—say, to return to my home in Devonshire—could I leave my mother here at Eden Court and be assured you would tend to all her needs?"

"Yes, mistress."

"I have your word?"

"You have it."

"Thank you."

He bowed out.

Abuzz with thought, Lilith turned, picked up the wood baton and tentatively tapped the great African drum. The sound resonated deeply through the room as she experimented with various rhythms—rhythms which seemed to trigger suppressed emotions within her.

We are both armchair adventurers. . . . Though neither of us will ever set foot there. . . . Charles' words vibrated in her mind along with the beat of the drum.

All her life she had waited. Through the years, she and her mother had waited for her father to return from his long, dangerous expeditions. With unfailing anticipation, she'd waited for his letters from the field. She'd waited for the day he'd promised to take her with him. She'd waited for her mother to regain her health. Even now, still she waited—waited for a husband who would never take her to his bed because he married her from duty, not love.

Standing before the giant drum, something snapped in her like a spring coiled too tightly for too long. She brought the baton down with a mammoth strike and the air shook with her decision.

She was done with waiting.

She was ready to study, explore, and discover—if not by Dunraven's side, then alone. She walked over to the desk and unrolled the parchment map, picked up pen and paper, and began writing down the coordinates of the Society Islands.

She must arrange her personal affairs, the main of which was telling her mother of her plans and having her promise not to tell anyone. Samara would balk at first, but Lilith reasoned she could somehow convince her, even if it took a few white lies. No matter the insurmountable barriers, as soon as possible, she intended to take passage on a ship bound for the South Pacific.

Chapter

3

The dinghy rolled and pitched on the storm-thrashed sea. Lilith huddled beneath a tarpaulin and waited for death. Had it been two days or two hours? She shook with chill and cursed the disastrous typhoon that had overcome the *Copra.* She'd been the only woman aboard the cargo sloop. For her own safety, the crew had sealed her beneath the tarpaulin in the lifeboat with a caged canary bird. She would never know what had happened to the *Copra,* for during the chaos of the storm, she had been set adrift.

The incessant downpour of rain pelted the tarpaulin cover and her cramped body ached. Soaked to the bone, she felt numb with exhaustion, not to mention a total failure as an adventuress. Too late, she realized how slim chances were of meeting Dunraven in the myriad of islands in the South Pacific. She might dive for diamonds in an oyster bed more easily.

She'd left England on the twenty-second of November last on the Dutch sailing vessel, *Lootpuit,* and arrived in Papeete, Tahiti the first day of March. The voyage had been marked by English cholera, stormy seas, and a superfluity of boiled onions.

Three weeks later, including an unproductive side voyage to Raiatea in search of Dunraven, she decided to follow the one bit of information she'd learned from a French pilot concerning Dunraven's whereabouts. Monsieur DeVilliers recalled dining with Dunraven in Papeete the evening of the twelfth of February. Dunraven had asked about passage to the Tuamotu Archipelago, a chain of islands and atolls stretching over five hundred miles eastward.

Brimming with impatience and against all counsel and common sense, Lilith begged passage on the *Copra,* a dubious sloop setting course through the archipelago to the Marquesas Islands.

She knew now the Pacific was much bigger than the globe in her father's library led one to believe, and in this miserable moment, she deeply regretted leaving the comforts of her English hearth. More painful yet, she faced full mirror her own stupidity. It was said that on the brink of death, people's lives flashed before them. But since her life had been deadeningly dull, nothing but her own ignorance flashed out. Like some lovestruck Drury Lane doxy, she'd thrown all intelligence to the wind and followed her true love to earth's end—a true love who cared not a whit about her.

She felt a martyr to love. Tears welled in her eyes. *I will die in this peapod on the sea, and Dunraven will not know or care. I am a hapless Ophelia.* Indeed, she contemplated with philosophic hindsight; the darkest hour is always before—before it goes completely black—

Time lost meaning. When Lilith came to awareness

again she could not breathe, and felt as if she were suffocating in hell. Gently, she tapped the bird cage to see if her small companion still survived. She heard a faint rustle, but knew the creature was suffering as much as she. Rain no longer pounded above her and the boat rocked gently in a calm sea.

Water. She licked parched lips. How she wanted a drink! She splayed her fingers against the tarpaulin cover and felt the violent heat of a tropical sun radiating through. Lashed taut over the boat, the tarpaulin had been her salvation in wild seas from being swamped, but now—

Unsuccessfully, she tried to slip her arm between the tarpaulin and the side of the boat to unfasten the lashings. Finally, out of desperation, she pushed against it with her hands and feet. There was no getting out. Oh, god! She would be cooked alive! More than frantic, she belly crawled the short length of the dinghy, searching for supplies. Surely a lifeboat would be stocked with water and food rations.

Nothing.

What would the resourceful Lyman Brazen do in such a position? Eat the canary? She certainly could not! If she had a knife she might cut through the tarpaulin and—What could she do after she'd freed herself besides roast in the tropical sun and pray for a passing ship?

I won't be defeated, she vowed. Tenaciously, her fingers went to her throat. The idea struck her that she might use the sharp pin fastening of her scrimshaw brooch to cut through the tarpaulin. Unclasping the brooch, she began working a hole in the tough fabric.

After what seemed hours, the circulation had drained from her hands and arms. She'd only managed to make a hole large enough for her smallest finger. She bit down on her lower lip and let her arms collapse onto her breast. Exhausted, she knew it was foolish to believe a passing vessel might rescue her. Suffering from heat and thirst, she decided to strip off her clothing. For better or for worse, her veil had blown away in the typhoon. Slowly, she worked the tiny jet buttons down the front of her black bombazine mourning dress.

On any excursion it is extremely important to dress for the climate, echoed the advice of Lyman Brazen. *One does not wear knickers to the Himalayas and only the most devout missionary would wear black bombazine in the tropics.*

Since Lilith was in mourning, she excused herself to wear black bombazine to the tropics. But as she lay suffering, the convention of mourning meant very little in the face of her own demise. In truth, writing about adventure was certainly easier than living it.

I should have remained in England, safe and cared for at Eden Court, she ruminated abjectly. A picture of herself and Charles Vivian rose in her mind. Together they could sit into old age, side by side before the fire, safely tracking and discussing Dunraven's exploits.

Finally, stripped down to camisole and petticoat, she gingerly touched a chafing rash on her arms. Another stone in her burden bag, the climate did not suit her. An anathema of skin eruption from the combination of tropical heat, humidity, and black bombazine covered her skin. She looked and felt like a smallpox victim.

She removed the remaining brass hairpins from her hair and attempted to straighten the unkempt black mass into a coiled loop. However, nothing alleviated her misery and her mind continued to wander. To bring it back to the plight at hand she began singing. Her talent for singing compensated for her lack of beauty. In a rich contralto she sang the rhythmic Turkish songs her mother had taught her as a child. The time passed. She hummed through her repertoire of English ballads until her throat tired. Then in silence, she rocked in her sea-borne cradle and listened to the creaks of the boat and the lap of the waves.

Suddenly, she heard laughter—bizarre, clownish laughter. It frightened her.

I'm going mad.

No, no, it couldn't be! deduced her saner side. Maybe it was just a sea bird flying overhead. But no, the sounds came from the water near the boat. She turned to her side and put her ear to the hull. She heard whistles, clicks, and then a noise like the rusty gate at Devon cottage. The rattling chuckles came again. The canary fluttered restlessly about in its cage.

Desperate, she called out, "Hallo."

More clicks.

"Hallo. Hallo," she continued to call.

The clicks ceased and the rusty gate sound came again.

Lilith thrust her two pinky fingers between her lips and blew a shrill whistle in answer.

She felt foolish.

Then she heard a pert whistle.

Quickly, she whistled three short bursts. The canary gave a weak chirrup.

This time the only answer was silence.

Her breath near halted as she vainly listened.

Nothing.

No, it was not her imagination. Someone or something was out there. The restless canary sensed it as well.

"Hallo," she cried out again. "Hallo. My name is Lilith Cardew. I have been cast away in a storm. Please, please, help me."

Yes, something was there. She could hear it now. She pressed her cheek to the floor of the boat and strained to hear the faint sound. Was it singing? It sounded like singing in a subterranean cavern. Mermaids?

Now you are being foolish, she thought, with self-castigation. *No matter what it was, it did give hope.*

She began tapping her foot against the hull in code. Since childhood she'd been very good at ciphering. Each Sabbath, she and an unknown person who sat about five pews behind had passed the paralyzing sermons of Vicar Heathcote Holmes in conversant subterfuge. She'd never been quite sure who had been her partner in irreverence. She guessed him to be Lady Oldfield's gardener, the one called Long Beard. He would be dead now—as she soon might be as well.

The singing faded away and her foot tired.

Hour to hour, she cautioned herself against being too hopeful and then she fell into a doze.

When she awoke again, she knew it was night. The tarpaulin was cool to the touch and the air was no longer stifling. She reached inside the canary cage. Her searching hand found the bird huddled in the corner. With a fingertip, she slowly stroked its breast and wing. Alone in the pitchy darkness, she'd never felt so forsaken, so abandoned, nor so frightened.

She thought, I don't want to die as anonymously as I have lived. Her mind called out, *I can't die! Somebody, something, help me!*

Sounds again. The rusty gate, the rattling chuckles,

and then the rhythmic clicks. Somehow the sounds were comforting. It was a responsive presence in the vast loneliness. She took off her shoe and began tapping code.

She tapped out, "My name is Lilith Cardew. Who are you?"

For a moment, nothing, then random clicks.

Of course, whatever it was, it would not know code.

She tapped out, "Water water everywhere, but not a drop to drink." There came the rattling chuckle. Perhaps it did understand.

The pulsing singing began again.

Fish could not sing—or could they?

The deprivation of being adrift in the sea for two days, maybe three, was muddling her thoughts.

She dreamed.

She was spiraling through fronds of emerald kelp in deep exotic waters. Sea creatures drifted past—shimmering, spidery-tentacled, cerulean jellyfish, schools of golden sunfish, and rainbow-scaled sea horses. None paused to remark on the oddity of a human being swimming deep in the sea—except the eye. The eye was connected to a sleek, silvery apparition that drew closer with the bare swish of its tail. The marvelous eye was just inches from hers—staring, even smiling. Looking into the eye she knew she was safe.

A thud!

She was no longer in ocean depths, but cramped in the dinghy again. Voices, she heard voices.

She stuck her finger into the tarpaulin slit and wriggled it desperately. Now she heard more cross flow of voices.

Suddenly, the tarpaulin lifted.

The noonday sun flashed over Lilith, her eyes watered and she squinted into the brilliance. Obsidian eyes peered at her from a brown face framed by a halo of white frizzy hair. Intricately tattooed, the face was a demonic mask. She forgot all of Lyman Brazen's rules of introducing oneself to primitives.

She opened her mouth to scream aloud. Nothing came out. She tried again, uttering a forlorn squeak. His thick lips curved into a fearsome frown. She felt suspended in time. Her heart stopped in her chest and she prayed. She prayed that this wild man was not a cannibal. She prayed he would take pity on her for the time being. But most fervently of all, she prayed that Adam Dunraven would miraculously sail forth from the horizon and rescue her.

The native continued to stare at her—

He might believe she carried a plague and was a castaway. Quickly, she must think, but she couldn't think. Her thoughts were muddled by the sultry air, the sound of splashing, the sun blinding her, and the incredible thirst. Mustering the last dregs of her strength, she pointed to the sun, and then to her face and arms. With great apprehension, she peered through her eyelids at the brown, tattooed man.

She wanted to swoon and would have, but for the still small voice of Lyman Brazen declaring in the back chambers of her mind. *It is of the utmost importance to maintain eye contact (except in those societies that consider eye contact impolite) upon meeting natives. Establish hierarchy by declaring one's title. The native respects confidence and lineage.*

She wanted to tell him about the storm, but she had no voice. She wanted to pound her fist to her breast with a show of fitness, but she could not lift her arm.

She cleared her throat to say *ia ora na,* a greeting she'd learned in Tahiti, but nothing came out save a pitiless whimper.

The fierceness in the native's face softened and his dark eyes glistened with moisture. Oddly, he seemed overcome with emotion, but still he said nothing.

When none speak English, the use of hand gestures, facial movements, and pantomime become appropriate. Most importantly, give them gifts such as trade beads.

She had no trade beads. She'd nothing to give. The canary could be dead. The brooch, she could give him the brooch. Barely grasping it, she raised the palm of her hand to his view. He caught the brooch in his hand, examined it momentarily, and then exclaimed loudly. He raised it high and spoke over his shoulder to comrades she could not see.

His strong arms reached for her. Lilith swallowed back her fear.

"Aue, aue, aue," he cried while embracing her heartily. Behind him erupted a clamor of shouting. This frightened Lilith even more. The shells and bones decorating his armlets and waistband clicked as he lifted her. She was doomed. He was a cannibal to be sure. He would take her back to his village and, in some primitive rite, torture her. Her father had once recorded an unforgettable account of an unfortunate explorer who had been skewered on a cooking spit over a smoldering fire, roasted, and eaten by savages layer after layer.

Other brown, tattooed natives were leaning and reaching to assist him move her. She felt the hands of men lift her from the dinghy onto a fine-size deepwater voyager. Frigate bird feathers adorned twin mastheads and carved tikis crowned upswept bow and stern, which were inlaid with mother-of-pearl motifs. She saw no fewer than fifteen people—including broad-backed men, ample-hipped women, and wide-eyed children—and a squealing piglet.

Mats were adjusted, provisions moved aside, and a space was made for Lilith to recline. A bare-bosomed, rotund woman knelt beside her and flashed a smile of shell white teeth. She placed the canary cage beside Lilith and a small girl intently peered at the drooping bird.

She said something repeatedly, her dark eyes full of concern.

The woman spoke to the girl. Then the woman gave her a piece of fruit that the child pushed inside the cage. The bird seemed indifferent.

Lilith was desperate for food and water herself. With a hoarse whisper she asked, "Water, please. Water, please."

"Aue, aue," sighed the woman, turning her attention back to Lilith. "My name Heikua. Thee safe," she announced in biblical English. Her hand gently patted Lilith's own. "Thee safe."

Touched, Lilith parted her lips to try to say more, but the woman already held a gourd in her plump hand.

She lifted Lilith's head and pressed the gourd gently to her lips. Greedily, Lilith drank, trying to quench her thirst. Never had water tasted so good. Heikua turned and took a leaf from her companions, then turned back.

On the leaf was a gooey substance. She dipped her two fingers in the paste and touched it to Lilith's lips. "Thee partake," she clarified. The taste was breadfruit. "Thee partake, become strong."

Lilith ate slowly, and then wished only for sleep.

Someone threw a plaited, soft leaf mat over her and she closed her eyes.

Later, she woke to singing. Feeling stronger, she sat up and looked about, marveling at the vastness of the sea and the resonant sweet voices of these strange people who had rescued her.

Echoing the rhythms of the sea everyone sang in a soft harmonic flow. An old man, wrinkle-faced and steadfast eyed, stood with his feet planted wide apart on the forward. Amid rolling seas, his only movement was an occasional gesture to the helmsman. The singing quickened.

"Reva Ra," announced Heikua with a pointing hand. Lilith looked beyond the outrigger. In the distance she saw a smoking black volcanic turret rising out of the sea. Beneath, an island sprawled like a napping sea monster whose dormant volcanic spires poked thousands of feet into misty clouds. The sea frothed against coastal cliffs and the setting sun illuminated the trees and tumbling dark green mountainsides. Oddly, a wave of emotion erupted within her, a lump rose in her throat, and tears welled in her eyes. She'd been adrift in the sea for so long that sighting landfall felt like a homecoming.

Finding her voice at last, Lilith repeated slowly, "Reva—Ra—" The word touched something lost, something familiar in her memory.

Her attention settled on the scrimshaw brooch. The woman Heikua had fastened it to a shell choker about her own throat. "Yes, Reva Ra." That was the inscription on the back of the brooch she suddenly realized! *Lily, Reva Ra, 1787.*

"Reva Ra," smiled Heikua. "Reva Ra, thy home. Lily return home." Her black eyes glistening with a wise knowing, she pointed to the scrimshaw brooch and pressed her warm hand to Lilith's heart. "Thy home."

In punctuation of this strangest of coincidences, a dolphin exploded out of the sea dangerously near the outrigger.

"Look, see," said Heikua waving her brown arm seaward. "Rangahua, Rangahua."

Again the Rangahua shot out of the water. The sleek form burst through the surface and arched through the air with serene assurance. The children squealed and clapped their hands with delight. The dolphin swam parallel to the vessel and whistled softly, opening its blowhole, then half closing it to emit a taut, brief trumpet. Lilith recognized these sounds.

"Rangahua, sea traveler," explained Heikua. "We follow Rangahua to sea of the moon. Find Lily."

The revelation, that the Rangahua somehow had relayed her plight to these people was difficult for Lilith to believe. The dolphin leaped near enough for her to glimpse into its alert eye. It was as if she again met an old friend. *I know you,* she thought.

The dolphin chirruped and submerged.

Heikua touched her hand. "Rangahua, keeper of sacred life breath. Rangahua save thy life."

Lilith looked to the exotic island beyond. Then her eyes drew back to the wild and beautiful people surrounding her. All her disbelief began to fade. In the shimmering golden light of the setting sun, Lilith felt as if she were entering another realm, a haven she had visited before—if only in unremembered dreams.

On steady track, the outrigger glided through a gap in the reef and headed for the sand line of the beach. The old wrinkle-faced navigator pressed an enormous conch shell to his lips. His narrow chest swelled and shrunk with breath and the horn of homecoming echoed across the lagoon.

A group of men waded out through the breakers, took hold, and guided the outrigger to mooring. Everyone hastily abandoned the outrigger and splashed ashore.

Heikua was at Lilith's side. "Come, come. We make big feast. Thee eat." She jabbed her finger into Lilith's bony hip. "Thee skinny skinny. Island womans no skinny. Come, Tiaro help thee."

Under the supervision of Heikua, the tattooed, white-haired Tiaro lifted Lilith in his strong arms. Once ashore, it was not a long walk to the village. The majority of houses were built on stilts, shored up with mangrove poles and thatched with palm fronds. Tiaro carried her to a large and lofty thatched communal house as the little girl ran behind, carrying the canary cage. The roof of the communal house soared upward to a crisscross of massive beams and the four sides remained open to the cooling trade winds. He gently set her on a mat in the center of the house.

Women greeted and grinned a self-conscious *Ia ora na*. Like the women on the ship, these women wore a wraparound skirt from the waist to below the knees made of bark cloth. On Reva Ra, there seemed to be no moral reason to hide one's body from the view of others. Lilith's upbringing caused her to lower her eyes with embarrassment.

Children peered at her curiously while preparations for feasting were in full swing. A gigantic fish tail was smoking in a pit oven beyond the communal house. Women prodded and stirred the fire while others wrapped smaller fish in carefully woven sheaths of palm leaves to bake in ashy coals.

A wide-hipped woman, whose hair frizzed a wild wreath around her face, announced something that brought three giggling maidens to Lilith's side. A half-dozen eager hands removed the pins of Lilith's hair and combed through the mess of tangles, deftly waving and coiling it into neat loops. The girls argued among themselves, not agreeing on the outcome. Water was poured into a large shell and gently sponged onto her face and bare arms. More discussion broke out when Lilith refused to allow them to remove her camisole top and skirts. She clutched the fastenings at her breast and shook her head emphatically.

The woman Heikua arrived and sent them off. "Thee sleep. Feast ready soon."

Lilith welcomed this reprieve and, feeling somewhat refreshed, she reclined into a restive posture with one eye cracked open.

Sometime later, she roused to the slow, hollow beat of a drum. An old man, flanked by two younger men who clicked split bamboo sticks together, paced the beginnings of a formalized ceremony.

Lilith suddenly found herself lifted up and supported physically on either side by two younger women who moved her to a more favored spot and ornamented her with chains of sweet-smelling flowers. Before her stood a line of handsome warriors, Tiaro centermost, who danced surefooted to the slow rhythms. Behind were adolescent boys moving gracefully in the shadow of their fathers with no show of self-consciousness. All the dancers wore swinging skirts of dried grass and on their heads were tall, feathered headdresses.

With the conclusion of the men's dance, the women

and girls swayed together in a circle of singing and hand clapping. Then Tiaro stepped forward and spoke in a ringing tone that reached the furthest ears of the assembly. After her stay in Papeete, Lilith's understanding of Tahitian was rudimentary. These islanders spoke a different dialect, but it was similar enough that Lilith felt confident she would eventually grasp it. Tiaro spread his great arms wide as though to embrace every person and pronounced a blessing upon all heads. Then, he embraced Lilith until she thought she would collapse. But all the while she was tremendously moved, nearly to tears. Truly, she felt the sincerity of their welcome even though she was quite undeserving.

Quickly, mountains of food appeared and were set out on the woven mats before Lilith. She looked on at the abundance of cooked and marinated raw fish, *taro,* and cooked breadfruit served on shiny leaves. Steaming baked yams with coconut were piled to one side of a smoldering roasted pig. Dubiously, she eyed the pig, avoiding the snout and focusing on the red hibiscus flower tucked behind its ear as garnish.

Rubbing her stomach and shaking her head, she whispered aside to Heikua, "I can't eat all this."

Heikua laughed and spoke loudly to everyone else and then they all laughed. "Thee partake. Thee finish, we partake."

She concluded it was either island etiquette or they were fattening her up in order to eat her later on. She could not be sure, but at this moment, she was very hungry and would deal with that event when it happened.

She ate—and ate.

All the while, the natives sat in a great circle around

her, singing songs and moving their hands in graceful movements to the soft rhythms.

She drank and drank. The drink served in a half coconut shell, Heikua called *kava*. It brought giggles to Lilith's lips and she felt better than she'd ever felt before. In truth it caused her to feel so wonderful she began singing with the others. At one point she could not quite remember anything—

Lilith jerked awake. Her eyes snapped open. Her body was damp with sweat and her heart was pounding. The nightmare—it was only the nightmare again. *There are no flames here, no smoke,* a faint voice assured, as her fears vanished into the clarity of wakefulness.

But where was she?

Her head throbbed and her mouth tasted foul. She groaned aloud. She could not have felt more repentant even when the first thing she spied was a wooden cross hung on a mat wall directly before her. Next, she realized that beneath the woven grass mat she lay naked. Her high-top leather shoes, corset, camisole, petticoats, and black bombazine dress were neatly stacked in a pile beside her.

"Ia ora na. Thee awake?" came Heikua's soft voice.

Lilith's eyes slowly searched for Heikua. She sat cross-legged on a mat beside a lap-high bamboo table, which accommodated a large Bible.

Her dark eyes turned from her serious perusal of the pages and she said, "Thee sleep. Wake in new place. Long time Jesus John house. He drown in lagoon." She gave a wide smile, exposing perfect white teeth. "We say we eat him. No more Jesus Johns come to Reva Ra."

Leaning her weight on one arm, Lilith sat up. The world swayed and then steadied. Heikua was at her side offering her something to drink. Lilith tucked the mat more securely about her and peered at the liquid narrowly.

"No more *kava*," smiled Heikua. "This *peepa* juice."

It tasted refreshing and seemed to smooth out the rasp in Lilith's throat. "Thank you," she managed.

"Thee welcome," returned Heikua. She reached as if to touch Lilith's scarred cheek. Her eyes held immense sympathy. *"Aue, aue.* This hurt much?"

"No—not now. I was burned in a fire as a child," said Lilith. Her eyes skirted the room as she felt exposed without her veil.

"All this time and scar no go away?"

"No," said Lilith, wishing to change the subject. She quickly asked, "How did you learn to speak English?"

Heikua pointed to the Bible. "I only one on Reva Ra speak English. Jesus John teach me read Bible book 'bout Jesus." She paused reflectively. "He love me."

"Yes, Jesus loves us all," confirmed Lilith, warmed by her simple faith.

"Nay, *Jesus John* love me—he love me everynigh'. He say, 'For the lips of a strange woman drop as an honeycomb, and her mouth is smoother than oil: Let her be as the loving hind and pleasant roe; let her breasts satisfy thee at all times; and be thou ravished always with her love. Prov. 5.'"

"He quoted this to you?"

Heikua smiled, her eyes twinkling. "Everynigh'. When he come to Reva Ra, we think he no man. He keep apart from us. No sing, no dance. I healer woman. I teach him to be man. In missionary church he no learn."

"Did his death make you sad?" Lilith asked, wondering if Heikua had loved the preacher.

She let loose a deep sigh, "I weep river Babylon. Tiaro tell me there are many fish in the sea. Tiaro tell me go fishing."

"So is Tiaro your—your husband?"

Her eyes lowered modestly. "Sometime. He chief have many concubines and children. Thou art his *tamahine* now."

"What?" Lilith knew *tamahine* meant daughter.

"He adopt thee."

"But why?" Lilith realized this could happen. Dunraven had been adopted by the Iban tribesmen, but thus far she had done nothing to merit adoption.

"You walk?"

"I—I think so," said Lilith.

"I show thee. Come."

"I must dress first." She reached for her camisole.

"Thee wear *pareo* like island womans. Much better," said Heikua pointing to a bark-cloth skirt that was laid out beside Lilith's clothing.

Lilith shook her head, but smiled so not to offend. "No. I don't think so."

"Sun hot on island."

"I'll be fine," assured Lilith, proceeding to lace up her corset. Lilith felt Heikua's disapproving gaze all the while she was dressing. Yes, she thought, this self-imposed imprisonment would seem odd to an island woman. Because of her scarring, she had always covered herself from head to toe and she could do no different on Reva Ra.

With the final fastening of her high-top shoes, Lilith came to her feet albeit a little unsteady. Heikua encouraged her to lean on her arm and led her through the threshold of the palm-frond hut. On the bamboo-poled porch hung the empty canary cage.

"Where is the canary?"

"I let go," said Heikua, her liquid eyes lifting to the treetops.

"What?"

"Fly away. Go free in Reva Ra. No need for cage."

"Oh, I—," Lilith began, then said thoughtfully, "yes, it would be better to let it fly free. Indeed, I think it has earned its freedom."

"Everything free on Reva Ra. Thee and I—birds, fish, everything."

Lizards skittered beneath fern canopies leaving tail squiggles in the fine sand, and unsettled wrens flew higher into the feathery casuarina trees. Heikua led her along a path of large-leafed breadfruit trees and into dense vegetation of pandanus, coconut fronds, and wild fern. Lilith breathed in the morning island air and felt revitalized.

Heikua paused to touch a brilliant orange orchid. "Good flower for heart sickness," she informed. Then she reached beside it and picked a few seed pods from a nearby tree. Turning to Lilith, she waved the pod over her hands and said, "This *ati* seed. *Ati* maybe help thee." She stuffed the pod in a pouch at her waist.

"I am afraid nothing will help me, Heikua. I have been to many learned physicians in England. No one has helped me yet."

Heikua frowned. "Thee has not been to me. I, Tahua, healer woman." She leaned closer to Lilith and reached up to lightly touch the disfiguring scars across her chin and forehead. "Sacred fire plant grow on Reva Ra, make thy scars disappear."

Lilith's lips tightened with disbelief. It would take a

miracle to wipe away those scars. In all her experience, she'd never heard of anything that could repair scarred skin, but she would not argue with Heikua. Since she was at the islanders' mercy, she could not resist their ministrations. She only prayed her attempted cures would not be painful and worsen her plight, as had happened so many times before.

Heikua stepped back onto the path and Lilith obediently followed. The sand gave way to rocky terrain making Lilith glad she'd worn her leather shoes. Still a little weak, she paused occasionally to catch her breath. As Heikua had warned, the sun was hot, especially as they broke from jungle foliage and climbed an upward trail cut in rough lava. The perspiration beaded on her forehead and she wished she'd worn something cooler than black bombazine.

"Not far," assured Heikua with a smile and assisting hand. "Here *marae,* holy temple."

Lilith felt nauseous from exertion and wanted to beg off trekking up Reva Ra's boulder-strewn slope until another day. A sound as of distant cannon fire rattled from the volcano's depths. Wind-blown smoke eddied and whirled, revealing glimpses of seething shafts of lava crawling down the mountainside toward the sea. Slowly the slope flattened and she stood before a pagan platform temple of tumbled stone. By brief estimate the platform measured about fifty by thirty yards. Here and there were stone seats, situated for ceremonial use. Behind an open-air altar built from hundreds of small black volcanic stones stood a large, squat-featured Tiki. The dark stain of blood left no doubt in Lilith's mind that the altar was used for human sacrifice.

A chill trickled down her spine and suddenly the atmosphere seemed oppressive. She wondered if the natives of Reva Ra still practiced this ritual and what qualified the victim. She did not relish being the most recent virgin added to the island population.

"Look," said Heikua directing her gaze beyond the sacrificial altar. Stepping forward, Lilith witnessed a view of the four directions that slowed her breath and stunned her with a heartfelt sense of wonder.

Just below and to the south lay the village and its calm lagoon; to the north emerged a rugged, rocky, wave-beaten coastline. To the west she saw waterfalls unfolding down verdant slopes, and bright rivers scoring lush rain forest.

"Moana-nui-a-rangi. The great ocean of heaven," said Heikua, with a wide sweep of her arm. She turned eastward and pointed to the emerald peaks of a neighboring low island. *"Tiaretapu,* sacred garden. In Bible book, name Etene. Adam and Eve live in *Tiaretapu.* Oro cast them out to sea. The serpent he become shark. He swim after canoe of Adam and Eve. He always hungry."

Lilith could not help smiling at Heikua's version of Genesis while her eyes explored the mysterious splendor of the sacred islet, a dazzling pearl on the coral reef.

"You promised to tell me why Tiaro has adopted me," reminded Lilith.

"Come, sit. I tell thee."

Lilith drew closer as Heikua knelt down before the altar. She picked up a small object from the offerings of shell, flowers, and carved totems at the base of the Tiki. She turned a serious face to Lilith and put into her hand a small object. On closer look, Lilith realized it was scrimshaw on shell, identical to her brooch which now rested beside it. But instead of a woman, the portrait was of a native warrior.

"He Tangii, great chief. He chief when sky bursters come long time 'go. Tangii father to Lily." Heikua picked up the other shell scrimshaw and held it in her palm. "Tangii begat Savai and Savai begat Tevake. Tevake father to Tiaro. When the *papalagi* sky burster leave, take Lily to England. She no return. Tangii wait. Before he die he tell Savai, one day she return. Savai wait long time she no return. He die. Tevake tell this story to Tiaro when he small boy. Three nights ago in dream Lily come to Tiaro. She tell Tiaro she lost on sea of the moon. Tiaro ask Rangahua to find Lily. Rangahua find thee."

Lilith took her eyes from the scrimshaw pieces and reluctantly met the earnest dark gaze of Heikua. "But Heikua, I am not Lily. I am Lilith Card—," she paused to correct herself. "I am Lady Lilith Dunraven. I was born in Devonshire, England."

"Thy soul is Lily. We thy people. Long time we hold thee in our hearts. Thee return."

The notion was beyond Lilith and difficult for her to accept. She realized as long as the natives believed this she was safe, but she had no wish to deceive them. "No, Heikua. I have never lived here before. I have come to the south seas in search of my husband, Lord Adam Dunraven."

"He lost, too?"

"No, he's here to research—" Heikua's facial expression told her she did not understand—"to see the fire walkers."

Heikua's dark brows knit together with questioning. "Fire walk?"

Lilith pointed to her feet and said, "*Ahi*—fire."

"*Aue!*" exclaimed Heikua. "*Ahitao!* We walk *ahi* on Reva Ra."

Lilith looked out to sea, not missing the irony. Here

she sat, exactly where Dunraven should be, but was not. Well, she would make the best of it. She would research the local herbs and, if the event rose, she would watch this native ritual of fire walking. When a sailing ship passed, she would return to Tahiti with her findings.

"Now thee daughter of Tiaro," smiled Heikua.

Lilith was not very ecstatic about it, but she had no choice in the matter.

"Come, we climb higher to find sacred fire plant." She returned both the scrimshaw pieces to the altar, taking care to lay them side by side. She moved awkwardly to her feet.

"Is it far?" Lilith looked upward to the acid-eaten cliffs and the vast clouds of pulverized ash screening the volcanic peak. She was enthused to see a plant which could survive in such hostile conditions, but she still felt weak. It was not a good day for her to be climbing mountains in search of rare specimens.

"It close. It grow by the lava river which come from the mouth of Reva Ra."

"Does it grow all the time?"

"It always grow, but never same place," said Heikua. "If thee tired I go alone."

"No, I'd like to see it. Just go slow."

Heikua took her hand and began the climb. After a few minutes the path, which skirted a glowing stream of lava, narrowed and Heikua released her hand and moved in front.

"I see!" she declared suddenly. With surprising agility, the barefoot Heikua moved across the sharp rocks and bent down on one knee.

Precariously, Lilith followed, glad again she'd worn her leather shoes. She knelt beside Heikua and peered down into a sheltered crevice.

The sacred plant was a funny-looking weed, spindly stemmed with red spidery branches. She was amazed it could grow so near the hot, acrid environment of the volcano.

Heikua snapped it at the base, taking the whole plant in hand. "This enough. I make paste. Thee must rub on thy skin for many day. Now we go swim. Sea, sun, and sacred plant make thee whole," she smiled.

Lilith turned her gaze down to the blue lagoon and white sand shoreline below. Just now, a cool bath in the sea seemed quite appealing in comparison to the nearly unbearable temperatures of the volcanic slopes.

"I do not know how to swim," she confessed as they started back.

"Does thee fear water?"

"No."

"This good. Jesus John, he fear water. That why he drown in lagoon. Come, I teach thee. Little time thee swim better than *ma'o*, the shark."

"Well, I hope I can swim at least faster," declared Lilith.

Heikua laughed softly and entwined her thick arm with Lilith's own.

Chapter

4

In the dazzling light of sunrise, before the heat of the day drove everyone into the shade of the inner-island forests, Lilith followed a narrow sandspit that reached out into the sea to her favorite early-morning haunt, Shark Rock. The tepid water lapped against her ankles, then fell away. At low tide it was a perfect time to stroll out to the rocky point. From a distance she would appear to be walking on the vast blue sea. She climbed around pinnacles of stone rounded down by the relentless wash of waves. In her hand she held a dolphin figure, carved from the gray wood of the *te itai* tree.

She slipped off her *pareo* and scooted down the rock face to immerse herself in deeper water. Like a child in the enchanted world of play, she plunged and skimmered the miniature dolphin through the warm water.

"If you call, the Rangahua will come," Heikua had

told her. And most mornings it was so, if she was patient enough.

Gazing over the shimmering scaled sea she smiled to herself. She had found paradise. She set the dolphin behind her on a rocky shelf. Her fingertips roved over the smooth, sunbrowned skin of her waist, then up to her dark honey shoulders—and lastly to her face.

The scars had disappeared. Heikua's cures had worked magic—unbelievable magic! It had taken only one passing of the moon before Lilith began to discover a change. She'd spent many days staring into the glassy reflection pools of the inner island to be sure.

She flung back her head, and with long black hair floating in the water, she began chanting the call to Rangahua.

Necklaces of shell clicked as she moved. The Lilith Cardew of a few months before no longer existed. She was called Lily, the adopted daughter of Chief Tiaro. Now, she chose to live as a native woman of Reva Ra. Corset and camisole had given way to *pareo* and bared breasts. She never dreamed she would do such a thing, but as her lifelong scars began to disappear through the healing herbs of Heikua, her inhibitions left.

At first she stripped off her clothing only in the seclusion of the inner-island pools where she could be sure no one would see her. Then, as the slow, sultry island days passed, she became more bold going down to the lagoon to practice swimming. And there on the beach she sunned herself until her skin became a golden, nut brown as flawless and smooth as Bordeaux satin.

What would her friends and acquaintances in England say if it was rumored she was running about nude on a tropical island like Eve before the fall? Well, she was certain of what Vicar Heathcote Holmes would say. She could just see him pinching his narrow lips tight and thumping the pulpit. "Nakedness is against God!" he would declare. An impish smile touched Lilith's lips. Vicar Heathcote Holmes would never know.

Still, she felt uncomfortable when the dark gaze of a virile island warrior lingered too long in her direction. But the islanders believed her to be the long, lost daughter of the ancient Chief Tangii and none would approach her without first speaking to Tiaro. To the rare stranger, she would seem no different from other women on the island, except for her clear English.

The rising sun, a golden flare stretching on the horizon, touched the lava spires of Reva Ra's mountains and steaming tropical foliage. Lilith flicked her fingers noiselessly under the water as Heikua had instructed. Nearby, she saw the dark dorsal fin of Rangahua slice through the sea. In a flowing, sweet voice, Lilith sang to the Rangahua. Her prayers had been answered. Tiaro and the villagers of Reva Ra had not boiled her in a pot as she had feared, but assuredly saved her life. In truth, she'd been given new life.

Her black eyes sparkled with anticipation. The dark shape glided closer. Lilith swam to meet it. She dipped her face under the water and burbled, *"Ia ora na!"* The male dolphin responded by surfacing and releasing a gust of air from its blowhole near Lilith's face.

She giggled and reached to stroke the smooth gray skin, soft as a babe's. Rangahua nudged her face with its upper lip. She delighted in this playful game. She hooked her arm over its dorsal fin and clung to its back as it carried her out into the lagoon. The

Rangahua shot through the water and Lilith felt light, free, and alive, more alive than the total of all her days as the English mouse, Lilith Cardew. She had no wish to see England or Englishmen again—well perhaps just one Englishman, the "Daring" Dunraven. Why did she love a man who did not love her? She had asked Heikua who was wise in matters of the heart.

"A man can no love thee when he no here," Heikua concluded practically. "Thee want him come? Call him. He come from sea like Rangahua. Thee need lots magic. He civilized man, no so easy hear heart call."

Civilized—yes, that was the problem—being civilized. But she was no longer civilized. The jet buttons of her black bombazine were now a necklace around Heikua's neck and the black bombazine, a *tapa* about Tiaro's hips. Her corset had become a swinging basket for fruit and her camisole a sieve for *peepa* juice. She now understood Dunraven's notorious reputation for "going native" and his own propensity for uncivilized women. It became an issue of liberation. In Reva Ra, she was liberated from the rigid boundaries of civilized society. Even though the islanders had their own taboos as strict as any Puritan code, here she was at last herself. No veil, no black bombazine, no Vicar Heathcote Holmes.

Yes, she'd listened to Heikua. Each night, as the silver moon rose over Pearl Lagoon and restlessness tugged at her heart, she went down to the beach and called Dunraven. With the tide lapping at her feet, she sang the chant to reunite estranged lovers which Heikua had patiently taught her.

Now, side by side, enmeshed, she and the dolphin swam past the reef. She clutched Rangahua with the reassurance that this wild creature was not wild, just as she had learned that the primitive natives of Reva

Ra were not so primitive. Overlapping somewhere in antiquity were man and beast. Unfortunately, she decided, "civilized" man chose to ignore this and, in doing so, acted more the beast.

A stream of spray and bubbles spouted from Rangahua's blowhole, a signal for more play. Lilith let loose its fin and paddled on the water as it circled her, then it darted beneath the surface. The moment passed, then she felt the intimate touch as the dolphin thrust its smiling bottle nose between her parted legs and lifted her out of the water. She shot forward into the air like a flying fish. Her arms spread like an angel of the sea.

In his adventurous life, Adam Dunraven had done, seen, and heard many things, but this was the first time he'd ever seen what he was seeing.

"What the devil?" he muttered. He adjusted the spyglass.

Captain Robert Lachlan stepped to the gunwale of the *Aberdeen*.

"Do you see the village?"

"More than that. I see someone out there riding on a dolphin's back."

"I told ye the island was bedeviled," laughed the captain, taking the spyglass in hand. "Reva Ra is like no other island. The devils still eat missionaries. There's a runnin' curse on any who anchor in these waters. Strange things happen—madness, plagues, evils beyond yer imaginin'. Legend tells that aboot a hundred years ago, explorers kidnapped a chief's daughter and took her back to England where she died in miserable conditions. I dunna want my men on the shore. The reef is beyond crossin' even in a light canoe. The natives call it the Reef of Spirits—one that eats canoes."

"Then how am I to land myself?" asked Dunraven.

The captain grinned. "Yer the Darin' Dunraven. Swim. Maybe the sea beastie will give ye a ride if ye flounder."

Dunraven squinted back to the sea and assessed the distance to the island. He calculated he could make it, barring a hungry shark or two. He winged his arms to limberness and looked back to Lachlan.

"And when are you likely to pass back through?"

"I dunna know. Six months, a year. These waters are off the main sea-lanes. If yer no in a cannibal stewpot by then, ask the natives to take ye to Tahaa. They're a canny lot aboot the sea. Now be off. I'll have no blitherin' savage curses on me ship and crew."

Dunraven stripped off his shirt and pants and secured them in his duck-cloth bag of belongings. He'd been traveling from island to island for months, trying to find the legendary fire walkers. He'd not be put off by a few tales. His pack in one hand, he climbed on the gunwale and prepared to jump the twenty feet into the warm tropical waters.

"Until we meet again," he touched his forehead, gallantly.

"I think yer a fool," declared Lachlan. "But luck go with ye."

Dunraven plunged feet first into the sea at the same moment the captain gave orders to full sail.

Though Dunraven was a strong swimmer, he'd not expected to be dumped miles from the island in the middle of the sea. His gray eyes scanned the sea. He saw only the distant fin of the dolphin and its dark-headed swimming companion. He took comfort in native knowledge that there were no sharks where there were dolphins. He attached a towline to his duck-cloth pack and began rhythmic strokes. As he swam, he mused over the novelty of a sea creature like a dolphin allowing a human to swim beside it. He'd once heard a tale about a dolphin rescuing a drowning sailor. Until now, he'd believed it only to be a tale.

After a time, he approached the fringe of reef. Lashed by bursting swells, the reef could be as unassailable to a swimmer as a ship. Had it been high tide, his crossing would be less precarious. But he was tiring and he could not wait for high tide to give him the advantage against the razor-edged coral. A few strokes and he hovered at the break of the surf. A sixth sense launched him forward at full speed. Beneath the swirling backwash of sea his feet touched the grating reef. He tried to hold his balance but the slap of a wave tumbled him upside-down. Twice he somersaulted, smashing against the domed coral daggers. He hauled himself, cut and bleeding, onto the dry reef where he caught his breath and surveyed his wounds.

He peered across the lagoon and saw that his arrival had been marked by the natives. Bedecked warriors lined the beach. He had no choice but to swim on. Over his lifetime, he'd ventured into worse circumstances without hesitation. He'd greeted a hundred chieftains in a hundred lands and had discovered people were much the same wherever he'd traveled. Myths, traditions, and gods were universal.

He adjusted the tow rope on his pack and dove into the calm waters of the lagoon. At a cautious distance, the dolphin and its companion swam parallel to him. Their wariness was evident.

He kept a watchful eye on shore, but his main

attention was held on the sea-borne pair now closing in on him.

He lost view of them in his peripheral vision. Then, explosively, they reappeared in the water within an arm's reach beside him. He felt the whip of a tail fin graze his leg. Abreast, a sleek snout and a dark-headed female form surfaced.

Awe washed through Dunraven.

The dazzling black eyes of the woman peered wonderingly over the shiny back of the dolphin. Bracing a brown graceful arm over its dorsal fin she floated like a sea nymph in a wreath of glistening obsidian hair.

He was stunned. It was a moment before he found his voice. *"Ia ora na!"* he finally said, though an inward voice declared, *Oh God! She is a vision!*

He fell into the depths of her eyes feeling as though he'd met someone raised from the dead. Overwhelming emotion gripped his solar plexus—he knew this woman. But where and how? Some unremembered soul connection was there in her eyes, her features, her essence.

Her full lips softened slightly with surprise and innocent allure, but she did not return his greeting. It was a rarity when he felt the need to make a good impression on a woman. Of course, there had been Lilith Cardew back in England. And why would Lilith Cardew come to his mind? He'd not thought of her in months. Despite leaving England, their meeting had lingered in the corners of his mind. Her words, her manner, her mystery had left him intrigued and unsettled. He had found himself reliving that afternoon in the library over and over. Though he was adept at keeping women at a courteous distance,

Lilith Cardew had been able to circumvent those defenses—like this woman before him now.

Breaking the spell, the dolphin's large mouth, lined with rows of diamond-point teeth, yawned open, made a rachetting noise, pushed ahead, and carried the woman off.

Dunraven's hands moved just enough for him to maintain himself in the water. His breath was even, but his heart pounded with the verity of a man awakened to life. He was not a toucher by habit, but he wanted to touch her. He was celibate, but in that split-second connection of eyes—and yes, soul—he no longer wanted to be.

Fastening her *pareo* around her, Lilith sprinted up the beach shouting with joyous disbelief, "He is here! He has come!"

She must find Heikua. Life could be gloriously magical. Her heart was doing cartwheels, as she excitedly contemplated announcing her true identity to Adam Dunraven.

I am your wife, Lilith Cardew, she would say.

Then, after her revelation he would take her into his arms and—

She stopped dead in her tracks.

No! He'd not believe her.

She'd no veil, no personal papers. Sweet heaven! The man had never seen her face. Of course, there would be hours of skeptical interrogation as she answered his questions.

And what if he did believe her?

Before, the necessity of true identity had not entered. As Lilith Cardew, she'd planned to meet up with him and offer her services not as wife, but efficient secretary. Dunraven was her legal protector and guardian; he could not refuse. But the worst might happen. He could ship her back to England posthaste.

The sea breeze splayed her hair as apprehension churned within her. Her hands clutched her breasts. Leave Reva Ra? Return to England? Become again the anonymous woman behind the anonymous veil? Could she? Never!

She looked toward the lagoon. The golden head of Dunraven moved through the water. Tiaro and his warriors lined the shore in a fierce show ready to confront this rare stranger. Would they kill Dunraven?

Lilith stood paralyzed.

Stark naked, Dunraven stepped out of the lagoon with the pack slung over his shoulder. He strode confidently toward Tiaro like a prince come home.

She watched as Dunraven sank to the sand, crossed his legs and made his two hands into a single fist. He spoke in a low flow of native tongue which Lilith could not hear. She had resided on the island long enough to know his traditional attitude placed him at the mercy of Tiaro. There was no abasement in the act, especially with a man like Dunraven. He might bow low but his body was arrogant and at ease. He was a man who could walk into a village of savages or the queen's court with arresting dignity.

Tiaro returned a brief introduction after which Dunraven took the opening to unfasten his pack and present a gift. When he took from his pack a dozen or so Tahitian red parrot feathers and held them in full view, a murmur of pleased voices rippled the air. Tiaro especially smiled. Lilith knew there could be no better gift to the chieftain than the delicate feathered symbol of the god Oro. The feathers were used in decorating tapa cloth and shell masks. A few fixed together with a twisted string made from coconut husk were similar in sacredness to a Christian cross. Such a gift would undoubtedly win Dunraven Tiaro's favor.

Tiaro urged him to his feet. Dunraven stood tall, sun golden and as sleek muscled as any of Tiaro's warriors. Much to Lilith's relief, Tiaro spoke a welcome. Dunraven was then presented a tapa which he immediately wrapped about his bare hips.

Tiaro gave a signal and the warriors encircled him. She lost sight of him as the group of men moved up the beach to the communal house.

Lilith felt sick and elated at the same time. She must go somewhere and think. What should she do? She turned up the path and ran straight into Heikua.

"Where thee go? Come see the *papalagi* who swim from nowhere."

Lilith shook her head and stepped to move on.

Heikua touched her arm. "What wrong?"

Of course, she must tell Heikua. "He my *papalagi*," she emphasized.

"Aue!" exclaimed Heikua. "I very happy. Thee call him. He come. Thee go to him."

"I can't!" Tears spilled down Lilith's cheeks. So long she'd imagined him coming and now he was here. The dream became just that, a foolish dream. When she'd faced him in the lagoon it had been almost magical. But, she sadly remembered their last discussion in the library at Eden Court—his avowal to celibacy, his maddening remoteness and self-control.

"Aue." Heikua's dark eyes were swimming with concern. "What wrong?"

"He does not know me."

"His heart know thee."

"No, Heikua."

"Tonight, when time to sleep, Tiaro will take thee to him. He know thee."

"No, Heikua!" she said adamantly. Heikua drew back. Lilith pressed her hands to her temples and said apologetically, "I'm sorry. There is much you don't understand. For Tiaro to take me to him would be a humiliation. Dunraven would—would send me away."

"Send thee away? *Aue. Aue,*" said Heikua shaking her head, slightly puzzled.

How could she tell Heikua that Dunraven was celibate? There was not a word in her language for such an unnatural state. Then she remembered Heikua's story about Jesus John. "Heikua, he does not choose to be a man."

"*Aue,*" she breathed, her brows lifting with comprehension. "This so?" Her lips curved thoughtfully. "Come, we go to the counsel house. I will see this one."

"You go alone. I do not want to see him."

Heikua leaned over and wrapped Lilith in her great warmth. "My Lily be happy. I Tahua of the heart."

Feeling comforted, Lilith returned Heikua's affection. "You cannot heal everything, Heikua. I don't expect it. I have made this muddle myself."

"We stay back. He no see thee. Come." Heikua took her hand determinedly into her own.

With great reluctance Lilith followed her down the crushed cowrie-shell path to the south entrance of the communal house. Inside, Heikua crept behind a pillar in the outer woman's circle and the pair sat down on the matting.

Lilith's eyes quickly settled on Dunraven's sun-freckled, broad shoulders. He faced away from her, sitting cross-legged before Tiaro. Around him, women were preparing a *kava* ceremony of welcome. The woman, Sua, spread a new mat on the floor and set out hand-carved wooden bowls. Her eyelids were half lowered in deference, but occasionally she gazed sidelong at Dunraven in a coquettish manner.

Lilith clamped tight her lips as a pang of jealousy niggled within her heartsick breast. Sua was a beauty and notably experienced in what the islanders perceived as the art of love. From early puberty, the secrets of love were explored and refined. By the time a young woman had reached marriageable age, she'd had a number of lovers. What if Dunraven no longer avowed celibacy and succumbed to Sua's charms? For Lilith, it became an arduous task just to remain sitting and watching. She wanted to leap to her feet and step forward to declare Dunraven to be her husband. But here she had no claim on him. If he chose Sua, she would please him—more than Lilith could do. His words echoed in her memory. *I have never been tempted to make love to a "civilized" woman, particularly an Englishwoman.*

Lilith studied the damp hair now bound at the nape of his neck. He was too, too arrogant. If he'd never bedded a civilized woman, how indeed could he pass such a judgment? That was a civilized man for you! Her frustration smoldered into anger at Adam Dunraven. She'd traveled halfway around the world on his account, suffered deprivation and near death, and all for what? A civilized, uncivilized man! And to think moments before she'd been weeping on his account. She was furious with herself for falling into such a foolish trap.

The *kava* maker, who had been vigorously working the pulp of the pepper plant with his knife, announced

80

it was ready to squeeze into the drinking cups. He clapped his hands sharply three times.

Tiaro promptly ordered, "Pour it out."

Sua, the cup bearer, gracefully approached. On the tips of her toes, she lowered herself with knees bent, both hands clasping the cup, and offered it to Dunraven.

He drank to the accompaniment of chanting and hand clapping. Sua took the cup to Tiaro. He drained it and tossed it spinning like a top onto the mat, declaring in a deep guttural tone, "It is dry!"

In a sentence, Tiaro invited Dunraven to speak. Leaning forward, Lilith strained her ears to follow each word.

"I have come a long way," came Dunraven's familiar voice. He spoke boldly and fluently in the native tongue.

You are not the only one, ruminated Lilith.

"In my own land I am a Tahua," he stated without modesty. Tiaro watched him steadily. "I am a keeper of sacred ritual." Here he touched the tattoo upon his cheek. Tiaro nodded with understanding, his heavy eyelids half-closed. "I journey over the sea seeking those brothers who have knowledge of the fire walk." He opened his pack and withdrew a compact leather-bound volume.

The book looked familiar to Lilith. Quickly she recognized the volume to be none other than her own *An Explorer's Handbook Out.* Her anger and irritation with Dunraven dissipated. He had credited her work enough to carry it thousands of miles around the world. The irony of it struck Lilith. Unexpectedly, she hiccuped—not a dainty hiccup that could be smothered by a lace handkerchief, but a loud croak of a hiccup.

Many heads turned to her unwitting disturbance of the solemn gathering, among them Dunraven's. She clamped her hand over her mouth and held her breath mightily.

Curious, his gray eyes held hard on her own. A shock flashed through her and set her trembling. Her chest jumping like a cricket, she ducked her head behind the pillar. Some part of her feared he would recognize her. He had, but not as Lilith Cardew or even Lyman Brazen. He recognized her from their meeting in the lagoon.

Lilith's legs tensed, ready to run from the communal house. Heikua held her elbow firmly and would not allow it.

At her ear, Lilith felt Heikua's breath and then the whisper of her voice. "This one see thee. This one know how to be a man. His eyes say so when he look at thee."

Lilith was not so confident as Heikua.

It was Tiaro who broke the spell by asking, "Does the Tahua come this far to gaze at the beauty of a woman, or does he wish to speak to me?" Tiaro's tone and meaning were not lost on Dunraven.

Recovering, Dunraven turned back and cleared his throat. "I wish to record the fire-walk ceremony in a book like this one. The book will be placed in a sacred temple of wisdom in my homeland, England."

"What power will you exchange for the knowledge of the sacred fire walk?" asked Tiaro.

Dunraven's features shifted with confidence. He picked up two ironwood sticks lying beside a hollowed-out drum. "The power of the drum."

The drum was Tiaro's own. Tiaro was the high Tahua, or shaman of the island. From her anthropological studies, Lilith knew that you didn't find a shaman without finding a drum. In that instant, she realized Dunraven, too, was a shaman. Late nights at Eden Court, his drum had sounded through the hallways. Born in civilized society, he was a shaman without a clan.

She watched. Without permission, Dunraven could not play Tiaro's drum. The two men assessed one another. Dunraven could offend Tiaro to such a degree that he could have his warriors kill him. Of course, Dunraven would have surmised this. Hopefully, he had read the section in *An Explorer's Handbook Out* that dealt with the consequences of offending one's host.

Tiaro's hands clapped together and another drum was brought and placed before Dunraven. Lilith's heart fell with relief, but the moment Dunraven struck rhythm, her senses entrained with the beat. Hearing these same rhythms she'd fallen asleep to those few nights at Eden Court, Lilith seemed to awaken. The barking click-click of ironwood sticks filled her ears and played her own pulse. She looked around and saw others connecting to these new rhythms. The women began clapping and the men stamping.

Time passed. The sun had risen mid sky. The knotted muscles of Dunraven's broad shoulders glossed with sweat and the veins on his forehead welted from the force of his concentration. He played wildly, with close-eyed entrancement, gifting the islanders with sacred drum voices from across the sea.

Abruptly, his hands halted and the spell of the drumming was broken.

Finally, Tiaro announced, "The power of the drum is enough." Admiration radiated from his black eyes and a smile spread his full lips.

The fare for a feast began appearing. Sua served popoi, a freshly baked breadfruit paste slightly fermented. With two fingers, Dunraven expertly consumed the whole bowl. This show of a good appetite pleased Tiaro. Soon the pair were elbow deep in other gastronomic delights such as mashed bananas, coconut puddings, and roasted fish. Traditionally, women were not allowed to eat with the men. So while the men ate, the women sang and danced by way of entertainment. Lilith stayed behind her pillar, but kept a discreet eye on Dunraven. Thankfully, he did not look her way again. His whole attention was focused on eating. How he ate!

The day wore into afternoon and still he sat before Tiaro matching him mouthful for mouthful. Lilith had witnessed this form of competition once before during a celebration. The voracious appetites of the islanders left no doubt that food was for eating. The abundance of the sea and land was a gift of the gods and the more one ate, the more gratitude was shown to the gods.

Occasionally, Dunraven would come to his feet, run in place and breathe deeply. This brought encouraging jests from Tiaro and his warriors and giggles from the women. As for Tiaro, he sat solidly. He rubbed his ample belly and unfastened his tapa for comfort.

In the end, it was Tiaro who flashed a great white-toothed grin and fell backward onto the mat in defeat.

Tiaro placed his hands on his own chest and uttered, *"Taio."*

Cheers went up all around.

"Aue! Aue!" murmured Heikua at Lilith's side. She urged Lilith to her feet. With her hand on Lilith's arm, Heikua led her out of the communal house.

"What has happened?" gasped Lilith.

"Bad for thee. Good for thy Tahua Tane. Tiaro make him his *taio.*"

"That is good," said Lilith, relieved for Dunraven's sake.

"For thee, bad. A *taio* like a son. Now he Tiaro's son. Now, he thy brother."

"Yes," followed Lilith.

"Thee and he, no make love. Big taboo for brother and sister!"

"But, he's my husband!"

"In England, maybe. Here, he thy brother."

"My brother! I don't want a brother," sighed Lilith.

"Thee have brother now." Heikua placed a wide-brimmed woven hat on top of her head. Sunlight filtered through the loose weave of pandanus, freckling her brown face. "Come. We go to sacred temple. I talk with gods."

Lilith stole one last parting glimpse of Dunraven. The effects of drumming, gluttony, and the heat of the afternoon left him sprawled spread-eagle on the mat beside Tiaro. She picked up a palm-leaf fan and proceeded to follow Heikua up the volcanic slope to the sacred *marae.* As always, Heikua would consult the gods of her people first. If this failed to resolve her quandary, she would then return to Jesus John's hut and consult the Bible book. In an odd ritual of divination, she would open the Bible and with her eyes closed stab the page with her finger. Whatever verse her finger settled upon was read aloud as an absolute oracle from on high.

"Could we not wait until sunset?" Lilith asked, the perspiration glazing her body. Though the soles of her feet were now callused from months going barefoot, the lava rock felt uncomfortably warm.

Heikua ignored her question and walked on. Since

the excursion was on her behalf, Lilith dragged forward like a reluctant postulant.

A ring of clouds napped on volcanic peaks. Higher up, a cooling inland breeze stirred the stagnant air. Fruitlessly, Lilith's eyes searched the sky for the reprieve of an afternoon rainsquall. The hairs on her neck prickled as she approached the sacred *marae*. Death hung in the atmosphere and draped the ancient stones stained dark from blood. Off to one side, facing away from the fierce-eyed Tiki, she chose a flat stone to settle upon. She did not like this place.

Heikua arranged an offering of white hibiscus flowers and sat cross-legged before the Tiki. She began softly chanting. From below, the roar of surf resonated to her voice. Lilith lifted her hair off her neck and fanned herself as she took a deep breath of thick island air. Like a queen, she sat atop a pinnacle of earthly paradise, her eyes drinking in the immense forests, tall and tangled, sometimes ablaze with flowering trees and dazzling silver waterfalls.

She glanced back at Heikua who appeared to be in a deep meditation. After a while, Heikua stirred. She opened her eyes and shifted position.

"I know what we must do. Thee listen."

Lilith set down the pandanus fan and leaned toward Heikua.

"Long time thy Tahua have no woman. This good."

"It is?"

"What is forbidden is more wanted. In Bible book, King David want Bathsheba because she another man's wife. Adam and Eve eat fruit of the tree because it taboo—forbidden by God. Thee forbidden fruit to the Tahua Tane. He want thee more."

"I'm not so sure, Heikua."

A mischievous smile touched Heikua's lips. "It *thy* turn to beguile the serpent."

"You do not know this man, Heikua. You saw him today. He is not readily beaten and quite beyond temptation. Besides, won't something happen if we break the taboo between brother and sister?"

"*Aue.* Thy Tahua will have his heart cut out on *marae* altar."

"*Aue!*" exclaimed Lilith. "This cannot happen!"

"This no happen," she assured in her soft liquid voice.

"But—" Again, Lilith was not assured. Her lips curled with distaste and she avoided looking at the blood-stained altar nearby.

Heikua cut her off. "Thee go to Tiaretapu." Heikua pointed beyond to the sacred island rising like a stunning emerald from the sea. "Thee stay on Tiaretapu until feast of the full moon. I think on way to end taboo."

Chapter

5

In the morning quiet, Dunraven peered through his spyglass at a dark fin circling in the lagoon. As was his custom, he'd risen early to run on the beach. The dolphin's appearance caught his attention. He raised the glass across the lagoon to the small island the natives called Tiaretapu, the forbidden garden. He scanned the line of white sand beach. A dozen or so bush birds and a blue feathered parrot winged up from a stand of casuarina trees. A woman stepped out from beneath the foliage of ferns and pandanus.

He adjusted his spyglass to sharpness.

He recognized her to be the illusive sea nymph. Since that first day of his arrival, he'd not seen her.

She tossed her head from side to side and her hip-length black hair caught the light of the rising sun.

He studied her lithe suppleness as she strolled down to the water's edge. She raised her graceful brown arms and clapped. The sound carried across the shared lagoon. The dolphin leaped from the water with trumpeting squeals in answer.

Dunraven was profoundly mesmerized.

Unfastening her *pareo,* she allowed it to drop around her feet. She bounded into the water and swam toward the dolphin.

He released a tense breath between his teeth, lowered the glass, and rested his elbows more comfortably on his knees. He was titillated and honest enough with himself to admit his need to observe her was more than from curiosity. He was acutely conscious of her femininity. Watching her grace and beauty revived within him feelings he'd adamantly wished to suppress.

From living the monastic life, he'd gleaned invaluable insight into himself and the world around him. During the past years, he'd learned control over the challenge of his desires, but he'd not transcended so far as to ignore them. The roaming and promiscuity of his earlier years had left him disconnected with himself and the cosmos. When he'd entered the monastery in Lhasa, his self-discipline had been hard won. He was a born hellion, and no one could dominate him in his youth—not the cleric, not the schoolmaster, not even his father. At sea, while serving as mast mate, he'd rebelled against the authority of the captain, and was shackled in irons for a time.

In the solitude of Lhasa, he'd learned to discipline himself from within. In the beginning, there had been no rules for him. His mentor was wise enough and knew human nature well enough that he gave him no boundaries in those early days. He presented him with a *damaru,* a hand-held drum. He said, "Simply tune yourself to the rhythm of life." Through drumming and meditation, he had eventually created balance in his life.

It was not the first time since his return from the monastery that he wrestled with his avowal of celibacy. His mind traveled to his wifely mystery, Lilith Cardew, who for all her propriety had questioned his very masculinity. She must be a damned Bluestocking to challenge him so. The remembrance caused him to laugh aloud. But he realized the last laugh was upon himself as he recalled again his feelings of arousal in her presence. Lately, that black-veiled shadow had been appearing in his dreams. He wondered why? He knew a man on a spiritual journey should never ignore the message of his dreams.

As the rising sun gilded and shimmered the water of the blue lagoon, he savored the distant dance of the woman and dolphin. In graceful synchronicity the pair surfaced and dove, spiraled, and circled through the sea like lovers. Like the dolphin, he wanted to swim in the sea with the woman. Even more—he wanted to make love to this woman in the sea. This intense awareness caused him to shift forward. He was not so shorn of desire as he avowed.

Sitting on his haunches in the coral sand, he felt the rising sun touch his skin with morning fire and ignite the primal lust he'd so long controlled. Like kindling in summer dryness, his soul felt parched from the absence of shared intimacy in his life.

Was there no way to be immune? He came to his feet thinking he would go inland to bathe, down to the frog pools. Tiaro said that frog sang the song that called the rain to earth. When ponds are dry, the frog calls upon the clouds to cleanse and replenish the earth with water. Like frog, he felt dry and in need of replenishment. Seeing this woman was like seeing water at the end of a long drought. He wanted to taste her in his mouth and swallow her essence—

Rising to his feet, he strode off. He was stupid to remain there, nourishing it.

"Ia ora na."

Dunraven looked up to see Tiaro approaching.

"Does the Tahua Tane wish to go pearl diving?"

He had seen the rare pearls found in these waters and hoped to try his luck. Dunraven did not hesitate. "I will go," he said easily in native dialect.

Tiaro smiled broadly and slapped Dunraven on his shoulder. "We will go in my *va'a.*"

Dunraven followed him down the beach to a ten-foot canoe, which seemed nothing more than a hollowed-out log. Pearl diving required little more, but when the natives wished to fish for bonito or albacore, they went out in the deep-water *pahi* canoes.

Pushing out the *va'a,* he leaped in after Tiaro. While Dunraven paddled, Tiaro directed him parallel to the shoreline in the opposite direction from Tiaretapu and the swimming woman. Sunlight threw sparkling pinpoints and sheets of flashing silver on the sea all around. Tiaro's experienced eye guided the *va'a* near the band of high reef. Dunraven continued paddling. Then, upon Tiaro's order, Dunraven ceased paddling and the boat came to a rocking halt.

"I dive first. You watch," announced Tiaro. He sprang into the water, holding his spear attached loosely to his wrist with a piece of twined *copra* and a small woven basket.

Closely, Dunraven watched the place where he dove in. The water was crystalline clear and he could see the shadow of Tiaro deep below the surface. Seconds became long minutes and he wondered at the ability of Tiaro to control his breath for so long. Explosively, he splashed to the surface and tipped the basket of oyster shells into the *va'a*, then dove again.

It was obviously not an easy task. Dunraven kept his eyes on the water. The afternoon wore on until the floor of the *va'a* filled with oysters.

At last, Dunraven spoke to him. "I will dive now."

Effortlessly, pulling himself over the side with powerful arms, Tiaro climbed back inside the *va'a* while Dunraven steadied it.

"Good place to dive. You will find many oysters straight down," said Tiaro, unfastening the basket and spear and giving them to Dunraven. Tiaro stayed in the boat while Dunraven took to the water, plunging in with a splash of enthusiasm.

Long minutes later, he broke the surface and shook his head, scattering sparkling droplets all around in a glistening spray. He grinned triumphantly.

He held up the largest oyster yet to be found.

"Tahua Tane find old-man oyster," laughed Tiaro, taking it from his hand and tossing it on the pile. A half-dozen times more Dunraven dove, but came up with nothing.

Tiaro motioned him back inside the *va'a*. "We will open the oysters and find our pearls."

Somewhat winded, Dunraven climbed back into the *va'a*.

"We open this one last," decided Tiaro putting the old-man oyster aside. Using his single-pronged spear, he opened an oyster and handed it to Dunraven to probe for the small treasure. He felt a little disappointed because halfway through the pile, he'd found only three small pearls.

While the two men worked, the conversation meandered from diving techniques to fishing with a spear. Then during a lull, Dunraven asked Tiaro, "Tell me of this woman who swims with the Rangahua?" Tiaro gazed past Dunraven, his face empty of expression. He said nothing nor did his eyes register that he had heard.

Again Dunraven repeated his question and still Tiaro did not respond. Very puzzled, Dunraven was sure Tiaro had heard him. Changing the subject he asked, "Are these oysters edible?"

"Very good. If you are hungry, eat now." Tiaro invited readily.

Dunraven knew Tiaro had heard him before. He suspected that for some reason Tiaro did not wish to speak of the woman who swam with the Rangahua. Apparently on Reva Ra, if one wished to avoid a subject, it was politic not to speak or hear.

Dunraven pulled the moist meat from the shell and slipped it into his mouth. He was fond of oysters complimented by a pint of ale. Here he must settle for *peepa* juice.

While he ate, he watched Tiaro, wondering why he would not speak of the woman. Why had she not been in the village since that first day? He knew women lived apart during their menses, but he was sure this woman lived alone on Tiaretapu.

His curiosity overriding, he knew he held the advantage of being ignorant of custom. So without diplomacy, he pressed the issue.

He lifted his arm in a broad sweep toward Tiaretapu. "Tiaro, who is the woman who lives on the small island?"

Tiaro's full dark lips pushed out in a scowl and his eyes glimmered with disapproval. He said nothing.

Dunraven knew he must finish what he had begun, no matter how angry Tiaro became. "I am curious about the woman who swims each morning with the

Rangahua. If you do not wish to speak of her, I will honor your wish, though I have many questions about the island and the woman."

Displeasure continued to darken Tiaro's face. After a moment he said, "I will speak. You will listen. The island is taboo for the Tahua Tane. It is a sacred island of the gods from beforetime. The woman—" his eyes pinioned Dunraven—" the woman is my daughter. Because you are my son, she is taboo to you. We speak no more of this." He clamped shut his lips as tight as the unopened oysters at his feet.

Dunraven lowered his eyes knowing he would receive no more information from Tiaro. For now he would bide his time and ask the more talkative Heikua his questions.

Tiaro tossed him the large oyster. "Now Tahua Tane open the old-man oyster."

Dunraven braced it between his knees. He slipped the spear point between the lips of the oyster and twisted it slightly. After a moment of prying, the oyster opened. Grinning with anticipation, Dunraven thrust his fingers inside and probed the slick pulp. There was something—something larger than a pea, more like a—

"Good Lord!" shouted Dunraven. He held it up to the light. "It's black! I've found myself a black pearl!" It was nearly the size of a gooseberry, not perfectly round, but jet black. He handed it to Tiaro, who promptly put it in his mouth to polish it with his saliva.

Spitting it out into the palm of his hand, Tiaro said, *"Aue! Aue!* You are a proper island boy when you find a black pearl. We will make *kava* and celebrate."

After the celebration that evening, as the tide turned and the tiny brown-speckled crabs began their exodus down the beach, Dunraven climbed to Shark Rock to contemplate the sunset and watch the torches of the youths night fishing out on the reef. He skirted around the pinnacle to a chair-shaped dip in the rock. He had eaten and drank too much. He sluggishly climbed to the shelf of rock.

At the beginning of the feast, Tiaro had given him a small feathered pouch to keep the pearl in. On a length of finely twisted *copra* it hung around his neck. He fingered the feathered pouch with the prized pearl and thought of the woman. His eyes traveled across the water to the mountains of Tiaretapu purpling in the evening twilight. He never anticipated that a woman he had never conversed with could hold so much interest for him. Oddly, she held more attraction for him than his research on the fire walk. Some abstract sense told him there was more to the mysterious woman and the exotic isle of Tiaretapu than Tiaro would ever admit. His eyes moved idly for a long time, but always they returned to the wave-lapped shore of Tiaretapu.

The ocean turquoise stretched away to the vivid purple of the horizon where the morning sun rose out of the deep currents of the coral sea. The sky was a subtle forget-me-not blue merging into the soft violets of sunrise. The air was cool and a rousing southeasterly wind rustled the arching fronds of the shore trees.

While Lilith momentarily rested in the eddying currents at the base of Shark Rock, she saw Dunraven walking along the beach where the white sand ended and the coral flats began. Ocassionally, he would pause, bend down on one knee, and study a foraging creature or some notable natural phenomenon. How beautiful he looked, like a golden castaway of heaven.

His hair had grown until it drifted in fine waves below his shoulders. Most of the explorers from her experience wore a beard—her father, for instance—but not Dunraven. He had the quality of appearing groomed even in a mudhole.

She saw Dunraven rise to his feet and disappear into a stand of palms. She felt disappointed. It was still very early and nothing but a few pigs and chickens was astir in the village. The moment was short as she deliberated, but just as quick she climbed out of the sea and up onto the rock. Leaping along jutting outcroppings and down to the beach, she followed his footprints in the sand to the point he had turned inland. She listened, hearing only the warbling of birds and the rustle of foliage.

Carefully, she followed. His direction led down an overgrown path into a dark hibiscus grove. She heard the pulsating flow of water and knew his destination to be the frog pools. Framed by a dense growth of fern and the green tangle of jungle, the frog pools became a magical, secluded haven.

Morning sunlight sparkled across the emerald water. She parted the drooping fronds and spied Dunraven. He poised on the cliff side of the upper falls. He had shed his *tapa* from his hips and tossed it down to the lower pool beside the spyglass. Lilith felt no shame in studying his male anatomy. Her sojourn on the island had demolished false modesty. In truth, she found exquisite pleasure in seeing the play of line and curve of flowing muscle knit arousingly into his well-carried, sensuous masculine frame.

He arched, and in a sleek dive, cut through the waterfall's vaporous cloud into the tranquil pool. When he surfaced, sunlight dappled his muscular arms and touched his gold-burnished head. His hands slicked back his dripping, curling hair. Water trickled in small rivulets over his broad, sun-freckled shoulders.

She shifted and a twig crackled beneath her foot.

He turned as if sensing her presence. His gray eyes pierced the jungle foliage and near into her very core.

Her breath caught.

A frog's deep-voiced croak vibrated the air. He turned to the sound.

Lilith let out a slow breath of relief.

Plucking a fragrant-plumed plenaria, she retreated into denser cover and crept up the slippery stones to a cliffside perch above the pools.

He was floating on his back now. His eyes were closed with the contentment of a man with no time schedule. The imp in Lilith let a palmful of petals rain down upon him. His eyes flicked open and a faint smile touched his lips.

"Ia ora na," he said aloud.

Lilith dared not answer, but her heart paced with mischief. The shrill call of a kula bird filled the air. She opened her mouth and let loose a poor imitation.

He laughed. "Might I suggest singing lessons. Do you wish to scare me away?"

She smiled as well, but still dared not speak.

"Who are you?" He said this twice, in two different native dialects.

Lilith wanted to reply, "You are just too, too clever," but instead she reached above her head and plucked a scarlet-flamed hibiscus flower. She dropped it over the edge where it landed upon his chest.

He caught the flower in his hand and tucked it behind his ear. "You tease me, Woman Who Swims With the Rangahua."

Of course he knew.

97

"Why do you not show yourself?"

While he spoke, he had drifted out of her sights. She leaned precariously over the edge.

With shock, she realized he was climbing the waterfall face. Looking to her right, she glimpsed his golden head just below. He was in the process of entrapping her. Part of her wanted to stay where she was, but good sense told her this flirtation must be conducted from a safe distance.

Taking a lung-inflating breath, she leaped to her feet and dove into the large pool below. She swam underwater to the far end of the pool and surfaced. She looked about but saw no trace of him.

Within arm's reach she spotted a ripple of bubbles. Like a patrolling shark, he darted just beneath the surface. His fingers caught her ankle, then she felt strong hands grip her waist. With a squeal, she made to twist free and scramble out of the water, but he held her fast. Her heart raced.

He surfaced, his face within inches of her own, the wet spray of his released breath sprinkled her cheek. Masculine, dangerous, and unfamiliar, his face held clean-lined composure. His eyes widened slightly, and light speared the gray filaments of his irises. The nostrils of his sovereign nose flared for more breath while his cavalier lips parted victoriously.

Indeed, he held the advantage now.

She'd forgotten how menacing the serpent tattoo made his demeanor. It coiled on the sharp line of his arrogant cheekbone like a threatening scimitar.

Truly the air vibrated.

Against her bare breasts she could feel the hard crush of his chest and the rise and fall of his breathing amid the faster beating of his heart.

Beneath the hammering of her own heart she felt

the thrilling drive of her rising desire. Sweet heaven! She was next to him—and naked! Never in her wildest dreams did she believe it would ever happen—

It should not happen, she realized.

The reality that she was stark naked and so was he added to the awareness that she should not be there at all.

Panic shot through her.

She pushed off from him. He relinquished his hold on her easily.

"Don't fear me, I have no intention of harming you," his sober voice assured her.

For a second she paused, glancing over her shoulder at the sincerity of his arresting face. Fear of him had nothing to do with it. She wanted to stay. But no, it would be too hazardous—she must honor the tribal taboo.

Hastily, she pulled herself over the rocky edge of the pool and disappeared into the forest. Backtracking, she ran down the slippery path toward the beach. She clapped her hands to call the Rangahua and leaped back into the sea.

Dunraven did not follow.

While he gathered himself, Dunraven winged his legs and arms slowly through the tepid water. Good God! What was he about, chasing after the woman like a pubescent youth. While his senses remained volatile from the brief contact with her body, he raked his mind for understanding. For the first time in his astute life, he was learning self-doubt. And he was finding this tutelage sadly compromising. His motives, his feelings, even the core of his philosophy was being overturned, like some revolution of the soul.

He hadn't meant to frighten her. In the all, she had

frightened herself. Why had she come, if not to meet him? Why had he chased her, if not to capture her? She seemed shy, yet bold. Mysterious, yet transparent. His own transparency in the matter afforded him no comfort.

The scarlet hibiscus floated in the water. He caught it up in his fingers and climbed out of the pool. Sitting down to dry off in the sunlight, he turned it slowly around. He knew one had to look deeply into things to see. If he wanted to understand himself and why he so desired this woman, he could not just stand outside as an observer. He would have to enter deeply into a relationship with her to really understand. He must give up his hard-won self-possession, his avowal of celibacy. He must learn to feel all over again, to know the exquisite pain of suffering, the ecstasy of pure joy. He must love her. He had never accomplished this with anyone—perhaps he never would.

He dropped the flower aside. Standing, he wrapped his *tapa* around him and tucked his spyglass at his hip. At a leisurely pace he walked down the trail to the beach. He discovered her footprints in the white coral sand heading down the shoreline to Shark Rock. He knelt to study the pressed sand concave left by her hasty passage. He traced the outline with his forefinger from slim toe tip to tapered heel. It was unusual for an islander to have such a narrow foot. Most spanned double wide over the average European from never being confined by shoes. He spread his hand above the print. He realized he could comfortably hold this delicate foot in one hand.

He rose and scanned the lagoon. She had returned to Tiaretapu. His own binding quandary gnawed at him. He needed to be alone to meditate, to reestablish his discipline which provided the balance in his life. To sort it out he would leave the village. It was time for him to travel into the island's interior. He would take his drum and go into retreat, beyond the village, away from the ever-present distraction of The Woman Who Swims With the Rangahua.

The sun peaked in the arc of hot noon. The day was cloudless and snapping blue. A slender ribbon of surf undulated along the distant beach of Reva Ra. The sand was hot on Lilith's feet. She walked to her hut with the catch of shellfish she'd searched out in the exposed rocky crevices at low tide. She dropped them on the ground, took a drink of fresh water from a coconut shell, and rinsed her hands. With the minimum of daily foraging, Tiaretapu provided all her needs. Occasionally, Heikua sent someone across the lagoon with other provisions or came herself to visit, but mostly Lilith remained isolated, but not alone.

Her early mornings she spent with the Rangahua. She shared her midday meals with sidestepping beach crabs and red lizards. In the evening she strolled with the black and white pelicans on the sandspit. Always, she looked across the lagoon for a glimpse of Dunraven's golden head, but for many days she'd not seen him.

She began feeding dried grass and branches into a little roasting fire in the scant midday shade. Soon she buried the shellfish beneath the coals and sat down on a mat in the cool of her hut. To pass the time, she had begun cataloging flora for medicinal reference in an empty journal found in the hut of Jesus John. Though she'd found no ink, Heikua gave her a black concoction made from the sap of the *fe'i* banana that the

101

natives sometimes used in ornamentation of tapa cloth. She began sketching plant specimens and writing descriptions.

"Ia ora na," came a friendly voice.

Lilith looked and saw Heikua's brown face smiling at her.

"I come, thee lonely no more," she said. In her hands she carried a huge basket that she promptly put down.

Lilith jumped to her feet to embrace her friend. *"Ia ora na,* Heikua. Oh, I am so glad you have come. What have you brought me?" She nosed into the basket. "Heikua, turtle eggs! I can make an English omelet. What has been happening on Reva Ra?"

"Aue, aue," she lifted her hands before her to slow so many questions. "I sit first. It hot day."

Lilith quickly remembered island etiquette. "We will eat. Then you tell me." She went and fetched *peepa* juice for Heikua to refresh herself. She scooped the shellfish from the coals and in no time placed before Heikua a hospitable welcome of fruit and shellfish.

Lilith was more anxious for news of Dunraven than she was hungry. She suffered through Heikua's slowly chewed repast, answering her queries about herself and her herbal findings.

She held up a leaf she'd found in abundance around a remarkable temple site in Tiaretapu's interior. The leaf was heart shaped and grew on medium to tall shrubs covered with flowers. The flower held a faintly pleasant odor, but the leaf was bitter to taste.

"What is this, Heikua?"

"Ahh—" grinned Heikua, between mouthfuls. "This *yaona.*"

"What do you use it for?"

"This for lovers."

"An aphrodisiac?"

"Aue," she nodded. "We chew little bit and mix with milk of coconut. I give to Jesus John to help him become a man."

Lilith bit back a smile and entered Heikua's description neatly in her journal. Poor Jesus John had no chance whatsoever against the wiles of Heikua! She pressed the leaf between the pages and closed her book. Heikua was finished eating, and she could finally ask her about Dunraven.

Unfortunately, Heikua pushed back and reclined into a comfortable position and said, "I sleepy."

Lilith felt somewhat exasperated as Heikua fell into a snoring nap. She would just have to wait. One did not rush islanders. After clearing away the food, she too stretched out comfortably on the mat beside Heikua to rest.

Dozing off, she heard Heikua's voice, "Thy Tahua Tane—he want thee now."

Lilith's eyelids flicked open, not sure if she was hearing right. "What?"

"In beginning I think I must use *yaona* on thy Tahua Tane. But not now."

"How can you know?"

"I know. I Tahua of the heart."

Lilith turned on her side and faced Heikua. "You always say that, Heikua. I don't always believe it, you know, but then I know you really are a Tahua. So, how do you know he wants me?"

"He go."

"He go?" Lilith echoed with alarm. "Where?"

"He go into jungle. Long time, many nights pass." There was a long pause, then she said, "Sua, she go to him."

Lilith's heart fell to the pit of her stomach. She sat up. Here she was moldering on this island while Sua—

"He send her away."

"He did!" she breathed with immense relief.

"He tell Sua, he no want woman. Not true. He want thee, not Sua."

"How do you know that?"

"He know thee here, thee know he there. Magic time."

"I want to be with him, Heikua. I'm tired of waiting."

"He Tiaro's *taio,* it still taboo for thee and he to be together. At the full-moon celebration, thee must choose one of Tiaro's warriors."

Lilith's mouth dropped open with shock. "No! I am already married to Tahua Tane. Tell this to Tiaro."

"Then he kill Tahua Tane."

"Kill him? Why?"

"I think he fear the Tahua Tane will take thee across the sea once again, never to return."

"It is true that when he leaves I will go with him. I love him. Since I was a child I have loved him. As long as Tahua Tane is alive, I could never choose one of Tiaro's warriors."

"If Tiaro learn this, he kill thy Tahua Tane."

Lilith ran her fingers through her hair with distraction. "Then Tiaro must not find out. You are the only one who knows. Heikua, promise me you will not tell."

Heikua touched her hand to her lips. "My tongue will not speak of this." She sighed deeply, and said, "We must speak of other things. Watch sky, when the moon full. Time for celebration. I come to prepare thee." She reached into the great basket and retrieved a *pareo* of special design. "Thee must bathe in the pools. I will rub the oil of coconut over thee, until thy skin shines like the shell of the abalone. At sunset, a *pahi* paddled by Tiaro's warriors come across the lagoon. Thee will come to celebration and begin to court thy chosen one as do the island women."

"How am I to do this? My chosen one is taboo to me!"

"*Aue, aue,* my child. Thee must have faith in Heikua. I Tahua of love."

Chapter

6

When Dunraven emerged from the jungle, he was no longer caught in the brutal web of his own contradictions. The surf crashed against the jagged turrets of Shark Rock with resounding clarity while the sky snapped radiance in the noonday sun. Jade mountains frilled with white sand rose out of a brilliant world of blue. From this vantage point he saw the sea's white spume splash the southern reef with jaunty bravura, while deeper than any dream, more flamboyant than an artist's pallet, the island of Tiaretapu leaped before his eyes and senses like an exotic, perfumed dancer.

He spied a small *va'a*, tipped turtle fashion on the beach. Hoisting it onto his shoulders he strode down to the water, pushed off, and jumped in. He had shaved, bathed, and anointed himself with coconut oil until the hair of his body glistened like gold dust against a bronze relief.

Five days he had fasted and meditated in an attempt to clear the woman's image from his mind. But each night, she returned to seduce him in his dreams. Two days and nights he drummed, journeying into the dreamtime in search of the indelible truths of his past. On the seventh night of his journeying, the Rangahua appeared in a vision, giving voice to what on one level Dunraven already sensed. He and the woman were inextricably linked on the deepest level of the soul. He now understood his awakening desire for the woman and the need for union. Each held the pieces to joy and happiness that the other was missing.

With purpose, he paddled the *va'a* across the serene lagoon, peering down into the water at the many-hued coral castles lit with skeins of sunlight. Feeling vibrantly alive, he looked to the bow and saw the sleek, silver-shadowed flash of the Rangahua. A good omen.

He eased the *va'a* through the glistening shallows and onto the beach. He stepped upon the warm sand and looked around. The island held a magic like no other, but where was the woman? Beyond the beach, the vegetation was lush and lovely. He walked slowly along the pink-tinted coral sand, heading for the line of parasol palms.

He remained circumspect, savoring the beauty of his surroundings, marveling at the myriad of shells sprinkled over the sand, and the variety of rainbow-plumed birds winging through the trees.

He wound his way past armadillo-barked pandanus and large-leafed breadfruit trees laden with dull yellow globes of fruit. As he walked through long grass with the occasional tangle of passion-fruit vines he watched in the periphery of his vision for the half-hidden appearance of the woman. He made his way to a clearing where the sun more easily penetrated the umbrella of foliage. Breaking out of the vegetation, he found a hut walled with bamboo and thatched with coconut fronds.

"Ia ora na!" he called, hoping to rouse his shy hostess.

His only answer was the tinkling of a shell wind chime hanging above the doorway of the hut.

He peered inside. Food and drink were laid out on a mat of coconut fronds. Had she prepared for him a hospitable welcome, or was she just sitting down to eat when he arrived?

"I am quite hungry," he announced.

To his left and behind, he thought he heard the rustle of foliage. He did not turn to the sound.

He stepped inside the hut, sat cross-legged on the mat facing the doorway, and selected a pale orange passion fruit. He poised the fruit carefully before his lips between thumb and forefinger and deftly popped the skin so that only the honey-scented seeds flowed into his mouth.

He sucked into his mouth tiny orange explosions of sweetness and exclaimed in English, "Good Lord, ambrosia!"

No denying, he heard a muffled giggle from the bushes to the left of the hut. The woman was there! Her mirth sparked his own playfulness. He leaped to his feet, ducked through the doorway, and dashed after her. She flickered past his vision and disappeared into long-armed ferns.

In Borneo, he'd learned a successful hunter made his way through the forest by never looking at his feet. It was by looking at the feet that the hunter stumbled and fell and made a lot of noise.

Expertly, he gave chase. He kept his eyes and ears intent on the slightest sound or movement. She was leading him into the interior of the island where trees grew close together and the undergrowth was thick with creepers. He had to push and scramble to break path while his illusive quarry threaded her way just beyond his view. Once he saw her poised on the trunk of a felled tree. She appeared temptingly alluring in her neatly wrapped *pareo*. He realized she waited for him with the intent he should not lose her. He could no longer hear the sea. Where was she leading him?

His curiosity increased when he climbed a massive boulder that blocked his way. He caught his breath at the scene that came to view. Above the tangled canopy of jungle the spiraling pinnacle of a shimmering temple emerged. It looked like a Triton's trumpet shell, high spired and stepped with a series of whorls, and faced with an intricate mosaic of shell. Dunraven never expected to see such a magnificent relic of ancient architecture in these islands. Climbing down from the boulder, he moved forward. He parted the overgrowth of vines and touched the rough stone surface in wonderment. There whispered a rustle of wings that sounded like a cryptic, sacred chant. A score of slender white cranes took flight.

"It very beautiful, yes?"

Startled by the woman's voice, he stepped back and looked about.

"I here," she said.

His eyes riveted to an archway. She stood within the opening, a quizzical smile upon her lips.

His own mouth felt dry with the nervousness of at last coming face-to-face with her. "You speak English."

"*Aue*. Heikua teach me from Bible book."

His gaze traveled the length of her, taking in her slim, shapely body, the rum-rich shade of her skin, and the dainty swelling muscles of her calves visible just below the hem of her *pareo*. She was lovely.

"Do you wish me to speak to you in your native tongue or English?"

"English, please."

"Very well," he said, agreeably. "But if you do not understand what I say, then ask me to repeat myself. It is important if you wish to better your English. Is that clear?"

"*Aue*. It clear." A small smile teased at the corners of her mouth. Oddly, he had the distinct feeling that she was toying with him.

"Do you know who I am?"

She lowered her delicately shadowed lids as if to search her memory. "Thou art the Tahua Tane."

"Yes, I am. And you—who are you?"

She did not answer him right away. Like a child reciting lessons, she pursed her pliant lips for a moment.

"I am—I am Lily," she finally said.

"Lily." He rolled the feel of her name over his lips. Then asked, "Are you afraid of me?"

"No."

"Then why do you run from me?"

She raised her beautiful dark eyes to his own and said cannily, "Thee know as well as I."

Her forthrightness caught him off guard. He gave a humorless chuckle. Indeed, he knew as well as she. Rather than go into all that, he changed the subject. "What is this place?"

"This place from beforetime. God live here once. Heikua say this Garden of Eden."

"I could easily believe it. I never thought such a place existed on earth." He gazed at the temple and jungle appreciatively. He turned back and looked at her endearingly knowing that the real treasure here was not the ancient temple. At close quarters, she was even more beautiful. Slim hipped with a graceful stance, her almond eyes glistened like obsidian.

"Well, Lily. I take it you are the guardian of this temple. Will you show me inside?"

"Thee must promise not to tell anyone. Temple secret thing."

"I promise."

"I show thee."

He followed her across the threshold. Again, his breath slowed at the vision that met his eyes. The circular internal chamber was more inlaid mosaic of pearl abalone. Light poured through many diagonal slits whorling the height of the spire and illuminating the interior. But, more amazing, in the air he now heard the whispered ebb and flow of the sea. It was like holding a sea shell to one's ear. The builders had ingeniously imitated the natural world in design.

"By God! What a find!" His words echoed upon themselves with acoustical perfection. He clapped his hands in a staccato refrain. It sounded wildly exhilarating. His first thought was of drumming in such a place. His second was of his colleagues at the Royal Geographic Society who would be most impressed by this discovery. Architecture of this sort had never been found in any of the Pacific Isles.

After the sounds died, Lily said in a whispered caution, "Remember, thee must not tell anyone."

"Yes. I understand."

An incidental movement of her head sent her shining black hair over her shoulder like a caress. He almost reached out a hand and touched it.

"Heikua say this temple sacred place. She say this place temple of love."

His attention was unabashedly back to the task that brought him to Tiaretapu in the first place—her, the mysterious Woman Who Swims With the Rangahua. His every nerve was alive and jumping as he looked at her.

"Is it?" His voice was playful, as though he spoke to an imaginative child. "And what do you know of love, Lily?"

Her delicate features relaxed and again the secretive smile teased the corners of her lips. "I know from Bible book, love forbidden fruit."

He laughed. "More is the pity. The first rule when one learns to read is not to believe everything one reads."

She raised a disarming dark-winged brow. "Heikua say, forbidden love best love of all."

His eyes narrowed intently and he affirmed in a low constricted voice, "Heikua is right."

"Thee know of forbidden love, Tahua Tane?"

"I know."

After a long aching moment, she said, "One day you teach me of love, Tahua Tane?"

His senses soared at the thought. "Yes, Lily, one day I will teach you."

"But not now, Tahua Tane. To you, I forbidden fruit."

Good Lord! For him she assuredly was! Shaking his head he began to laugh and again she let flash that impish, provocative smile.

Yes, she was created for love. And damned unfortunate for them both. Without touching her he felt the stinging attraction of her nearness. His eyes traveled over her face, marveling at the sooty lashes self-consciously lowered against dark-honeyed cheek-bones, and the perfect nose whose polished nub begged for kissing. Even more so, he was aware of the pleasure promise within the sensual curve of her mouth.

"Has the forbidden fruit ever been kissed?"

Her lashes lifted, a glint of surprise lit her liquid eyes. "No, Tahua Tane."

"Do you wish it?"

"Wish what, Tahua Tane?"

A patient pause.

"Wish to be kissed?"

"By whom, Tahua Tane?"

"By someone who wishes to kiss you."

"Aue." Another impish smile. "Would it be forbidden love, Tahua Tane?"

"No. It would be a simple kiss."

"Then, I wish to kiss someone who wishes to kiss me. Does thee know of someone, Tahua Tane?"

"Yes, Lily," he said, very carefully. "The someone is myself."

"Thee?" Puzzlement glinted in her eyes.

"I must warn you, Lily. I have not kissed anyone for a very long time."

"I wish," she said in a small halting voice, "to kiss someone who has not kissed for long time."

He stepped closer, letting his gaze play lightly over the winged arch of her eyebrows and lashes and her lips, with their softly pliant satins. His upraised hand gently drew away her hair. "Some believe there is an art to kissing. I might have forgotten how."

Lilith truly did not care about the art of kissing, or if he had forgotten how. She only wanted to know that he knew how. Her heart was hammering like the bells of Westminster while her senses quivered like a row of puddings on market morning.

His head inclined slightly, and she saw that his gaze had narrowed drowsily. One hand cradled the curve of her neck beneath her ear; the other cupped her chin and cheek as his lips sought hers. "Give your lips to me, Lily," he breathed. "Give me the nectar of your mouth."

Lilith knew she would give him anything he asked for and more. She had waited all her life for his kiss. A part of her could not believe it was truly happening. Was she really in his arms?

Then, she felt his languid, soft kiss pressuring her lips. Yes, there would be no denying she was at last in his arms. He kissed her, lushly and long, with a caressing intensity that left her limp everywhere. His thumb began a slow compelling rotation at the pulse of her throat. Seeking to steady herself, her hands grasped the hard line of his sleek hips.

Her mouth soon parted to his pleasuring, drinking the aqueous, erotic dew of his breath. She did nothing artful upon her part, she merely kissed and was deliciously kissed in return.

When he released her lips from the mastering bondage of his own, she gave a deep, heartfelt sigh.

She felt as if the whole world spun in a new direction. If one kiss could leave her reeling, what would happen when they came together in complete union of body, mind, and spirit? Surely, the heavens would burst and the earth shift upon its axis.

"Thee has not forgotten," she said, breathing unevenly. In her mind, she knew this one simple kiss had bound her heart to him forever.

Holding her in a gently sardonic gaze, he said, "I had thought not."

He laid careful hands upon her waist and nuzzled the velvet skin of her neck. "Lily, sweet Lily," he whispered her name ever so huskily into the veil of her hair.

A wellspring of emotion brought the sting of tears to her eyes. Again she realized how long she had loved him! Again she doubted that he held her in his arms. She near whispered, *Is it really you, Dunraven?*

Heikua had known he had changed, but how and why?

Her arms coiled to embrace him while her cheek rested against the warmth of his bare chest. They stood together feeling the reliable course of each other's pulse until she felt so overcome with the wonder and ache of this forbidden love that she felt as if she would retch. Too much, too fast—and fear.

Even in the midst of this fleeting glimpse of heaven she worried that someone might come and discover them together. Uneasy, she had no wish to endanger him. What if someone saw his *va'a* on the beach?

Summoning her power of will, she separated herself from him slightly. "Thee must go." The last thing she wished to do was send him away, but he must leave for his own safety.

Dunraven knew it was time to stop as well, and as will and common sense coalesced, he pressed her urgently closer and lay his forehead softly against hers. "Lily, I searched you out knowing you were taboo to me. I am sorry. We are in the thick of it now." Drawing away, he released her.

She smiled. Her smile pleased him enough to smile himself.

"We are," she echoed sadly. "I thank thee for thy simple kiss, Tahua Tane." And with those words, she stepped back through the threshold.

Wishing to forestall the moment of parting, he followed her. Outside he looked around.

She had disappeared.

Sometime later, after plowing through vegetation that raised way above his head to obscure his view, Dunraven managed to find his way out of the dense island interior. He took care that no one should see him near the isle. Following the less visible southern shoreline, he slowly paddled the *va'a* in a circuitous route around the lagoon to Reva Ra. He pondered his visit with the woman. The simple kiss would dwell with him a very long time. Silently, he made a vow to return to Tiaretapu very soon.

Chapter

7

With the last lights of sunset the island drums awakened. A single, throaty whoop exploded across the lagoon. In counterpoint to its sister rhythm of the surf, a pulsing tattoo spread tentaclelike into the sultry night air. Quickening, a deeper, booming beat burst as if from the jungle's heart.

The vibration touched Lilith where she stood on the edge of the lagoon watching the torchlit canoe of warriors paddle toward her. She smelled the fragrant white gardenias that wreathed her head. She felt the sensuous rustle of the dry grass skirt about her hips and the cool-petaled kiss of wild mountain orchid leis against her bared breasts.

Lilith Cardew was no longer a "civilized" woman. Beneath her veil of reserve and reliable practicality, she was a bubbling cauldron of hot emotion. Her passionate nature had been bottled up inside for years. Tonight she would explore the mystery of her own existence and allow passion to rule. This night she was Atua Tamahine, daughter of the gods.

Heikua stood beside her, watching the warrior canoe that would carry them across the lagoon to Reva Ra. Like a queen's attendant, Heikua had prepared her for the celebration, bathing and washing her hair with scented herbs. She had rubbed her body with coconut oil until her now-flawless skin shone like polished, dark amber.

Lilith breathed deeply, her whole body tingling like coral chimes in an ocean breeze. She raised her arms above her head and reached to embrace the expanse of heaven and earth. Welcoming the canoe, she let loose a joyful, *"A haere mai!"*

Tiaro's warriors let out a series of excited whoops and cries in answer. She studied their noble faces as the canoe scudded to shore. Tiaro would have her choose one of these strong and virile warriors to be her mate. Who would she choose? Vahiki, a tall, well-mannered youth who had taken her fishing once? Or would it be handsome Pauro, the heartthrob of every maiden on Reva Ra?

All kept their eyes downcast. It would mean bad luck to meet eyes with the Atua Tamahine before she had made her choice. She stepped into the canoe and kneeled in the center beside Heikua. The warriors took up their paddles, dipped them into the obsidian sea in a unified thrust, and began a soft chant.

The daughter of the sky she comes,
The daughter of the sea she comes,
The daughter of the earth she comes.

Dunraven sat with the drummers, his fingertips tapping out the slow, sensual rhythm of celebration.

His eyes were on the *va'a* gliding across the mirror waters of Pearl Lagoon.

The woman was coming.
The Woman Who Swims With the Rangahua.
The woman who ignited warmth in his chest and fire in his loins.
The woman was coming.
The woman who was taboo to him.

He watched her step to shore. He watched the tantalizing swing of her full grass skirt as she walked to join the circle of women. His eyes followed her and her alone as the group moved up the beach toward the communal house. In greeting, Tiaro touched noses with her and enfolded her in a full-arm embrace.

The feasting began. Nine courses of food appeared and disappeared, being consumed with great relish and enjoyment. Gourds spilling with fermented drink passed hand to hand. Dunraven ate nothing, drank nothing. His focus remained on his drumming and his eye steady on the Atua Tamahine. She did not look his way. However, Tiaro did. Dunraven knew tonight he would be observed.

The festivities wore on. The warriors danced before the Atua Tamahine together, and then one by one. Dunraven took heart that her beautiful eyes remained downcast, never lifting to single out any man in particular. He'd witnessed these mating rituals in various forms often enough. Tonight, more than ever, he wished to take part—to leap to his feet like a peacock and flaunt his virility before her.

The warriors retreated and the women came forward. The Atua Tamahine stepped within the circle to initiate the beginning of the women's dances. Along with the other drummers, Dunraven's rhythm softened to accommodate her slow, artful movements and the sweet-voiced singing of the other women. Her dance was singly feminine, gliding and well marked. Her hair was black as a Nubian diamond and, in the torchlight, flowed down her back like molten midnight. The supple sway of her hips and languorous grace of her hands mesmerized him.

The singing told the legend of Lily, the beautiful and beloved daughter of the chief Tangii. Because of her beauty, Lily was kidnapped from her father's house by *papalagi* who sailed off in a sky burster. Brokenhearted, Tangii waited, but she did not return. On his deathbed, he prophesied one day she would come home.

The women sang,

The daughter of the sky she comes,
The daughter of the sea she comes,
The daughter of the earth she comes.

Then all the women moved to the center and began dancing. Beginning slowly and tenderly, they swayed in a sweet harmony of song and motion.

Abruptly the singing stopped. The drummers wound to a halt. Momentarily, silence reigned. In this silence, the choosing would take place. Without a spoken word, the women and men would link eyes and hearts. The wind rustled the palm fronds and the sound of surf swelled and fainted. Dunraven was tense; he wanted her.

At last he touched gazes with her.

When their eyes met, they met fiercely.

She spoke with her eyes. Without doubt, he knew she chose him in the reverberating silence of lapse of tide and crash of wave. Confident enough in his own masculinity, he did not feign surprise. Yet, all knew he was taboo to the woman, and she to him.

Heedless, his eyes smoldered his answer.

Explosively, a wild whoop erupted. The warriors sprang forward to entrap the women. The Atua was left alone. Dunraven's eyes shifted to Tiaro to discover his attention was on Heikua. She was offering him something to drink, which he laughingly gulped down.

The drumming resurrected into full life. Instinctively, Dunraven's body erupted with that power, but he could not act upon it. Instead, he began beating out a strange, throbbing, deepening cadence that became intoxicating.

Like a shock, the pulse of the dance animated wildly and the women and men gave way to the powerful hip-snapping *tamure, tamure*. With lascivious movements, partners teased and entreated and pursued each other into the jungle shadows.

Holding Dunraven's gaze, the Atua Tamahine turned her back to all others. For him and him alone she danced—quivering, suggestive, and seductive. Her smile gleamed over her white teeth. Her black eyes sparkled, lowered, and flashed up again to inflame him and enslave his senses.

More couples disappeared into the night.

The ebb and flow of her pliable body challenged each strike of his drum. She molded herself to his every rhythm, tempting, leading, seducing until the demon within him struggled to break through. Sweat glossed his body and lust fired his loins. He felt an overwhelming desire to possess, touch, caress, hold, and subdue this exotic creature flaming his thoughts.

All caution, all reason, all oaths of abstinence withered on the pyre of his passion to possess her. His eyes devoured the taunting quaver of her nipples as beading moisture glittered like gold over her full breasts. Her dance was a burning poison igniting his desire in red and fiery explosions. His own need snapped as she, with a glance so wanton, slipped out of the circle of torchlight into the darkness.

His hands froze in midair, though his heartbeat paced with the drumming. He looked over to Tiaro and met the sparkling eyes of Heikua. In her lap, she cradled Tiaro's head, his features clouded with the bliss of a man drugged. With a conspiring smile, Heikua gave Dunraven a nod of encouragement. Eyeing those around him, he rose to his feet. Assured all were self-absorbed, he disappeared into the shadows of the night. Behind him the drums throbbed a reverberating warning—taboo, taboo, taboo.

Caught in sublime insanity, he sprinted after Lily, heedless that possessing her was the highest risk. His blood pulsed to some ancient primal urge. His nostrils flared and his chest heaved like a jungle cat, stalking the forbidden prize of her flesh.

He sighted her moving down the path to the frog pools. She paused, hearing his step. She turned expectantly, her eyes glittering flares in the night. She was the embodiment of every love goddess down through the ages. He felt himself lost in the mysterious underworld of her spell. She unfastened the *pareo* at her waist and let it fall.

In a single gesture, he dropped the *tapa* from his hips.

They looked at each other and dared to smile. Her pearl white teeth flashed. His own conspirator's grin gave answer.

He stepped forward. She did not retreat. Desire

raged between them in skin-tingling currents of body heat. She raised her arms and lifted over her head the fragrant leis twined around her neck.

She leaned against him and he felt the soft brush of her nipples upon his chest. She smelled of seaweed, flowers, and recklessness. His heart clamored like a closed fist against a sealed door. Enticingly, she looped the flower leis over his head and shoulders.

"Ia ora na," she said in a soft, honey voice. "Art thee the serpent come to beguile me?"

His bold gray eyes pinioned hers. "I am he."

His arms moved to encircle her, but she ducked from his hold. He embraced empty air.

Like an elusive shadow, she had disappeared.

Her taunting laughter slashed through the emerald jungle with promises of sweetness and pleasure.

Accepting her challenge, he muttered into the night, "It is I who am beguiled, Woman Who Swims With the Rangahua."

In that instant, he became owner of his own darkness. His brash savage heart wanted her—wanted her all to himself. His throat opened and he let loose an earthy cry. It ripped through the jungle air like a typhoon of untamed desire wild to mate with the thrusting drumbeats vibrating in the night. Gone was the proper Victorian gentleman who politely chatted at genteel soirees. Gone was the celibate monk who had prayed away the hours in quiet meditation.

The chase was on.

He sliced through the undergrowth with the stealth of a feral hunter. Enough illumination for passion's errand, stars and moon glinted through the green-leaf foliage.

He heard the gentle rain of a waterfall, the dull

croak of frogs, and the humming of a woman's sweet voice. He parted the fronds of fern and saw her silhouette against the pools.

She turned.

This time he stood his ground realizing he walked a tightrope over a void. She might bolt, but then he knew as long as she led the chase, he would follow.

"Do you want me?" he asked.

"I want thee."

There was no stillness here with hearts thundering, blood pulsing, and breath coursing.

"Come to me."

She came.

On her naked body, shadows painted traces of heaven, stars, moons, and suns. Her eyes shone like beckoning twin flames. Like benign serpents, her arms embraced him. His arms crisscrossed the warmth of her body. He leaned into her, seeking to know the scent of her. She writhed her hips against the heat of his own, and her grasping fingers caught hold to the soft coils of his hair. His turgid manhood arched against the dusky damp of her belly, and he felt as if he were climbing into a higher heaven.

He bent his head and captured her pliant lips with blazing pleasure. Her lingering juices blended in his mouth with infinite taste. A warm heat spread its sweet desire through his veins and he ravished her with sweet, dark kisses of possession.

From his mouth his breath, his essence, his fire poured over her. His kisses traveled like golden lava down her neck and lower—

Laughing, she slipped from his grasp.

He cursed under his breath.

"No hurry. The sun still sleep, Tahua Tane," she

said, sweet amusement peppering her voice. She dove into the pool and disappeared beneath the surface.

No hurry! She wasn't the one who had spent the past years of her life in contemplative abstinence— few islanders did! His nostrils flared as he watched the moon mirroring ripples. No hurry! But gallant reason reminded him she was a virgin. She was the chief's virginal daughter. She was the bewitching forbidden fruit that lived apart on Tiaretapu. Her first kiss had been innocently awarded to him and now—here he was, panting like a wild boar on the scent with no control.

Damn! He knew one learned to pleasure one's partner before pleasuring oneself. This applied especially when one initiated a virgin into the mysteries of love.

He let loose a slow, calculating breath. Control was slowly returning to him. Good God! What was he thinking of when he ran after her?

He swallowed hard. He watched her sleek shadow ripple beneath the surface of the pool. He wanted her. In Tantric tradition, the ritual of initiation took many nights. Tonight should be but the beginning—

He dove in after her. The tepid water slowed the throb of his loins, though not the ardency of his desire. He caught her spiraling body in his arms and pulled her to the surface. Her laughter burst like fountains of water as she gave mock struggle in his arms. Her naked silken body nudging against his further inflamed him.

"There are many fish in the sea, my temptress. Do not be too slippery."

Her black-winged brows arched with flirtation. "A good fisherman have spear."

He pressed his hips to hers. "Rest assured, I am a good fisherman."

Her legs coiled around him provocatively.

"Aue. Aue. Thee does not lie."

Pleased by her banter, he put his hand to her chin and tilted her face to his own.

"I never lie." Without taking his eyes from hers, he said, "Truthfulness is one of the few things in this world I hold in high regard. I will never lie to you, Lily."

She lowered her lashes, remaining silent.

Her features seemed troubled. Briefly, he scrutinized her face. She was indeed beautiful—and irresistible. He kissed her full on the mouth, a wild, devouring kiss that left him pulsating and breathless. Her response was innocently subdued. When his lips left hers, he noticed tears gathering in the corners of her dark eyes.

"What is it? I did not mean to overwhelm you. I want you."

"No, no." Gathering herself, she blinked back her tears. "I like this kiss. I am happy. So happy," she returned.

He hugged her to him, kissing her forehead and hair. His manhood pressed between the satin crevice of her thighs. His lips tasted the savoriness of her skin. By God! To have this woman, he would transgress a hundred taboos!

Lilith was not a liar by nature. Deception did not come easily to her, but the grim reality of the moment was that she must continue the charade. But was it really a charade? Truly, she was no longer the woman who left England those long months ago. For love she came to the South Pacific, for love she lied to Dunraven, and for love she would risk all to win him.

Now—this instant—he held her in his arms. She was happy. So long she'd waited. She would not waste precious time in useless reflection. Her awareness of his body against her own was so acute, it was almost painful. As Heikua told her, she must follow her instincts. And her instinct was to give herself to love.

She embraced him wholeheartedly, melting against his warmth and virility. She felt his hands travel slowly, feeling the curves of her hips and waist. He lowered his head and kissed the honey-dark curve of her shoulder. With his tongue, he traced lower, to the waterline that lapped over the swell of her full breasts. His mouth dipped beneath the water and he caught the nub of her breast between his lips and gently suckled her.

Her breath stopped. Sweet, sweet heaven! How could anything feel so good? She near swooned.

He lifted his face back to hers. "You are beautiful, Lily," his deep voice purred. "When I first saw you swimming with the Rangahua, I thought you were a sea nymph. Since then, each morning when I see you swimming, I have admired you. I have been very jealous of the Rangahua."

"I think Rangahua jealous, too."

A chuckle vibrated his chest. "For good reason, my exotic Lily." His mouth covered hers.

Her lips clung to his while his hands traced the smooth flow of her hips and cupped the nest of her womanhood. Again, sensations tingled through her like morning chimes. Loving did feel wonderful, and to think she might have stayed in England and never known any of this—

Nearby, the lighthearted banter of a man and woman rustled the air. Lilith tensed. She broke the kiss and looked around nervously.

"Quick," said Dunraven. "We must not be discovered."

Lilith did not hesitate. She swam to the edge of the pool and scrambled out. At her heels, Dunraven followed.

Into the jungle they ran, she in front and he behind. The drums pounded in the distance. Lilith felt the blood rush of danger and reckless risk. What would happen if they were found out? Would Tiaro truly kill Dunraven? She glanced back over her shoulder to assure herself Dunraven was still coming. She thrust her way through slapping fronds, taking no notice of direction. Her ears throbbed from the sound of her own breathing and her heart cartwheeled from the exertion of flight.

She broke from the jungle, feeling the fine sand of the beach under her feet. The thick smell of seaweed replaced the musky fragrance of vegetation. She scanned the expanse of beach and, to her delight, saw that it was deserted. The hot-moon night touched her senses like a clash of thunder. Boldly, she turned to him, caught his hand, and together they ran down to the sea.

Like aqueous children returning to the deep, they plunged forward, tangling legs and arms, rolling and frolicking in the lagoon. Waves splashed over them like veils of night black spume and their lips met in abandoned, soul-devouring kisses.

How warm the sea felt. How warm were his lips. Lilith floated on her back. Her breasts were small islands in a caressing, velvet sea. He was beside her. One of his hands supported the small of her back while the other cradled her hips. His hair flowed in tawny waves from his temples, an inflaming gaze lit his eyes. The swell of wave lifted her and tumbled her against him. She loved him—she loved his hands upon her and his lips above hers and his eyes smoldering into hers.

He was virile, he was primal, and he was beautiful.

"You are a sea goddess," his voice was low and endearing. "A sea goddess must be made love to in the sea."

His intent caused Lilith to laugh. Only the Daring Dunraven would be so outrageous. The sea swallowed her laughter, but not the playful promise his words evoked.

"The Tahua Tane must hold breath long time," she challenged.

"What better way to drown than to drown in love," he teased back. And then he seemed to gather himself, his face losing all flippancy.

Leaning down, he kissed the center of her forehead. "Awaken your mind to love."

He lowered his mouth to hers. Lightly, he touched the moist, soft sides of her lower and upper lips. A full grin relaxed her mouth. She felt his tongue pause. She nipped it playfully. Taking the opening, he slipped his tongue inside her mouth, past pearl white teeth. Slowly, he ran its tip across the roof of her mouth and licked the satiny folds of her inner cheek.

An exquisite ticklish feeling rippled through Lilith as a subtle wetness suddenly watered her mouth like warm dew. Sweet heaven! The man knew what he was about! She sighed a slow breath of surrender and boldly laved the slick heat of his cunning tongue.

While kissing her, he bestowed continuous caresses with the palm of his hand over her shoulders, following the full swell of her breasts down to the soft flesh of her belly where the seawater lapped and pooled. Lilith felt poetic, and wanted to spout odes of love, but her tongue was mesmerized by the intimate stroking of his own.

With the lightest brushing of his fingertips, he circled the soft indentation of her stomach, moving down to the secretive nest of her womanhood. His touch pleasured Lilith. He aroused her in ways she'd often imagined in dreaming moments, but never experienced. He pressed gently with the heel of his hand on her woman's mound.

Fire shot through Lilith. On her watery bed she arched to the pressure of his palm as she felt the strengthening support of his hand on the small of her back. Holding her, he began a barely perceptible rocking motion that stimulated her to the extreme.

He withdrew his lips from hers and kissed the hollow of her throat. In a hoarse, passion-skirted whisper, he said, "Open your voice to love."

More lines of flowery verse flooded into Lilith's head, but she knew she could speak none of it. Yet, she wanted to speak. His lips had touched her, and in some mystical way had given her permission to voice the intimate thoughts of her heart.

"I love thee, Tahua Tane." At last she said the simple words. For years she had loved him in secret, between the shadow and the soul.

"And I—I desire you," he declared, omitting the word of love she so coveted.

If she could have spoken from her heart she would confess the depths of her love—a love like a wildfire burning in a forest. But this was not a night for confessions.

He buried his lips into the furrow of her cleavage and kissed the pulse of her heart. "Open your heart to love."

Though she tingled from his kiss, she knew her

heart had been ever open to love. . . . And then his tongue traced down to the pooling water of her belly. His kiss was long and deeply sensuous as if he sucked into himself her very essence.

"Awaken your womb to the seed of life."

And then his golden head went lower. She felt the pressure of his hand lift and then she felt the hot heat of his breath upon her woman's mound.

His voice was barely audible to her ears. "Open the lotus of your womanhood to love."

He kissed her then—in that hidden place she'd never known to be kissable. She felt like a goddess. He became her lord and lover, opening within her the wellspring of life and ecstasy. Tenderly, she reached her hands out, cupped his golden head, and drew his face up to hers. His arms encircled her. He pulled her upright from the water and held her close to him. She found a stable foothold in the sand. The waves swelled against her buttocks, as though prodding her into love's shimmering net of completion. Her eyes searched the steely-fired depths of his. They were silvered haunts of passion. He sucked gently on her upper lip, using his tongue and lips to imbibe the moist, pulpy under flesh.

Lilith felt as if a golden thread of pleasure ran down her body, connecting her mouth and womb. Each kiss she felt not only upon her mouth, but between her thighs. He was a magician of love to stimulate her so—

And then it began—the explosion of constellations, a thousand Southern Crosses bursting in her veins. Thick heat traveled from the center of her thighs like the moon multiplying on the glass blue lagoon.

Her fingers gripped his muscled torso and she threw back her head and moaned. He cupped her buttocks in his hands and pressed her against him. She leaned into his body, hungering for the hard swell of his loins. Her senses gyrated around and around. A secret clarity began opening within her like dancing light. In this bliss she held him, she held everything alive—earth, sea, and fire. She was alive. She ached—for him.

"I love you," she rasped as if she were dying.

She heard his indrawn breath and his eyes flashed the color of the night and scalded her with their intensity. A hand caressed her cheek. He did not answer with words, but another kiss. A devouring kiss, born of sunrise and lightning bolts—

Reluctantly, she broke the kiss.

Panting for breath, she leaned her cheek against the firmness of his chest and gave way to the slowly eddying pulsations. Her knees felt weak and she believed she'd collapse if she tried to stand alone.

She felt demolished by passion.

Again, he kissed her forehead—he kissed her throat, and stroked the wet black tangle of her hair. His eyes were shadowy and shining. "Your pleasure is my pleasure, Lily."

But Lilith wanted to return the pleasure. She wished more than ever to please him. A strange heat still fired her blood and she became bold and kissed him as he had kissed her—meeting his tongue, moving her lips against his.

Dunraven's desire was intensely heightened by Lilith's release, yet now he craved his own. She was an island and he a drowning man. He stood pressed against her, his manhood hungering for the deep body of her womb.

Done with years of constraint, he commanded huskily, "Love me, Lily." He cared not for expertise, but prayed for the wantonness of inexperience. The woman had beguiled him not through artifice, but innocence—and in innocence she would pleasure him.

The sea lapped at his knees and at the thick cloak of her hair that clung to her naked torso.

"I do love thee, Tahua Tane," she breathed with the sincerity of angels.

He believed her. And like the plant that never blooms, he knew love lived darkly in his body. And he knew he did love her without knowing how, or when, or from where. The mystery of it drove his fingers into the voluminous strands of her hair to draw her nearer.

Her lips were at his throat, then his chest. When her pink tongue circled his dark nipples, he moaned with pleasure and a fathomless expectancy settled into the depths of his heavy-lidded eyes.

Down, down she traced to press a kiss upon his naval. When she settled to her knees and the blue salt waves washed against her shoulders, he tensed with anticipation. She surrendered her lips to his thighs and set her fiery tongue free. His breathing deepened in quick and steady arousal.

She took full possession of him.

He closed his eyes. His fingers coiled into her hair. He muttered oaths of lust in which men speak the ancient mystery of flesh, blood, and desire—

Amid the undulations of foam, wave, and sand, their stolen moment of loving became a journey with water, stars, and carnality.

Like a pair of castaways they collapsed in each other's arms into the surf, lying together awash with the repleteness of love.

Shockingly, the light of a bamboo torch on the beach cauterized the moment.

The sharp voice of a warrior brought Dunraven to his feet. A tremor of dread shot through Lilith, and she forgot herself. "God in heaven, no!" she muttered.

Luckily, Dunraven missed the clarity of English in her voice as he turned. Rising, Lilith slipped behind him, wishing to disappear into the sea. But it was too late. They had been found out. But how? Then, lurking behind the warrior, she saw the graceful silhouette of Sua.

Dunraven's hands reached protectively for Lilith as two more warriors splashed through the surf and arm gripped him. Lilith clung to him and looked at the men with confusion.

"You break taboo," one announced, his dark eyes potent with accusation. "Tahua Tane, now die."

"No!" cried Lilith. "No! He is my—" she dared not finish.

"I love him. Let him go."

"He break taboo," he repeated. "He die!"

Chapter

8

Her face stone solemn and as pale as death, Lilith plodded up the volcanic slope of Reva Ra to the sacred *marae*. Tiaro's priests shuffled in front, chanting and pounding a heavy cadence on hourglass drums. Her eyes held on the broad shoulders of Dunraven who, hands tied before him, walked ahead of her. She wiped tears from her eyes that already burned from too much weeping.

It must not happen!

Soon, Tiaro would strike Dunraven down and the warriors would throw his body into the fiery cauldron of Reva Ra. She felt sick with anxiety and remorse.

It was her fault. She had—had beguiled him. Played upon his senses and vulnerability. She had followed him to the frog pools that early morning. She had tempted and teased him during the full moon celebration. But he alone would pay. The Daring Dunraven would come to his end all for a woman.

The procession snaked on to the plateau. Bamboo

torches were placed around the *marae*. Tiaro began imploring the gods in a monotonous chant.

Dunraven's face and body had been painted in swirling serpent designs with plant dye and black ash. Lilith watched in agony as he was led to stand before the stone god. Since the night before, Dunraven had not spoken to her. She had been exiled to the hut of Jesus John while Dunraven remained tied to a stout pillar in the round house. Following tradition, Heikua had expertly painted his body through the afternoon in preparation for the sacrifice.

"He does not speak," declared Heikua upon Lilith's queries. "He goes within to prepare for his ordeal. He powerful Tahua."

He stood erect, his shoulders iron straight and his features schooled with steely gravity. On one cheek coiled the serpent tattoo while on the other a black and red pinwheel was brandished. Lilith watched his gray eyes slowly survey the scene from the plumed heads of the warriors to the shell-jeweled women. Clearly, there was no mark of fear in his stoic expression. She realized he had totally detached himself. He was now the academic, coolly observing his own ritualized demise. She almost expected him to turn to Tiaro and ask for a quill pen and parchment book to record the last sacrificial moments of his life. The event could be posthumously presented to the Royal Geographic Society.

Look at me! She inwardly demanded.

His eyes slipped past her as if she were a formless spirit. Had they given him some herb to dull his awareness? She had read of primitives doing this to their victims. Or was he the other Dunraven now? The rational scholar-explorer whom she'd first met in England on her wedding day, the man who politely bowed and withdrew. Gone was the primal male who had stalked her through moonlit jungle and star-kissed surf.

It couldn't end this way. She was swamped in desperation. The devil take his pride!

In the form of Tiaro, he near did. The sacrificial moment arrived. Two warriors stepped on either side of Dunraven and held his arms secure. Gripping a great stone, Tiaro stepped behind Dunraven. He poised his hand above the nape of Dunraven's neck, the proper point for a lethal blow. Dunraven's face showed no fear.

Her stomach sickened and her heart near burst.

"No!" she shrieked out. Her cry ripped above the drumming and the rumblings of Reva Ra. She vaulted forward and fell to her knees clasping Dunraven's legs.

"Aue! Aue!" she moaned. "I beg thee, please don't kill him. Take my life instead. Kill me. I will do anything—anything—please, don't kill him," she sobbed.

The drumming halted.

Reaching down, Tiaro pulled her to her feet. "Do not disgrace yourself, daughter," he counseled. "The Tahua Tane broke the taboo. He must forfeit his life. There is nothing you can do."

Suddenly, Heikua stepped forward. She sank to the ground, crossing her legs and making her two hands into a single fist in obeisance. She spoke in a clear voice for all to hear. "There is one thing, my Tahua. The fire walk. If the Atua Tamahine is willing to walk the lava flow of Reva Ra, she can redeem the life of the Tahua Tane."

Cold fear seized Lilith. Her head jerked up. The thought terrified her. She couldn't do it! The fear flashed back. She was again a child, screaming for help, suffocating in smoke and flame.

"No!" she heard Dunraven's voice shout emphatically. He broke away from the warriors. The passive scholar had retreated. The possessive, primal male returned. He stooped to his knees before Tiaro in petition. "It was I who broke the taboo," he announced in a dangerous tone. "If anyone is to walk the fire, it shall be me!"

An expectant murmur rippled the ash-flecked air.

Tiaro frowned deeply. He looked intently into the faces of those kneeling before him.

Finally, he spoke. "You have no say in this, Tahua Tane. The woman must choose for herself."

Disregarding Tiaro, Dunraven riveted his thunderous gaze to Lilith. "You will not do this!" he ordered in a voice he could not keep in perfect control.

In God's name, she didn't want to do it! Her senses recoiled with the thought, and her already parched throat felt as dry as kindling. Tears stung her eyes. The air was foul and she felt weak and on the edge of a swoon. But if it was the only way to save him, she must do it!

She shifted on her knees to fully face him. Placing her palms on his muscled chest she asked softly, "Understand me, Tahua Tane."

She looked with serious, imploring eyes into his glowering face. Torchlight played on the curve of his tall cheekbones and the tight set of his firm chin. She might be smaller than he and a woman, but she was in no way cowed. Her strength of will would match and surpass his own if it came to the contest of saving his life.

She asked through a dry throat, "See me."

Would he see her? Could he see the woman she

really was? Would he see the woman he married in Saint John's Kirk a half a world away and more?

"I see you," he said, giving her a hard look. The gray silvered irises with spokes of black seared her own. "I see you to be a fool. To offer your life for my own is idiocy. I want no such sacrifice on my behalf!"

His ego was talking. Lilith had always noted that explorers had inordinate amounts of ego. She near muttered, *You want all the glory yourself, I suppose.*

Then allowing her frustration to dissolve, she gathered herself and said slowly, "I love thee, Tahua Tane. If thee dies, I die."

His features seemed to slightly soften, then as merciless as a guillotine, his eyes sliced through her. "Forget me," he said flatly.

How could he expect it? After last night she was his—heart, mind, body, and soul.

"Never!"

Her fingertips still pressed to the warmth of his chest. Her black eyes probed the fathoms of his own as she leaned to touch her lips to his in declaration of her love.

His lips did not relax against hers. Moisture stung her eyes at his lack of response. Confused, she looked straight into his eyes a long probing moment, then drew away. She knew his false indifference was meant to save her, but she would have to abide such a parting. She had made her decision. She stood. In a steady voice she proclaimed, "I will walk the fire."

Dunraven's eyes widened and his jaw clenched with adamant disapproval. He was rarely outdistanced. "My life now depends upon you risking your own. I won't have it!"

"Accept it. It is my gift to thee," said Lilith.

His blackened chest rose and fell with pent emotion. She had never seen his features so intense. "Then, I ask to be freed that I might drum with the others when you walk the fire."

Lilith's eyes flew to Tiaro hopefully.

Not pleased, he gave a reluctant nod and the warrior standing behind unbound Dunraven's hands.

"You have my gratitude," said Dunraven rubbing his wrists.

Lilith wanted more than gratitude. She looked at him intently, then said, "I only ask this from thee. Thank me not with words."

"Then how?"

"I would have thy love, Tahua Tane."

His hard impassive face seemed to flicker, betraying an unfathomable emotion. He confessed gently, "I do not know what love is, Lily. I cannot give to you what I myself do not understand."

"If we both survive this night, would thee marry me, Tahua Tane?"

For long seconds his penetrating gaze studied her face. The rumblings of Reva Ra burst and shattered the air like cannon fire.

She tried to read his thoughts. Was he thinking of the wife he left in England? With the fierce countenances of Tiaro and his warriors glaring at him, would he dare say he was wed to another?

"I will," he said finally in a quiet, sincere voice.

Knowing his life hung in the balance, the Atua Tamahine forgave his duplicity. But could she, Lilith Cardew?

"I will draw upon the strength of thy promise, Tahua Tane." She turned back to Tiaro and lifted her chin. "I am ready."

"It begins!" declared Tiaro. "Come."

A procession formed to move higher up the mountain nearer the crater's edge and main lava flows. The wind-blown smoke eddied and whirled, revealing glimpses of fire and flame and showers of rock in the crater's depths. Gaseous clouds constricted breathing and Lilith felt as if she would pass out. Sweat broke out on her skin and her heart palpitated with fear. No, she must not pass out! She must not succumb to her fear.

A fork came in the path. Heikua led her away from the others, up the left-hand track. After a few steps the ground leveled slightly. Lilith faced the wide glowing stream of molten lava she must walk across to reach the others.

Smoke and crimson light danced over their features making them appear like dreaded demons. But for the beloved visage of Dunraven, she felt as if she were in hell. He stared back silently, his eyes glittering in a strange way. Her skin clammy under shivering fingers, she hugged herself and tried to swallow back her fear.

She whispered urgently to Heikua beside her, "If I fail, you must throw me into the volcano as well. If he dies, I will die too."

"Thee will not fail," assured Heikua.

"I must not fail—for his sake," she breathed, feeling smothered with fear. "What must I do?"

"You must become one with the fire. Listen, listen to the drum of the Tahua Tane." Heikua pointed across the tongue of lava where Dunraven stood with the others, drum in hand. "The drum speak to Reva Ra. The voice of the drum becomes one with the fire."

Suddenly, Dunraven let loose a bloodcurdling whoop and the drumming began. An entrancing beat dominated the air. Lilith stared at the molten fire a few feet away and began swaying to the pulsing of the drums. She felt the heat on her skin and forced away the memory of the long months of agonizing pain after the cottage fire.

At her back, Heikua continued to whisper encouragement. "Face thy task squarely, with pure intent. The fire can either burn thee or purify thee. Let thy fear boil. Look to thy feet, which are the symbol of thy power."

Perspiration beaded over her body and dripped between the cleft of her breasts. The sound of Dunraven's beat lulled her fears, mesmerizing her until the fire pulsed through her veins.

"I am right by thee," assured Heikua.

Lilith looked at her feet. Orange radiance danced up from the earth. Stilling her heart and breath, she fixed her sights on Dunraven.

Their eyes locked. Without a blink he matched her gaze with the shrouded fascination of his own. Like a dark sorcerer, he willed her forward.

She lifted one foot—

She felt cold, not heat.

Another step—still only a cool kiss of fire touched her feet.

In the timelessness, she began to pull herself toward Dunraven. Every face, every sound faded, except for his. She felt like a wind gently lifting and falling as she moved along the molten lava—toward him and only him.

Angst sharpens the features of most men; it was not so with Dunraven. The sober bones in his face relaxed into something akin to optimism and reassurance. His hair was saintly golden, but his eyes willed her forward with near demonic force.

And she was there—across the tongue of earth fire.

The muscles holding up her knees turned to clabber and she reached for him.

She had done it! She had done it.

Dunraven flung his arms around her. He cradled her as she slowly sank to sit on the ground. He pressed his lips to her hair as she dropped her head down on her knees. In a monumental effort, he blinked back the emotion tearing his eyes. No one had ever put their life on the line for him like this. Crouched before him was this beautiful, delicate creature who, out of love, had risked all on his behalf. He felt in awe, as well as unworthy and undeserving of such sacrifice.

Until now, his study of the fire walk had been purely academic. How could he ever objectively write an account of what he'd just witnessed? After a lifelong quest he had at last found in this amazing ordeal the key to every philosophical question which had ever eluded him. At the core of all existence was selfless love. So simple, why had he never understood before?

He felt connected to her like he'd never felt to anyone on earth. This innocent, uneducated woman had become his greatest teacher. His embrace deepened and he whispered, "I love you, Lily." And then his wonder turned to concern. Gently he took a small foot in his hands to examine it to be sure she was not suffering. "Are you all right? Are you burned?" he asked.

Oddly her feet felt cool to his touch.

"I am fine," she murmured, leaning into him.

He slid his arms under her knees and shoulders and lifted her up. Holding her in his arms he turned full circle and announced, "She is not burned."

Tiaro came first to inspect. He took each delicate foot in his hand and dusted away the ash. Relief crept over his face and as he turned to the others, pride swelled his voice. "The Atua Tamahine is not burned! The taboo is broken."

Everyone let out whoops of delight.

Heikua came and embraced both Dunraven and Lilith in her great arms. "Does thee believe me now, my little doubting Thomas? I Tahua of love. I make all things right."

Tears trickled down Lilith's cheeks.

With her in his arms, Dunraven proceeded down the face of Reva Ra. Her head lay against his chest and he felt her breath soft upon his skin. The others followed, singing and laughing as if the whole affair had been nothing more than an evening jaunt. It was difficult for Dunraven to believe his life had ever hung in the balance. Yet, with every breath he blessed the woman in his arms who had saved him and unlocked the wellspring of loving in his own heart. He felt overwhelmed and as smitten with love as a schoolboy.

He felt her breast convulse. She was sobbing now, undeniably with relief.

He held her closely, "Hush, hush. It's over now. You were magnificently courageous."

She turned her face up to his and began giggling, between a hiccup or two.

He chuckled, realizing she wasn't crying after all. "Do you always hiccup?" Oddly, the veiled image of Lilith Cardew flitted through his mind. He thrust her out of his thoughts like a hot poker. This was no time to think of her.

"When I am nervous."

"Are you nervous now?"

"Yes."

"Why? Your ordeal is over."

"*Aue,* but now a new one begins. We will be united in a great celebration."

"That should not be an ordeal, but a wonderful event." Again, like a nagging specter, Lilith Cardew's image came to his mind. What was happening to him? Had the awakening of selfless love also awakened his conscience? Could he really marry Lily when he knew he was legally bound to another woman in England?

Lily's eyes lowered, the dark lashes dusted her cheeks. He wished he could read her thoughts, but was thankful she could not know his.

They had reached the frog pools. In a tender, careful gesture, he set her down beside the water. He unfastened his *tapa* and slipped into the pool. He took her small foot in his hand and began a soft exploration of her toes as he washed away the soot and ash. She stayed silent and he sensed some inner turmoil.

"What are you thinking?" he asked softly.

Her black eyes lowered to his. But still she did not speak.

"Be truthful," he encouraged.

Almost timidly she said, "Thee does not have to marry me. I do not wish to entrap thee."

There was a slight hesitation of his fingers. He dropped her foot and his hands went quickly to her waist. "Come here, my sea nymph." He pulled her gently into the water so that she was leaning heavily against him.

Looking straight into her midnight eyes, he said, "You have entrapped me, but I wish to be entrapped. I wish to love you, live with you, die beside you." He brushed his cheek against the softness of her own. "Believe me."

Her head tilted to rest on his shoulder and he glimpsed glistening tears in her eyes. Again, in a ruthless flash of conscience, the veiled form of Lilith Cardew came to him. What was he promising the innocent beauty in his arms? Could he keep this promise? He was an explorer, a wanderer by nature, he had never settled in one place for long. He was a man married to another woman a world away.

Good Lord! A mammoth quandary began to knot in his solar plexus and then, as he allowed himself to face the fear—the indecision for what it was, and only that—the misgivings slowly dissolved. No matter the obstacles, with a surety he could not explain, he knew this woman and he must be together.

In the face of his love for her, he cared nothing for exploring, nothing for honor. He cared only for her, the woman who had saved his life, the Woman Who Swims With the Rangahua.

Lilith awakened to the booming of drums. Within a few seconds, the women around her stirred from sleep with happy morning greetings of *ia ora na*. Today was her wedding day. She had passed the night in the women's house, while Dunraven had stayed with the men.

She lay still tingling with anticipation and joy. She listened to the chatter of birds in the trees, the distant rush of the sea, and the stirring of tousled children, their voices still dreamy from sleep. The village was athrob with preparation. The huts had been decorated with flowers and fronds. Enormous quantities of meat had been cooked in earthen pits.

She heard Heikua calling her name just as the horn of a conch shell echoed through the air.

"Will thee sleep through thy wedding day?" exclaimed Heikua, her gestures urging Lilith to animation. "Quickly, quickly, we all must bathe."

Lilith slowly sat up and stretched her arms high above her head and gave a nubile yawn. She brought her arms down to hug herself, all the while grinning with self-satisfaction. "I have no intention of missing my wedding, Heikua." She came to her feet. "Have you seen my bridegroom this morning? How does he look? Is he as happy as I am?"

"I think he happier," assured Heikua.

Lilith turned a doubtful eye to Heikua. "Are you sure? I feel like the happiest woman alive!" She bit her lower lip with sudden panic. "What if he has changed his mind in the night?"

Heikua began to laugh. "Change his mind? I no let him. I give him *yaona* to awaken him from such foolishness."

"*Yaona?* No! Heikua, no. I'll not have the man I love tricked into marrying me," she cried with castigation, then added under her breath, "The first time was enough."

"*Aue, aue.* Thee need not worry," calmed Heikua, her hand reached out to comfort her. "The Tahua Tane loves thee better than his life. Come now, we go with the other womans down to bathe."

In a long line of silent women, Lilith proceeded down to the sea. Morning mists were lifting. The tide was in and the sun beginning to rise. White pigeons swooped above the group of men a few yards down the beach. Her senses quickened as she saw the golden head of Dunraven among them. Heikua had explained that the men and women would not bathe together, nor would she be allowed to speak with Dunraven until after the ceremony. But still she hoped to briefly catch his eye, just one glance of reassurance.

Lilith slipped off her *pareo*. The shallows were warm and welcoming as she submerged herself in the luxury of the sea. Heikua attended her, briskly rubbing sand, the island version of soap, on her legs and arms. Soon, she emerged glowing and refreshed, and was guided back to the women's house to be dressed in island wedding finery.

"And when is the ceremony?" Lilith asked impatiently as the woman threaded tiny shells and flowers in her hair.

"Soon," said Heikua, straightening the folds of Lilith's sky blue *pareo.* "The men must give the Tahua Tane instruction on conveying his feelings to thee."

"He needs no instruction. He is very expert at it," Lilith declared, just as three orchid leis were placed around her neck.

"Aue, aue. Thee speaks true, but he must convince Tiaro he desires thee."

"I should think Tiaro is convinced enough. The Tahua Tane endangered his life out of desire for me," returned Lilith, still in awe of the course of fate. She had pined for him half her life and even in her wildest dreams never imagined he would love her as well as she loved him. He had been an idol, a god, beyond her reach.

"Be patient."

"I have been patient, Heikua. I can no longer be patient."

After a final touch of ornamentation, Heikua stepped back and perused Lilith from the crown of flowers on her head to the shell strands adorning her ankles. *"Aue, aue, aue.* Thee art beautiful."

The other women surrounding her cooed in agreement.

Their praise overwhelmed Lilith. Never had she been told she was beautiful. Never. Tears trickled down her cheeks and she felt undeserving.

"It is time," announced Heikua, taking her arm.

Lilith brushed away her tears as her pulse hastened

with an expectant thirst to see Dunraven again. The night had been vacant without him.

Dunraven awaited her. In the communal house, he sat beside Tiaro in a sky-blue ceremonial loincloth. The ends hung down in front and behind. Bracelets adorned his biceps and rings circled his calves. A headdress of feathers and a cape of long fine feathers completed his bridegroom's costume.

He heard sweet singing as the women approached. A conch sounded—and he saw her.

His breath lost rhythm and he rose to his feet. He had walked five continents, sailed seven seas, but never had he seen such a woman. In her form, he saw the beauty of creation.

"Are you pleased?" asked Tiaro, rising beside him.

Dunraven could not speak. His eyes were hooded fires, a knowing smile lingering on the surface of his lips. He knew his lifelong search had led him to this woman. He near bowed down to the universe in gratitude.

Tiaro said, "She is beautiful, isn't she?"

"Yes," said Dunraven softly. "She is very beautiful, I think she is the loveliest woman on earth."

She was before him now, her eyes lowered. He devoured her delicate features, her perfect figure, her grace and noble bearing. She began to dance before him. Her slow artful movements were lithe and eloquent, but her face remained impassive and grave.

Tiaro said, "She dances very well."

"Yes! She dances very well indeed," he agreed enthusiastically.

"You think she is very pretty?" interrogated Tiaro again.

"Yes, she is very pretty." Dunraven felt to call her

pretty was to understate the matter, but he would follow Tiaro's lead.

Tiaro now touched his forearm. "She is my daughter."

"You didn't tell me that you had such a beautiful daughter."

"I will tell you now, and if you ask for her, she is yours."

Dunraven shifted to face Tiaro and then knelt down on one knee in the customary stance of humility. "Tiaro, I ask for her."

Tiaro placed his hand on the crown of Dunraven's head. "She is yours, Tahua Tane."

He lifted his handheld scepter of carved ironwood and addressed Heikua as the emissary of the women's quarter. "I have given my daughter to the Tahua Tane. Bring her."

The women came forward, the Atua Tamahine taking position directly before Dunraven. She kept her head down, but in a swift stolen glance, she briefly struck gazes with him. Her eyes were bright fathoms of promise.

In an atmosphere of solemnity, the finest matting, lengths of cloth and flowers, were spread between them. Behind him the men stood in a crescent line while the women stood surrounding the Atua. Then some women came forward with food and offerings that they placed in the prescribed ritual in front of the bride and groom.

Tiaro took Dunraven's and Lily's hands. He held them between his own and made a short speech. The shorter the better, as far as Dunraven was concerned.

A few prayers were chanted with much whistling and stamping from the men and then, with an expansive gesture, Tiaro released the islanders to get on with the real business of celebrating.

The assembly fanned out and into a standing crowd before the bride and groom. The first notes of the *warup* chopped the air. Compelled by the slow, hollow beat, Dunraven jumped to his feet before his bride. Since the night of the full moon celebration, he had wished to dance for her; now he would.

He produced an astoundingly loud and vigorous note that seemed to burn straight out from the very depths of his soul. He removed his headdress and swung off his cape in a flourish. He began twisting his hands and slowly his body started to move with the pulse.

A high mating cry of a laugh rang out from somewhere at the back—a signal to the men who moved behind him in five long lines. Their palm-leaf skirts swayed as they began mimicking his weighty movements. Then he gave a series of quick turns and wild springs. His hand reached for a spear and he began performing daring maneuvers. Lilith drew back with surprise and fascination. The spear's tip flashed in the light of the noonday sun to the rhythm of the music, attacking, countering, thrusting, fending.

Sweat glossed the muscled contours of his sun-bronzed body. And then suddenly, he thrust the spear in the earth before her with whapping force. His glowing gaze held her in trance. He caught her hand and pulled her to her feet.

In a fleeting, lucid moment, Lilith heard the voice of Heathcoat Holmes preaching against the sins of the heathen. But for her there was no turning back, for this day she would dance like a heathen, love like a heathen, and mate like a heathen.

The energy of the celebration soared when she faced him. She undulated her hips slowly at first, her slim arms wreathing to the sky. Around her, the drums sounded and the islanders chanted bawdy innuendos. Her face flushed, not with embarrassment but with the fever of desire.

He circled her, his muscular legs lifting to the pulse beat of the drumming. Wild whoops erupted from the men, encouraging him to close in on her. His eyes never wavering from hers, he danced, steamy sexuality exuding from every pore. Lilith thought that from the dark intensity of his eyes, it would have been impossible to tell whether he was making love or war.

Her dancing quickened with the galloping rhythms, one wave after another. In the flashing of shadow and light, his hands caught her hips. Her hands fell to grasp the sleek hardness of his shoulders. She breathed the thick fire of his moist breath and felt the brush of him as he thrust seductively against her own undulations. Exertion silvered her body, dewing her from the furrow of her cleavage to the dark hollow of her thighs. Together in heat, in hips, in heart, the earth shook beneath them in the scorching atmosphere of a hot noon mating.

Then his mouth covered hers and the fire in her own flesh flared to meet his, connected, and flamed. Shifting, his hands clasped the rounds of her soft hips, synchronizing them against the roll of his own. Her hands looped around his neck and she twined her fingers in his hair.

In front of all, his primal sensual ferocity overtook her. She felt his tongue thrust deep, where his manhood could not, spearing fiercely inside the moist folds of her mouth. A low rough sound rumbled in his throat.

He drew back.

Her breath was coming in short gasps.

The black spokes in the sea of gray that were his eyes whirled. In a whispered rasp he said, "Come, now."

Joining hands, they fled the celebration and raced off to the beach. Amid excited laughter and calls and pounding drums, all followed—fathers, brothers, sisters, children, and dogs.

A garlanded *va'a* sidled on the beach. Dunraven had no need to urge her faster. She clung to his hand, leaping to keep up with his long stride. He glanced back, his teeth flashing white in an encouraging smile. The world swirled around her as he swept her into the *va'a* and pushed it into the churning surf.

In short, easy strokes, he paddled toward Tiaretapu. Off the bow, the Rangahua vaulted and dove, an exuberant matchmaker of the deep. The diamond-speckled sea quivered around them and Lilith looked across the *va'a* to the chiseled line of Dunraven's face—

His fathoming eyes poured sun into her senses—

They were together, and that was all that mattered.

Chapter

9

Lilith kneeled in the bow while Dunraven steered safely through the reef-blotched waters. Looking beyond the northern tip of Tiaretapu, she saw an enormous black cloud gathering. An afternoon squall was imminent.

"It's heading this way," he affirmed.

"Thee must paddle faster. When it breaks, the boat will swamp."

His pace quickened. Her eyes held on the expanse of his bare chest. His muscles rippled and knotted with each pull on the paddle. She looked to Reva Ra and saw that the celebrants were scattering for cover. The *va'a* slugged onto the beach while myriads of raindrops shimmered down from the mist-swirled sky. In a sudden, drenching release, the rain poured a blinding deluge of water over sea and land.

"Quick," he shouted. The raindrops dripped from his nose and chin. He jumped from the *va'a*. Giggling, Lilith took his hand and they raced like a pair of drowned specters up the beach, through the trees, and into the cover of the hut. Amid bursts of laughter, they flung themselves down on the mats.

She turned to him and he to her. She rested her weight on her elbow and looked at him. He smiled, his eyes speaking a thousand embraces. It was miraculous —his being beside her, their being together in this place at this time. What if she had never left England? What if she had been content to live her life as a reclusive spinster?

He reached out and cupped her cheek in his hand. "I believe we are two people who are meant to be together, Lily."

She lifted her hand to caress his own. "I believe this, too, Tahua Tane. We have not now met, we have been with each other all along," she spoke truthfully.

Simultaneously, arms and lips reached for each other. Lilith felt as if she had come home as her arms encircled him. Flowered leis crushed between breast and chest while rain-slicked lips melted into sweet union. Yes, she thought, it was a wedding day so different from the first. This was the kiss he had once withheld from her, and now no wedding day could be as perfect—or as promising.

When his lips withdrew, his eyes held her own.

"I think I am in a dream, Tahua Tane," Lilith whispered.

She felt his hold deepen. The pulse of his beating heart thrummed against her ear.

"In a loved one's arms, we are all dreamers. Close your eyes Lily, and dream," he said, lying back and cradling her in his arms.

"I pray this is a dream from which we will never awake."

"This is a waking dream. We have found paradise. I

have spent my life looking. Until now, I never found it. My search has taken me where no man should have to go."

A part of Lilith's own heart nearly broke upon hearing the desolation that etched his words. "But thee has found paradise," she said, her lips lightly dusting the hollow of his throat.

His hand stroked her back. "I heard once that you must lose your life to find it. As I walked up the mountain to the *marae* that night, it happened with me. I did not fear death. I feared being parted from you. Like yourself, if I could not have you, my life was at an end. I stood in a morass. The event of being tossed into the heat of the volcano was nothing to the fires of despair every time my eyes settled upon you. I did not look your way, because the pain was too great."

"Oh," Lilith sighed sadly. "My own heart was breaking, because thee did not seem to see me anymore. I thought—"

"I did not love you?" he interjected.

"Aue—"

"I had believed myself to be a man incapable of love."

"And now what does thee believe?"

"I believe I love you."

Her breath stopped.

He loved her! But whatever happiness she received from his confession resurrected myriads of complications. Whom did he love? Lily, or Lilith?

Bittersweet tears slipped down her face. "Love me, Tahua Tane. Love me now."

A half laugh slipped from his lips and he nuzzled her hair. "Lily, I will love you now, and tonight, and at dawn, and at noonday, tomorrow and tomorrow and the day after tomorrow. I will love you slowly and carefully, for in paradise there is no time, only time for love."

His arms held her with the warmth of the sun and his lips pressed a soft kiss to her forehead. "I will worship you with my love and my desire and my lust. I will court you, explore you, win you, and woo you, but in my own fashion. I am no island boy. Now sleep, Lily, rest. I want to lay beside you and watch you dream."

Lilith snuggled into the curves of his hard body. It was enough to be in his arms. She did feel extremely tired and was content and grateful to sleep. "Kiss me, Tahua Tane," she asked, timidly. "I want to carry thy kisses into my dreams."

Her eyes focused on his lips as they curved into a smile and then she felt them warm upon her own. His essence surged into her like bursting clusters of sweet *wongai* fruit, and soon she fell—into dreams, and dreams, and dreams.

"Lily, wake up," she heard her voice being called through some distant mist. A heady fragrance encircled her nostrils and she opened her eyes to discover a gardenia lay upon her breast. Dunraven knelt on one knee, his eyes alight with a warm greeting. "You will sleep your wedding night away. Come, let's go down to the beach and watch the sunset."

She stretched, then tucked the single gardenia behind her ear. He reached for her and raised her up into his arms. She felt a sweet rush of happiness. Her dreams could not compare to truly being with him, awakening to him. She kissed him, lightly.

He returned her kiss with a lush, lingering response and declared, "Lily, I will never see or smell a gardenia that I will not think of you."

They just stood, holding one another in a communing embrace.

"I am hungry," she said, resting her cheek against his chest.

He drew away. "Good, I have prepared a feast for us on the beach."

"Thee has?" Lilith grinned her pleasure, taking his hand and following his lead out the doorway.

"While you slept."

Hand in hand, they picked their way over the bony red mangrove roots and down a sandy slope and onto the beach. The western sky blazed crimson as the low-riding sun washed the trees, the sand, the rocks, the sea, in dazzling golden colors.

"It's beautiful."

"I didn't want you to miss it."

She squeezed his hand with affection while reaffirming he was flesh and blood.

"Good Lord!" he cursed, dropping her hand and sprinting down the beach.

"What—" She ran after.

He reached for a palm leaf and began waving it wildly over the neatly spread banquet he'd prepared on the beach.

Lilith began laughing. An army of small speckled crabs had invaded his hospitable repast. Undaunted by his threats, most remained while a few merely sidestepped with bits and bites of fruit and fish like adroit thieves.

"Prepare a pot," he crowed. "If nothing else, we shall have crab for supper."

Lilith could do nothing but laugh at the spectacle of

Dunraven shooing off myriads of crabs that would have nothing of his intimidation. Raising stiffened pinchers in outraged challenge, the tiny fellows held their ground.

"Damn!" shouted Dunraven. A David to his Goliath had actually pinched a finger as he reached to snatch a morsel of papaya.

Lilith stepped to his side, tempted to recount to him the advice in *An Explorer's Handbook Out* concerning the precaution of protecting one's food from scavengers as well as underestimating nature. Instead she offered, "I am not so hungry now."

Dunraven gave a boyish smile of defeat and stepped back. He glanced at his finger while eyeing the devastation. Still smiling, he looked over to her. "Nor am I."

"I need no feast. I will settle for a walk with thee along the beach." She took his hand, raised his pinched finger to her lips, and lightly kissed it.

"I am healed by a kiss," he said softly, tracing the rim of her lower lip with his fingertip. A skittering feeling tingled over her mouth from his touch and her pulse skipped a pair of beats. Then his arm encircled her and she leaned into him, her own arm coiling about his lean hips. Enthralled with one another, they began a slow stroll down the beach. She felt hardly awake as if she were still in the realms of sleep fantasy, so dreamlike was the seascape and the joy of his companionship.

"Did I ever tell you how I rose each morning to watch you swim with the Rangahua?"

"No," she said, "thee never did."

"Well, I did," he confessed, his hand softly massaging the round of her shoulder. "You fascinated me from the outset. I could not believe my eyes when I first saw you through my spyglass from the ship. You must have been swimming since you were a child."

Lilith lowered her eyes. She hoped he did not expect an answer.

"In England very few people learn to swim, especially women. And then they must wear a bathing costume which covers their bodies like a dress. I don't suppose you can imagine it. But women would never bare their breasts in public as you do here. Womanhood is hidden beneath yards and yards of petticoats. I have always thought it a pity."

His candidness brought a smile to Lilith's lips. "Someday maybe thee will take me to England," she said.

He stopped, turned his body fully to hers, and tightened his embrace. "I don't really ever wish to return myself. It cannot compare to here. Nothing compares to here. Besides, I don't think you would like England, Lily."

"Why not?" she asked innocently, but thought of the predicament that would arise if he were to return to Eden Court with her, his native concubine. She played with the thought of being two women at once, the reclusive Lilith and the free-spirited Lily.

"It is civilized."

"Civilized." She said the word succinctly. The thorn between them pricked again.

"Yes, civilized. You are not civilized, Lily. And thank God for it. I am not overly fond of civilized women."

"Aue," she mumbled. "Why am I not civilized?"

"Because," he kissed her forehead. "You swim naked in the sea." His mouth lowered to her lips and she briefly felt his warmth pass to her before he drew away and asked, "Would you like to swim now? Call your Rangahua and the three of us will celebrate our wedding in the sea."

"I would like this."

With her agreement, his hands deftly unfastened her *pareo*, and she stepped away as it fell onto the sand. His own *tapa* slipped easily off his hips. He embraced her then, again only briefly, but her senses flamed like the fiery doubloon of the setting sun. Hands joining, they walked down to the returning waves and into the sea.

Lilith breathed deeply, and began singing the chant to call the Rangahua. She and Dunraven waded in the warm shallows of the sandbar, and then eventually began swimming slowly and luxuriously out into the lagoon. Within a minute, Lilith saw the Rangahua and then there was a resounding splash a few feet behind her back.

Dunraven felt an overpowering sense of contained excitement. He felt as if he were greeting an old friend. At close quarters, the Rangahua looked enormous, sleek, and utterly intelligent. Lily nuzzled her face against the everlasting smile of a mouth as it curved its sensual body around her. It eyeballed Dunraven with relaxed intensity, awakening in his heart a sense of warmth and involuntary awe of the beauty of the woman and creature moving together.

He found himself swimming after them, turning and twisting in the water as the pair intertwined. The Rangahua clicked and ratcheted, its black blowhole opening and puckering in a most suggestive manner.

The water slipped past Dunraven's skin. He glided in one motion ever so smoothly into the golden corridor that was flashed across the water's surface by the disappearing sun. In one measured passing, Lilith leaned from the back of the Rangahua and brushed her lips over Dunraven's own. Playfully, he reached to pull her off its back, but with a twist of a fin, the Rangahua changed direction. On a second pass, the dolphin locked eyes with him before it deliberately winked. He chuckled into the swelling breeze and realized the Rangahua was sporting with him.

The pair dipped beneath the surface and then something stirred in the water near his hand. It was the Rangahua. A sleek snout and one very bright eye hung back just a few feet. Lilith slipped off its back and swam into Dunraven's arms.

"I thought you had been kidnapped," he said, his voice an amused whisper.

"Never," she cuddled and kissed him. She stroked his hair and gave him a provocative and heartfelt gaze. "I would never leave thee, Tahua Tane." The water moved around them, as he enfolded her waist with his arms pressing the downy softness of her hips against his tightening belly.

Her long black hair tangled over his arms as she rested her head on his shoulder. In the wonder-spun expanse of sea and sky he held her like a rare treasure from the deep.

They floated, kissed and floated more.

Just after sunset, a conch sounded, and across the lagoon came an echoing salutation to moonrise and more celebration. The drumming commenced once again and sweet-voiced singing carried in the air.

Dunraven and Lilith moved toward the shore to languish on the damp sand left exposed from the receding tide. On their backs they reposed on the beach to watch moon and stars rise. He cradled her in his arms. Hearing the pulsing of the drums, he held her, all the while his desire rising.

Intimacy had been long absent from his life. Now, beneath the hot-moon heaven, he realized he'd banished the very heart of life itself.

This night he loved. This woman he loved. Kiss by kiss, he wanted to traverse her mysterious infinities, her gardens, her lagoons, her flowing waterfalls.

Slender and fine, the tenuous moonlight illuminated her. It fell upon her body, silvering her soft abdomen, and the two yielding columns of her legs.

He shifted. Then he nuzzled his cheek against her soft breast. He sensed the coursing of her blood and kissed the soft pulse of her throat and touched her face with the radiant heat of his caress.

"Come, Lily, I have prepared a place for us this night in the sacred temple."

She sat up and smiled, "How did thee know I, too, would wish this?"

"I knew it was where we first truly met and kissed. For us, it is a place of love and magic." He came to his feet, drawing her up with him. He began to lead her up the beach.

She halted. "There is a short way thee does not know."

"Hah!" he declared. "I knew you purposely tried to confuse me that day."

She giggled softly, her eyes twinkling lights of mischief. "Come, I show thee."

First he went for a torch. When he returned, he followed her through the jagged shadows onto a narrow sandy pathway between palms and mangroves. Beyond the palms they entered into a thickly wooded area, impenetrable unless one knew the path. In only minutes, Dunraven realized she had led him to the heart of the island. The coral temple spiraled white in the moonlight. He put out the torch, realizing it served only to blind them from the natural luminescence of the night sky.

The rainsquall had left the jungle cleansed and vibrant. Heavy, fragrant scents touched Dunraven's nostrils like warm velvet while the far-off sound of drumming pulsed gently in his ears. Earlier, he had come and laid out matting on the temple floor and strewn it with flower petals, creating a sanctuary of love.

"I have never been here at night," said Lilith, taking his hand as she moved closer.

"Are you frightened?" His large hands moved around her slim waist protectively.

"No, I find it very beautiful, and Heikua has told me this is an ancient temple of love. There is nothing to fear in love."

"Nothing," he affirmed softly. He could feel the sense of sacredness. When they entered, he said, "Lily, may the love in our hearts now fill and abound in this space."

He guided her to the center, where the pearl-shell inlay of the walls shimmered in the filtering moonlight. Facing her, he took hold of her hands and breathed deeply of her essence. Her eyes reflected the radiance of a thousand stars.

When Dunraven's arms slowly encircled Lilith and enveloped her like a gentle cloud, she nearly melted away. Each time she touched him was like the first. She closed her eyes, her breathing full and deep while she nested her breasts against his chest. With the slightest of pressure her hands tentatively caressed the flesh and bone of him. Her pelvis relaxed and moved forward, meshing with his own. Thighs and bellies met and then she felt Dunraven's hand slip over the curve of her waist and down, to cup the round of her buttocks, lending her balance.

She was grateful for the support. She feared she might swoon.

Their bodies liquesced into each other, giving over to an unending embrace. Their breathing harmonized and their heartbeats entrained in soft crescendo within the temple chamber.

"How are you feeling, Lily?" His voice was endearing.

"I believe I am dreaming."

"We are both dreaming—a waking dream. Are you nervous?"

She hesitated, then decided to tackle her main point of disquiet. "I am," she confided. "I am afraid thee will think I am too civilized. Thee does not like civilized women."

"How—where did you? . . ." He was taken back by her admission.

"Thee said, thee was not overly fond of civilized women."

"I spoke true. But you are not civilized, Lily."

Lilith did not know what to say to this. Instead, she asked the question that had plagued her from the first night of their acquaintance. "What is the difference?"

He cleared his throat, the melting hug no longer so melting. "The difference is—," he paused, then began again. "The difference is—just believe me, there is a difference."

Lilith realized she could not continue making love with him until this was settled. Her own insecurity would not allow her total surrender to him. "Thee must tell me the difference," she pressed.

He sighed deeply and let loose her arms. "Let's sit down, Lily." Lowering to the mat, he faced her. He took her hands in his. He seemed quite perplexed.

Lilith pursed her lips with seriousness. He did not know the difference, she realized.

"The difference is that civilized women do not give themselves over to love. They are taught love is at best for procreation only."

Lilith nodded her head slowly, "I see. Does thee speak from experience?" She wondered where the foundation of his bias originated.

"Yes, I do."

"Tell me."

"Tell you what?"

"Of this experience."

He gave a half laugh. "It is highly improbable that I will recount to you—especially on our wedding night —my bedroom escapades."

"Why not?"

"Because, it is in bad form."

She could not resist. "Maybe the Tahua Tane is the one who is too civilized." And then, amazingly, she heard herself say, "If we truly love, we must share from the heart."

He did not immediately speak, but held her gaze. She was asking him to be starkly honest with her, something she had not been with him. Should she tell him now who she really was?

His hand slowly lifted, came to her cheek, and traced the hollow of shadow. "Lily, I could believe you have never spoken an untruth in your life. For one not in the habit of lying, it is easy to share from the heart. For me, it is very difficult. I've been schooled in a world of survival of the shrewdest and fittest. But you, Lily, you are without guile."

He leaned into her and she, almost penitently, to him. She would not tell him tonight, or any night soon. The truth would not, could not, be told. Too much, she feared losing him and yet despised herself for her deceit.

His arms were around her again. His lips drank from hers, insistently tasting her flesh with his open mouth.

"Never, never lose innocence," he whispered.

Her eyes fell shut, clamping back the hot stir of guilty tears. Her lips parted for him, her breath wantonly uneasy. With his kiss, she abandoned her conscience and surrendered to the growing pressure within her body that hungered for him. She turned her head weakly to one side, skimming her lips over his shoulder. He brought his hands up to stroke tenderly the length of her hair. He pressed his face into the black mass and inhaled its fragrance.

"You smell of sea and sand, and something more—yes, I recognize it now—Rangahua," he chuckled.

She drew back. "Is that bad?"

"No, no. It is good. Maybe an aphrodisiac, but I would never need one being around you. Whatever it is, I like it." He drew back and took her hands again. "Look into my eyes, Lily. I want to gaze into your soul."

Shyly, she lifted her eyes. Always aware of the shock that his glance summoned, she looked into his eyes only to die and resurrect, then die again.

Between them an intangible connection began to form. Lilith began to feel as if he were part of herself and allowed herself to be drawn completely into the deep fathoms of his eyes.

She was no longer a dreamer dreaming dreams. He was here and she was here, alive—together. She felt a sense of newness. She felt innocence and freshness flood her. She was looking into a mirror that contained everything and nothing. She was awakening, ready to celebrate her fullness and womanliness; ready to unlock the mysteries of the universe.

"I see and honor you," he said quietly.

Exhaling slowly, she returned, "I love thee, Tahua Tane. I have always loved thee."

"We have been in each other all along."

"I believe thee," she affirmed.

He released her hands and lay her back, gently guiding her beneath him.

He began kissing her all over, carrying her spirit higher than heaven, where existence meant only the wet hot ecstasy of his next kiss upon her flesh.

She felt his hands spreading the strands of her hair. He caught up the soft cascading weight and rubbed it over his chest, her breasts, his lips, her lips. "Let your hair be my own small night," he whispered huskily.

One of his hands smoothed over the round of her shoulder, while the other moved under her hair and caressed her neck. Lowering his head, he brushed his lips across hers, his tongue dragging a lazy tracery to the hollow of her throat.

Then his hand left her neck, wandering downward through the silken tangle of her hair until his fingers cupped the fleshy swell of her breast.

"Let your twin breasts fill my mouth," he breathed.

She arched to him. The damp fire of his tongue circled her nipples as his careful suckling brought her near rapture.

"Oh—love," she moaned, sighing deeply.

His hands moved over her body, a delectable exploration, massaging, caressing, igniting, readying her for sweet union.

Until now, most of love had been in the waiting. She could wait no more. Her hands clung to the lean hardness of his hips and instinctively she began opening her thighs to him.

He met her wantonness with his own urgency. And then, gathering her body into his arms, he eased himself into her. He entered slowly, very slowly, secretly foraging his way into her deepest heart, straining against her silken, virginal cloak of last resistance. His lips descended to hers. His kisses possessed her. His breath possessed her. His body possessed her.

Between breath and sigh, he burst like a violent sea into the dark magnolia of her womb, overflowing with exquisite and exultant muscular force, simultaneously strong and soft, potent and yielding, alive and present in his every thrust. His heart unbound, he was free to love her with nothing withheld.

She felt melting surrender and full-bodied joy. An overwhelmingly blissful explosion rushed with delicious force in all directions of her body, pouring and soaring up and up, up through her heart, flooding her head, rising and rising, pulsating out and out. She floated on the currents of eternity, swooning, expanding like a thousand-petalled lotus—out and out.

"I love thee, Tahua Tane, I love thee . . ." she breathed, feeling the vital drops of warm erotic liquid slipping between her thighs amid eddying waves of winging ecstasy.

"And I love thee . . ." he whispered, overwhelmed by their intimate link of mind and body and celebration of undiluted love.

Chapter

10

Through the next moon's passing, Dunraven lived the life of open-faced happiness on Tiaretapu. Each morning he arose beside Lily, an awakened heart. Each day became a matter of dawn, swimming in the sea together; morning cool, eating fresh fruit together; heat of day, napping together; sunset, walking on the beach together; and night, moonrise and more loving.

All their needs were provided for by the islanders, though he took to fishing during low tides and ventured with Lily into the inner island to collect plant specimens. He knew little of botanics himself and rarely thought about the future. He lived life in the present without ever a thought of returning to England.

Then, one night he dreamed of his father. Or was it a dream? He could not be sure. His Lordship, in top hat and cloak, seemed to stand right in the middle of the hut, beckoning to him. Instinctively, he knew his father was dying. After two more appearances on the following nights, Dunraven paddled across the lagoon to consult Tiaro.

"Your father is dying, Tahua Tane," agreed Tiaro. "He calls you home and you must go. Such a visitation cannot be ignored."

"But I have no wish to leave. Lily will be heartbroken. I cannot leave her. You are more my father than he," Dunraven confessed.

"It makes no difference. He calls you. If you do not go, he may curse you and his curses would bring you misfortune."

After a night of restlessness and a day of beach walking, Dunraven gathered the intent to speak to Lily about it.

One afternoon while they were fishing, he finally spoke.

He was baiting his lure with a rather smelly parrot fish head. After casting, he turned to her and said, "There is a problem."

"Yes?" she said, her eyes innocently curious. He wedged the lure between the rocks and took her hands in his. Looking soulfully into her eyes, he said, "Lily, I must return to England soon."

Dunraven's revelation shocked Lilith. Her heart plummeted while her eyes searched his in confusion. Yes, she had noticed a difference in his manner the last few days. Once at night, he'd awakened and left her side, not returning until dawn.

"Is thee unhappy?"

His hands moved up to her shoulders and he embraced her gently. "No, no, Lily, I have never been so happy. Everything I have ever wanted is here on Tiaretapu."

"Then why?"

"My father is dying."

"How does thee know?"

"He has come to me in a dream three nights in a row. I was never close to him, but he calls me back to England. I must make peace with him before he dies."

"You know this all from a dream?"

"Yes."

Lilith's fingers curled over his forearms. "Can I go with thee?"

His hands dropped from her shoulders. Sunlight reflected off the sea like sharp daggers causing her eyes to crinkle in a watery squint. Her own intuitive sense told her his answer before he spoke.

"No, Lily. You cannot come with me."

The fishing line went slack. She opened her mouth to draw it to his attention, but realized by the intensity of his features he was not interested.

"Why?" she asked, her voice barely audible.

He sighed deeply. He clasped his hands together and leaned his elbows on his muscular thighs. Staring out to sea, he said, "You cannot go back to England with me because . . ." His words faded away. His gaze held on the far-off horizon.

"Because why?" Lilith prompted softly.

"Because I am lawfully wedded to another woman in England."

His confession did not shock Lilith, so much as that he had made it. At the same instant, she realized that now was the time to confess as well. She would declare that she was that other woman in England, indeed she was truly Lilith Cardew. The world would now be set to rights and they could live happily ever after on Tiaretapu.

But before she gathered her wits to speak, he said, "You must be patient, Lily. I intend to annul the marriage when I return to England. The woman means nothing to me. I married her out of obligation to her father. I must return to England alone and settle my affairs."

Something—call it pride or mortification—halted Lilith's tongue. He planned to annul their marriage because he had no feeling for her. What would happen if she now told him she was Lilith Cardew? Would he reject her flatly? A wave of insecurity flooded over her. To keep him, he must love both Lily and Lilith. But how would he ever learn to love Lilith? No matter the cost, she must return to England with him.

"I want to come with thee," she placed her hand on his shoulder.

"No," he said, insistently.

"If thee leaves, thee may never return."

He gave her an even look. "I give you my word, Lily. I will return to you."

Lilith lowered her eyes dejectedly. She was thrust into turmoil. She wished to speak more directly, more openly, but she realized as Lily she could not speak her mind.

Though the sun was shining full, a pall touched her heart. Paradise had ended.

Within the week, Dunraven spoke with Tiaro of his decision to return to his dying father. Tiaro began arrangements. A deep-water voyager was prepared and larded for the open-sea voyage. The destination would be Tahaa, the nearest island in the main shipping lanes.

Lilith sat cross-legged beside Dunraven in the communal house, her heart grieving. Around her the women sang melancholy songs of parting while the men, their faces painted with charcoal and wearing skirts of shredded leaves, drummed the ground with

173

lengths of bamboo. It was hard enough for her to face the sadness of Dunraven's imminent departure without the added burden of her fears of the dangers involved in traveling around the world. It could be a year or two years before she saw him again, if ever.

And what will happen when he returns to Eden Court and finds me gone? How long before he discovers I am not in residence in Devonshire?

All this and more plagued her thoughts. She had begged and pleaded of both him and Tiaro to let her go with him, but to no avail. Tiaro would never allow her to leave Reva Ra under any circumstances.

Food and drink appeared before Lilith on the mat of coconut fronds: pork wrapped in banana leaves and roasted in an underground oven, baked taro root, and sweet potato. To complete the meal *poe* was added, but Lilith had no appetite for any of it. Dunraven ate unenthusiastically, though this would be his last meal before he and the other men chosen for the voyage embarked.

"Eat," encouraged Heikua, as she piled more food before Lilith.

"I cannot," she replied, verging tears pooling in her eyes.

Dunraven's arm encircled her comfortingly. She leaned into him, sensing he too found little pleasure in this last feast before parting. Her head resting in the crook of his arm, she tilted her face upward to meet his warming gaze. Careful fingers reached to stroke a drift of hair from her forehead, while his lips brushed lightly across her cheek.

"The time will pass swiftly, love. I will have returned before you miss me."

"How can that be? I miss thee now, and thee has not even left."

"Do not fear it. We are destined to be together, you and I."

"Then take me with thee."

"No." His tone was flat and she regretted asking. She did not want to sound as pestering as a spoiled child.

The blare of a shell horn vibrated the air and Lilith's breast contracted. It was the call that the tide was turning and the voyagers must leave.

Neither spoke as Dunraven folded her tenderly in his arms and pressed his cheek to hers. Her skin melted against the heat of his own and she felt his chest, moving only slightly as he breathed. All of her wished to be suspended in time, forever in his arms.

He released her then, and abruptly came to his feet. She wanted to cling to him, grovel after him, plead one more time for him to stay with her, but she, too, had pride—somewhere. This moment, it had all but dissolved.

She walked beside him as he passed out of the communal house. The progress was slow as men, women, and children moved to embrace him and the others, showering him with flowered leis. Tears of farewell stained brown cheeks. Everyone wept energetically.

When at last she and Dunraven reached the beach, he touched her shoulder and said, "I have a gift for you." He took off the pouch that held the black pearl and placed it around her neck. "This is yours and it will be a symbol of my promise to return. I love you, Lily. We are linked together in spirit and body. Until I return, hold me in your heart."

Clutching the pouch in her hand, she looked up at the smoky gemstones of his eyes, trying to imprint their depth of assurance in her mind. All the while her "thank you" remained unspoken, trapped behind the gigantic swell of emotion blocking her throat. She felt like she would never be able to speak again.

Lightly, he brought the back of his hand slowly down the side of her face as if he, too, were tracing and fixing her image to memory. His hands slid around her again and she melted into his embrace another time. The tears began streaming down her cheeks. She inwardly cursed herself. She had planned to be very collected.

Then he shifted, looking away from her to the others who were climbing into a small *va'a* that would carry them out to the deep-water voyager. Catching her shoulders in the drape of his arm, he urged her a few steps further down toward the water. She clung to him, while the tide washed over her feet.

"I must go now, and you must let me." He put his fingertips to her chin and tilted it upward to him. Gently, he blotted the droplets of tears trickling over her lips with the soft flat of his thumb. "One last kiss?"

She nodded faintly, still unable to speak. His other hand pushed through her hair and caught the back of her neck.

Lilith blinked to see his face through the blurring tears. But it did not matter whether she saw him or not when he laid his lips on hers. Her eyes closed, the tears seeping from the corners while she swam in the bittersweet pressure of their farewell kiss. When he drew back, she let go a small involuntary sob.

Murmuring softly, "I love you, Woman Who Swims With the Rangahua. I love you," he pulled her back to him and held her close.

Then, he released her. She watched in abandoned silence as he walked away from her and into the sea.

In the following days, Lilith discovered all too quickly that, without her lover, paradise was a lonely place. Daily, her gaze stretched across the turquoise ocean beyond the soft violet of the horizon. She was learning that an island could be as expansive as the breadth of the universe or as imprisoning as a gaol.

Walking the island became an exercise in solitude. Her mind wandered with her feet. A full day would pass and she could remember only that the sun came up and that it now was setting. Heikua came often, bringing food and insisting she eat it. She did eat, but only indifferently. Her swims with the Rangahua became rare while a part of her fantasized climbing upon its back and riding all the way to England. And indeed, the time came when the idea was no longer a fantasy.

One cloudless day out of many, before the monsoons, Lilith found herself strolling the slender ribbon of sandspit at low tide. Black and white pelicans patrolled the tide line, hoping to be served up a proper tea of whelk and sand crab. She kept her eye on them as a pair launched into the air, a magnificent dance of wing and wind. Following their flight, her eyes were quick to notice a distant, unfamiliar shape toward the western horizon.

Her first thought was that it might be the islanders in the deep-water voyager returning from Tahaa. Her second thought was a hope that perhaps Dunraven would be with them. Unable to bear separation from her, maybe he had decided not to return to England after all. Hope awakened. She hurried back to the hut to fetch Dunraven's spyglass that he'd left, along with his copy of *An Explorer's Handbook Out.*

At first she walked tentatively, then picked up pace. She was positive the shapes were sails. Reaching a lookout point, she stopped, raised the spyglass to her right eye and adjusted it. In a split second she recognized a ship. Not a deep-water voyager, but a three-masted sailing ship of European variety.

She dropped the spyglass. Without any thought in her head but to get closer, she ran down to the water's edge and began clapping her hands.

"Rangahua, Rangahua," she shouted, repeatedly.

Maybe she'd been out in the island sun too long. But whatever the impetus, when she saw the black fin of the Rangahua slice across the lagoon, she dove into the water and began swimming toward the deep channel that was the portal to open sea.

The Rangahua trailed her in a playful and benign mood. It whistled and clicked, passing closely with an occasional nudge to her thigh. Today she had no wish to play and continued to swim. She prayed the Rangahua would follow her and eventually carry her through the hazardous currents of the channel.

She was tiring and finally took a handhold on the Rangahua's dorsal fin. An unspoken connection between them enjoined. As if by preappointment, the Rangahua ushered her through the channel and out to open sea.

Running away to sea, Lilith felt no fear. She trusted the Rangahua implicitly to take her to the sailing ship. She rode its back, lying just beneath the surface, the warm waves lapping over her like a comforting blanket.

Soon, the ship loomed gigantic before her. The name *Aberdeen* was scrolled across the bow. Hanging over the gunwale, sailors whistled and called. She lifted her arms and hailed them happily. The Rangahua kept distance, giving the ship an evaluating sweep. Its blowhole opened, then half closed with a sporadic trumpeting.

A line was thrown out. Lilith caught it and then, before she swam forward, she turned back to the Rangahua and pressed her cheek against the bottle nose.

"Thank you and good-bye," she said aloud, feeling an undying bond with the animal.

In an instant, Lilith began to realize that the vociferous greeting from the seamen was more than a friendly welcome. She had been uncivilized so long, she had forgotten the reaction civilized people had to uncivilized people—especially uncivilized women.

Half a dozen hands reached to assist her over the gunwale, but a sharp full-bodied voice bellowed a halt. "Keep yer mitts off her, lads. The first man who touches the lass will feel the crack of my cane. I'll no' have a mutiny on my ship over a bare-assed lassie."

His threat brought Lilith full around to the perilous predicament she entangled herself in. She was standing naked before a ship full of female-starved sailors. Looking into their faces, she could predict their thoughts to the man. For a split second, she almost turned around to leap over the ship's side back into the sea.

It seemed an eternity, but she gathered herself and drew up with all the dignity a well-bred Englishwoman might muster. Clearing her throat she sought the sunburned face of the man who leaned upon a blackthorn cane and whom she supposed to be no less than the *Aberdeen*'s captain.

In her most clipped aristocratic tone she announced, "I am Lilith Cardew, daughter of the renowned explorer, Andrew Cardew." She dared not use the titled name of Dunraven for fear it would bring forth too many questions she was not prepared to answer. "I have been shipwrecked. Please be kind enough to give me safe passage."

Her words as well as her cultured tone had the desired effect as visible surprise registered on all faces.

"Jamie Strahan, give the lass yer shirt," ordered the captain.

The black-haired Jamie Strahan was out of his shirt faster than a mosquito at swatting time. Lilith took it in hand and before all onlooking eyes, lifted it over her head. It fell just below her thighs.

The captain stepped forward and in a warm voice said, "Captain Robert Lachlan, at your service. I will hear yer full story in the privacy of my cabin below. Come with me."

That night, Lilith lay on a rude-smelling, lumpy mattress on the floor of the ship's storage room. Feeling the roll of the ship and hearing the faint stir of rodents, she massaged her temples, trying to ease away the first headache she'd had since setting out for the Pacific a lifetime before.

She had not told Captain Lachlan the full story. She only detailed the storm and being cast adrift as well as being found by the natives.

When he asked if she had seen Adam Dunraven, she pled ignorance. And then he shrugged and gave a queer grin saying that he could understand why the natives might eat Dunraven and not her.

He promised her safe passage, but only if she remained below until the ship ported in Papeete. There, he felt confident, she could take passage back to England.

Feeling as if she'd made the wrong decision in leaving the island, she fingered the small pouch at her neck. She already felt homesick for Reva Ra, its freedom and beauty and, most of all, the islanders who had become her family. Would Tiaro ever forgive her for leaving without even a farewell?

And, more saddening, would she ever return? Tears rose in her eyes and she curled over on her side and wished and wished and wished to be back on Tiaretapu in the arms of Adam Dunraven.

Chapter

11

Adam Dunraven stood as stationary as one of the statues that dressed the tombs of Kenne Kirk cemetary. The dull thud of earth hitting coffin wood broke the midday silence. The villagers, the tenants, the staff, and the steward of Dunraven Castle had performed their obligation and returned home. He remained watching the gravediggers fill the six-foot hole with the dark-clay earth that his ancestors bid claim to for centuries—earth that held no attachment for him.

He lifted his eyes above the tombstones, past the kirk's bell tower, beyond the village rooftops to the turrets of Dunraven Castle. He was the last in the line, the one responsible to continue a noble heritage. Yet, he felt no connection here, only duty to provide an heir and now that he was no longer celibate, he could very well do so. His thoughts turned to his beloved Lily. He had promised that in time he would return to

Reva Ra. Soon, he would keep that promise no matter the cost.

"Adam, the coach awaits, whenever you are ready," came the voice of Charles Vivian from behind.

Dunraven turned to his longtime companion who had been inside the kirk speaking with the cleric. "Yes, well, I've done with saying my few farewells. I never knew my father, so you might say my grief is prosaic."

He adjusted his cape to warmth. He remembered that even as a child he never reconciled with the cold damp of the north country. A brief flash of snapping blue skies, coral seas, and the woman assaulted his mind. Again, he felt the interminable prod of wanderlust that never ceased to dog him when he spent any amount of time in England.

Charles stepped forward and Dunraven fell into stride. "You knew him well enough to return to his bedside after being visited in a dream."

"True. But I am hastily regretting it. I vow never to sit at a deathbed again. Such activities have drastically complicated, even ruined, my life. First, Andrew Cardew's plea that I marry his daughter, and now my father's last lucid breath in which he begged me to sire a child of Lilith Cardew. Tell me, Charles, do I look like a stud in the Royal Stable?"

Charles stifled a chuckle. "Not if you are still celibate."

"I am not."

"Good God! What precedes this miracle?"

"It is a long and romantic story. While we ride back to London, I shall tell you in detail. Suffice to say, I am now a bigamist."

"A bigamist!" Charles' amusement dissolved.

"I am a man wedded to two women—one from duty, the other from love."

"I need not ask which woman is which, but I will say I am shocked to the core. You have scoffed the notion of romantic love lifelong. Now, you tell me you have fallen in love and succumbed to the most ignoble of deeds, bigamy. I thought you a man of honor, Dunraven. From celibacy to bigamy! I am appalled."

"I do not excuse myself. I am well aware of my ignominious behavior. I wrestle with it hourly, daily, and nightly. When you hear the full account of my situation, perhaps you will understand—and, in some part, counsel me."

"I will state on the outset that any counsel from me will be biased. I am extremely fond of Lady Dunraven. I have met her but twice and those meetings left me inspired and covetous of another man's wife."

Dunraven looked over at Charles with surprise. "In truth?"

"In truth!"

"Charles, now I am the one shocked."

"Have no fear, I will not press suit to a married woman, especially my best friend's wife. But you see my position."

"Clearly. It may give you hope to know that I had considered asking for an annulment upon my return."

"You have not spoken to her?"

"No. She has left Eden Court. I was told she was in residence in Devonshire. I wrote to her informing her of my return. Even with the event of my father's death, in these three months, she has not responded to my communications."

"Nor has she mine," added Charles, his expression puzzled.

"You have tried to contact her?"

"Indeed, I—" Charles cleared his throat—"I found her to be an enjoyable companion."

Dunraven bit back a wry smile. "And I believed her to be a recluse by nature and habit." He remembered that day when she had blatantly asked if she were required to remain celibate as well. He looked sidelong at Charles and speculated the possibility of . . . No, Charles was much too honorable for an affair. He continued, "Nevertheless, I intend to go to Devonshire and meet with her. After I explain things, there is a good chance that she will agree to an annulment."

"And if she refuses?"

"Then I must keep my word to Cardew, my father, and to Lily, the woman I love."

Charles laughed outright. "Such a feat is beyond us mortal men, but you—you might just succeed." He shook his head and asked, "Tell me of this other woman, Lily. I gather you met her in the Pacific? Is she native?"

"Yes."

"Then you wedded her in tribal tradition, not under English law?"

"Correct. But I am bound to her far beyond the narrow confines of civilized law. She is my twin soul, Charles—"

"Twin soul? Have you been reading the Romantics? What is a twin soul?"

"I know you do not subscribe to the Eastern notion of karma but, believe me, this woman and I are bound together heart, mind, and soul. You speak of the Romantics, who idealized the meeting of a man and a woman whose spirits rush together in joyful recognition, and inner knowing that only through each other can they hope to find wholeness. It is not just an ideal of poets, Charles. It has happened to me."

"You weren't chewing island hallucinogens, were you?"

"If love is a hallucinogen, then I am guilty."

Charles shook his head and sighed, "I will take your word, though I freely admit these mystical things are beyond me. Where is she now, your twin soul? The island?"

"Yes. And I intend to return to her as soon as possible."

"You amaze me. I cannot believe all that you have told me."

"I do not give a preacher's damn whether you believe me or not," shrugged Dunraven. "I have explained as much as I will to you."

The two reached the coach. The horses, sensing their approach, shook impatiently in their halters as the liveryman tipped down the steps and opened the door.

"We're to London now, m'lord?" asked the coachman, reining back the horses.

"Aye, Matthews. To Eden Court."

It was half-past midnight when Lilith awakened—awakened to the deep, fine tones of *his* voice sounding through the garden court.

"Narota, bring Charles and myself some cold supper. We have not eaten. We made the journey in excellent time."

The Daring Dunraven had returned.

She sat up, straining to hear him. She loved that voice. Her senses soared. She wanted to jump from the bed and rush into his arms, but she could not. She was no longer Lily, the Atua Tamahine, but Lilith Cardew, the invisible wife of Adam Dunraven.

Only three days earlier, she'd returned herself. The voyage had been marked by calm seas, steady winds, and a brief stay in Southampton, where she'd had a new dress made—black bombazine with black veil. Her reintroduction to the corset had been harrowing.

Nearly a year and half after her late November departure she was again at Eden Court—a changed woman, a different woman. When she had arrived, Narota had greeted her with the news that Adam Dunraven had recently returned from his expedition to be at the side of his dying father in Yorkshire.

"It is proper you have come, Lady Dunraven," Narota had said. "The master has sent a note stating his intent to return to Eden Court after the affairs of his father are settled."

She listened. Dunraven's voice faded off. She heard their footsteps move down the colonnade and realized the men would take supper in the library. Dunraven's private rooms adjoined the library, not her own. Of course, in a loveless marriage, such an arrangement proved convenient.

Her heart beat erratically. She would not sleep again this night. She yanked aside the tapestry bed-curtains and came to her feet, crossed the room, and lit a candle on her dressing table. Her cheeks flushed the color of rubies in the mirrored reflection.

Who was the woman staring back at her with eyes haunted by love? Peering intently into her reflection, she traced a fingertip over her face. She was still amazed that her scars had vanished. In a slow dawning, she realized she was no longer Lilith Cardew— nor was she the Atua Tamahine.

She saw someone new emerging in her looking glass—a full-bodied woman, beautiful and statuesque, a woman who did not fear, but loved. The expectancy of that realization caused her stomach to feel like it housed a butterfly migration.

She turned away from her reflection, then turned back.

What should she do?

Should she reveal herself or continue to play out the charade? What if he never intended to return to Reva Ra? Would he be like a thousand travelers promising their hearts to native girls, never to return?

How could she judge him? Her own duplicity kept her from condemning his.

A despair weltered up inside her.

Could he love the woman she was becoming?

Questions, always questions circling in her mind like the sharks of Pearl Lagoon.

Looking around, her insecurities loomed as ominous as the demon ceremonial masks on the lattice screen walls.

The voice of fear became a relentless inquisitor. She should have never returned to England. She had entrapped herself monumentally.

Yet, amid all the harpies of her mind, the voice of her heart rose above the dissonant clamor. *Because you love, you will be loved.*

Outside the window the sky appeared as burnished gunmetal, while raindrops flung themselves against the windowpane like a scattering of transparent bullets. Lilith yawned, her eyes contemplating a tenacious tendril of ivy growing through the casing. She was again in the lush jungle beauty of Tiaretapu, plucking a handful of orchids to throw down upon Dunraven as he swam in the pools.

"Lilith? Lilith?" Samara's soft voice brought her back to the present. "Is that the end?"

Lilith's eyes refocused on page 543 in the book, *Tales of the Arabian Nights*. "Ah—yes, ah—no, mother. I'm not really sure."

"Well," sighed Samara, adjusting herself more comfortably in her bed. "If you cannot read to me properly, go to your husband. Rupee said he returned last night. He will expect a sweet reunion after such a long separation. Your father always did. Though he had no qualms about abandoning me long months, even years, for his adventures. I resented it, you know. I've never said it. But I did resent it. Our time together was usually so brief, I dared not complain. What man returns to a complaining woman?"

Lilith felt a rush of empathy for her mother. She knew what it was like to be left behind, and now after all these years, she understood clearly her mother's melancholia.

"Go tell Rupee to prepare my bath. I intend to take a lavishly hot bath. These cold fall rains seep into my very marrow."

"It is spring, mother, not fall," Lilith corrected.

"Really? Well, in England, one is the same as the other."

Lilith smiled lovingly at Samara. She shut the book and placed it on the bed table. "I'll come back later, mother."

"I do not count on it." Samara's black eyes became extremely lucid. "Where is it you disappear to, Lilith?"

"I suppose, mother," her voice wistful, "the same place you do."

"And where is that, my dear?"

"Paradise," she breathed softly. "Paradise."

She slipped out the door and proceeded across the

central court. She stopped and sat in a wicker chair. She breathed in the dusky smell of hothouse foliage, scanned the potted palms and spied a ribbon-tailed bird, and dipped her fingers into the dulcet-flowing fountain.

She wondered, could paradise be here, at Eden Court?

The tinkling bell of the morning post cut through the household quiet. A moment later, Narota padded through the colonnade, a tray of missives in his hand.

"Madam," he bowed, and offered the tray for her perusal.

Most were correspondence for Dunraven, but two caught her eye. One was addressed to Lord and Lady Dunraven, undoubtedly an invitation to some social affair. The other, addressed to her alone, was a packet from her publisher.

Lilith slipped it from the tray, nodding a dismissal to Narota. "Thank you, Narota."

"Madam," he bowed and departed.

She watched him go, wanting privacy while she opened the small packet. The publisher had forwarded a letter. It was neatly penned, imprinted with the seal of the Royal Geographic Society. Carefully, she broke the wax seal and opened it. Her lips moved as she read once, then a second time, a request that she—no, he—Lyman Brazen lecture at the Royal Geographic Society.

At first, she could not believe it. Then she realized the Society had no inkling Lyman Brazen was a woman. The sensible part of her knew she must send her regrets and a polite promise for the future. However, she could not forget the day when she went to fetch her father's belongings and the doorman would not let her pass. Well, she knew the assembly hall lectures were open to both men and women. Her mind began clicking. She was no longer a fraud. She had left England and could provide them details of legitimate experiences. Who among them had walked on fire? Yes, she would have an adventure to tell those aging, armchair explorers!

While she sat in her room at her desk composing an acceptance to the Royal Geographic Society, she felt a mixture of excitement and apprehension.

A knock sounded at her door. Her pen halted. "Come in, please," she invited, lowering her veil over her face.

Narota peeked through the door. "Madam, I am sorry to disturb you, but the master wishes an interview with you at your earliest convenience."

Nervousness stirred in Lilith's stomach and she wished she'd not eaten kippers for breakfast. She knew "earliest convenience" meant right away.

"Tell him, I will come soon."

Before Narota stepped out, she said, "One moment. Can you post this letter for me?"

"Yes, madam. This I can do."

She hastily made one last scrawl, a false but flamboyant signature of the renowned Lyman Brazen. She sealed the letter.

After Narota departed, she took time to steady her nerves and, yes, reach for the single perfume bottle on her dressing table that contained eau de gardenia. The day before she had visited three perfumeries to find just the right scent. She doused herself liberally and left her room. Her passage through the court colonnade left the air pungent with the full bloom of gardenias.

Her knock on the library door was firm and confident.

"Please enter," came his sovereign voice.

She entered, her veil hazing the rugged vitality of his startling features. He had lost the deep bronze island tan, but his complexion remained smoothly shaven and his hair shockingly golden. He was dressed as a proper gentleman, his coat a snug fit over his broad shoulders, while his black breeches outlined the muscular curve of his thighs. But, as ever, the serpent tattoo on his cheek blazed a reminder that he was not like other proper gentlemen.

Without inhibition she wanted to kiss him full on the lips, press herself to his hard male anatomy, and beg for the heat of his desire. Instead she seated herself primly in the overstuffed chair. Sitting there before him, she realized all too sharply that abiding in the same household with no love between them would be akin to living in hell.

Behind him, indigo flames danced in the hearth. He was half turned from her when she saw his chin lift and he sniffed the air. Then, quite abruptly, he riveted his attention fully to her, an expression of puzzlement on his face.

His brows knit slightly and his eyes were hard upon her.

Had she given herself away? A part of her hoped so; she wanted to be done with this disguise.

He bowed slightly. "Good day, madam. We meet again."

"Indeed, we do," she said softly. She knotted together her shaking fingers as tightly as silk tatting.

He continued conversationally. "I trust you and your mother are well?" He stepped closer to her, away from the heat of the fire.

"We are that."

"Narota tells me you have been residing in Devonshire while I have been away."

Lilith did not like to add lie upon lie so she said, "I offer my condolences over your father's death."

"I believe he has found peace." Dunraven's eyes lowered, and he momentarily fell into contemplative silence.

What would he say next, she wondered? Would he now ask for the annulment and confess love for another woman? Or would he skirt the issue altogether?

There was visible tension in the way he stiffly held himself. He appeared taller and more intense than she'd ever experienced him; to be so near him yet kept at a distance added to her turmoil.

"To speak forthrightly, madam. I have not."

"Ah?" Lilith paused, her attention on his body, not his words. "Not what?"

"Not found peace," he answered.

His fingers stroked his chin thoughtfully. "On his deathbed, my father asked for my pledge to sire an heir. You are aware that this is something of a burden to me, since I avowed to be celibate."

Was he using celibacy to cry off, she wondered? Would he lie to her?

His jaw clenched tightly, hollowing the tall cheekbones with distaste. "I have given this much thought. I respect you. I will not use you as a breed mare, no matter what my father's last request. I realize neither of us entered this marriage from love and I have no wish to sire a child without love. Consequently, since the marriage has never been consummated, I see but one avenue."

Sadly, she knew what card would fall next. Her heart churned, her hopes plummeted. No matter that she wanted to kiss every inch of his body; at this point she had no high moral compunctions. She would breed with him in an instant—here and now—on the floor of his library like a she cat in heat, if he so wished.

"I am asking you for an annulment."

She had known it, but knowing did little to serve her now. The fire crackled in the hearth. The room's atmosphere dragged like a Sunday sermon.

She sat quite still, allowing the silence to speak her answer. She still doubted herself enough that she feared the consequences of telling him who she really was. He was in love with Lily, not the veiled, civilized recluse, Lilith Cardew, nor the new woman that was emerging from the very depths of her being.

Finally, he cleared his throat and asked, "Are you agreeable to this?"

"Does it matter what I am agreeable to?" she asked in a slow voice.

"Of course it matters."

"Then my answer is no. I am not agreeable to an annulment," she said firmly.

"No?" His tone was clipped.

"No," she said firmly.

He turned his back to her. He put his hands on his hips and he gazed into the fire. She could almost see the wheels turning in his head. How was he going to extricate himself from this unhappy union? She could make it easier, but she would not. She would play it out to the fullest, for she had all to lose and nothing to gain.

He took his time before speaking, and when he finally turned back to face her, his tone was falsely patient.

"I see no advantage for you in denying me," he challenged with measured logic. "I am a wealthy man, I have no intention of leaving you destitute."

Lilith lifted her chin and the veil swayed slightly. She accused indignantly, "You offer to pay me off as if I were a harlot."

He visibly winced. "Forgive me, I did not wish to offend."

"Whether you wished to or not, you *have* offended me—deeply."

"How can you compare yourself to a harlot?" he asked smoothly, inclining his head with sincerity.

"I did not say I felt like a harlot, only that by paying me off, you were treating me so."

He shifted his stance. He lifted one foot to a Moroccan foot hassock and rested an arm on his thigh. "I made it quite clear from the outset that our marriage was in name only. I have acted honorably."

"Is it honorable to marry a woman with no intention of bedding her?"

He gave a half laugh and moved upright. "Hah! Most English brides would swoon with relief."

"Not I," she confessed softly.

He shrugged with disbelief saying, "I do not believe my ears. Your expectations for an arranged marriage are naive at best."

She unclasped her hands and with a vigorous thump on the arm of her chair, she said animatedly, "Three quarters of the nobility arrange marriages! I daresay three quarters of those gentlemen bed their wives and their houses multiply with offspring."

He was looking hard at her. Then his eyes narrowed, a canny light igniting in them. "You want children, don't you? Like all women, you wish to fill the full measure of your creation." His demeanor gentled. "Forgive me, I have not taken into account the feminine biological drive to maternity."

"Sweet heaven," Lilith muttered under her breath.

She rose to her feet and clutched her hands at her sides in an attempt at control. She put more distance between them. She glared out the small diamond-paned window to the street and then turned back to face him. "What I want is a wedding night! I want a night to prove that I can be wife to you."

His features impassive, he stood very still gazing at her through opaque eyes. It was as though he were seeing her for the first time. There was no point in trying to guess what he was thinking.

As for her, she had two choices. The first, reveal herself now and hope he would love her enough to forgive her. Or second, give him the annulment and then attempt to begin with a fresh palette.

Slipping his hands in his pockets, he took a compromising step toward her and said, "If I give you your *bedding* night, will you give me my annulment?"

His words stunned her. This surprising offer widened her options, but also made her mad. How could he propose to bed her when he loved Lily? Of course, she was Lily but he did not know that.

"I thought you were celibate."

"I was."

"You were?" Her voice held just a titch of jealous derision.

"No longer."

"May I ask what prompted this change of philosophy?"

"You may. However, now is not the time to discuss it."

His tone was polite, but something in his features warned her he would not be vivisected by her curiosity. And, at that moment, she hated herself unabashedly—for knowing and pretending not to know.

"What if I beget a child from this one-time union?"

"I will take precaution."

"But would that not enable you to fulfill your father's last request?"

"It would. But again, I am not in love with you. There will be no child from this union. I will guarantee."

At this point, Lilith would agree to anything he proposed just to be in his arms once again. She gathered up her nerve and said in a voice deceptively indifferent—which she hoped would fool him— "When do you wish to rendezvous?"

"Tonight."

"Tonight?"

"Yes. Tonight."

She knew it was not from ardor that he set the time so soon. She knew he wished it over with, wished her gone from his household.

"Where?" she asked, like an innocent pausing for directions.

"Here, of course, at Eden Court."

"I will not come to you. Give me my dignity in this one aspect, at least."

"It is given. I will come to you."

"Thank you for the courtesy."

"The hour?"

"Midnight."

"Midnight it will be."

He said nothing more. His striking features were relaxed, but his expression remote. With everything settled and by his failure to say more, she knew she must take her leave. Still, she stood, staring at him like a child stares at a glass jar of peppermint sticks in hopes one will be offered.

Finally, she turned to the door. He had the grace to move to open it. As she swished out, he said, "If you change your mind, send a note to me by Narota."

She paused, her back to him, and said clearly, "I will not change my mind, Adam Dunraven."

Chapter

12

⸺❦⸺

The night was very dark and a thin, cold rain was falling. Dunraven ran along the pavement, bare-headed and bare chested. He followed the north side of the river to the east of London Bridge. Realizing the time was late, he changed course and began his return route to Eden Court. He hoped the exertion would clear his head and somehow rectify the fact that soon he would be betraying the woman he loved with a woman he did not love.

Why?

How did he let it happen? He did not have to sleep with her to begin proceedings for an annulment. In fact, bedding her would complicate the business—the marriage would be consummated. Was it Lilith Cardew's Bluestocking impertinence that pushed him into agreement, or was he so love-sick for Lily that when the Cardew woman came into the room, the trigger of her perfume nudged him over the edge? Odd enough, in thinking back to that instant, he'd almost felt Lily's presence.

The drizzling mist touched his face like cool feathers and he longed for just one more kiss from Lily's lips. This night, what he wouldn't give for the mysterious woman behind the black veil to be the Woman Who Swims With the Rangahua.

Moving ferally, he dashed through the rain-slicked street and up the steps and across the threshold of Eden Court. He would bathe and prepare himself. Maybe the woman was having misgivings herself. With a little tact and sensitivity, he might gracefully bow out of the bargain. . . .

Lilith waited.

The clock chimed half-past midnight.

He was late.

The miasma of disappointment settled upon Lilith like a stillborn sea.

He will not come.

On the one hand, her heart rejoiced at his faithfulness to Lily; on the other, the thought of spending another night in the same house with him and not being loved by him was more than she could possibly bear. She had taken great care to turn out every lamp, bank the fire in the hearth, and secure tightly the tapestry drapes of the antique bed. She was in complete darkness. He would never see her face.

But would he guess?

Would he smell her scent? Were the contours of her body, the feel of her skin, impressed upon his mind?

She rested her head against the pillow, listening for the faintest sound of a footstep.

Please come! Please. Sweet heaven, she loved him! It had been too long without him.

You must come, Tahua Tane. You must.

Then it began, the drumming. Like the dream she'd had that first night in Eden Court, the rhythms snaked through the colonnades like an ancient litany, calling her. She sat up, pulled back the bed-curtains and moved to her feet. She wouldn't wait any longer. She would go to him in his library. She would stand before him, casting her veil aside, along with her pride and common sense. She would ask his forgiveness of her deception, and beg on her knees for his love, if need be.

She stepped across the smooth crush of the rug, pausing to light a small lamp, and stood before the full-length looking glass. Who was this woman staring back at her?

Lily or Lilith? Neither.

She unclasped her hair so it fell over her shoulders down against the folds of her ivory silk wrapper. She peered closer at her reflection, as if seeing herself for the first time. The pads of her fingers traced her cheek, her forehead, and chin.

Still flawless.

She wanted to dance for him again. She placed her hands on her hips and swayed provocatively to the steady drumbeat echoing through the night. She closed her eyes allowing her body to move with the slow, engulfing rhythm.

She wrapped her arms around herself and twirled slowly to the drumming cadence; that primal part of him embraced her as surely as if he were in the room.

She would go to him now, and face him at last.

The drumming stopped.

So did her heart. And then, in her breast, she felt the leap of hiccups. Her eyes flashed open. *Not now!* She swallowed seven times without breathing and prayed it would thwart the attack.

It did.

Rooted in place, she turned off the lamp and stood straining to hear in the sudden stillness.

She heard footsteps in the colonnade court. The hiccups gone, now her heart began thumping. Where and how should she stand? Should she go to the bed or remain standing in the middle of the darkened room? Lamplight filtered through the latticed screen walls. Perhaps it was only Narota in one last round of the household.

"Madam, I am without your door," came Dunraven's low voice. "If you wish me to enter, I would have you invite me in yourself."

Her words came out in a nervous hush. "First, I will extinguish the lamp."

"As you wish."

Darkness swallowed all light as her eyes dilated like a cat's at midnight.

"Enter—please."

The latch lifted and his silhouette passed through the doorway.

Lilith stood in the sooty shadows, enveloped in misgivings. The fear niggled that if she revealed herself now, he would reject her. She must wait. The time was not now. Perhaps after—after—

Within his lifetime, Adam Dunraven had bedded many women, yet he had bedded only one out of love. Tonight he would go through the motions of love without love. Playing the role of courtly lover, he would pleasure this woman with the artifices of seduction, but he would not love.

She lived as a shadow. Would she feel like a shadow in his arms?

Without being a lying hypocrite, could he tell her she was beautiful despite her disfigurement, that he desired her? He sensed she had no wish to hear such false bouquets from him. He would handle her gently, even kindly.

Good Lord! He wanted to turn back around and walk out.

Instead, he bowed to her with respectful grace. "Good evening, madam."

"And to you, Adam Dunraven." Her voice carried sweetly in the darkness.

"Pray, madam. Do you still wish for a night of love?"

"I do. We have made an agreement." Her tone assured him she would not renege.

"Then I am here to accommodate you."

Some sense told him she was coming across the room to him. He heard the rustle of her clothing and, again, the cloying scent of her gardenia perfume drifted to his nostrils.

"Where do we begin?" her voice was near, just in front of him.

"We begin at the beginning."

"And what is the beginning, Adam Dunraven?"

"To touch." His arms reached out and encircled her phantom form. He felt her fingers slip around his waist.

"Are you as nervous as I?" she breathed lightly.

He was nervous. She was undoubtedly a virgin. Along with civilized women, virgins were at the top of his avoidance list of intimate encounters—except for Lily. The mere thought of her filled him with unbridled longing.

"Dear lady, I would rather meet a hundred spear-hurling tribesmen than face you this night," he confessed truthfully, and then discovered his hands had wandered to stroke the filaments of her unbound hair. The texture and length held the echo of Lily. She pressed against him with a gentle fervency that he found endearing.

She gave a barely audible laugh.

"You don't believe me?"

"I do, indeed. But I am amused that the Daring Dunraven would confide such a fact."

"Amusing you was not my intent, but if it eases the awkwardness, then by all means, I am for levity."

"Myself as well. All and any," she returned amenably.

The steady pressure of her body against his own was a warm and growing connection. Despite himself, he felt tenderness for her. As he enclosed her in his arms, he sensed her vulnerability and her innocence, and realized there would be no shortcut to loving her this night.

Slowly, she pulled back from him and caught his hand. "Come to the bed. My legs are quite wobbly."

"As you wish."

She pushed aside the brocade curtains and sat down on the edge of the bed. Following her lead, he sat beside her, closely, decorously, but not intimately.

A strained silence fell between them. He had no wish to rush into lovemaking, yet he knew he must take the lead at some point and began a careful initiation. He should not have agreed to this.

Her soft breathing whispered to his ears and still he longed for Lily.

Where was she now? Swimming with her Rangahua, no doubt, in the Pearl Lagoon. Yearning shot through him and he felt his desire rise at the thought of her.

"This bed—it is very unusual," she remarked with obvious intent of moving things forward.

"Yes, it is from Tibet. Very old. I bought it in a market village near Lasli. It is said to have belonged to an ancient master of the Tantra and has mystical properties of bewitchment. I have never slept in it myself, but was quite taken by the craftsmanship and intricacy of detail. Do you find it comfortable?"

"Yes, very much so. Oddly, my dreams are extremely vivid—too vivid. I can believe the bed is bewitched."

"You don't become frightened, do you?"

"Oh, no. The dreams are not frightening, the dreams are—are erotic."

"Erotic," his voice held amusement. "I must try this bed out myself."

"What better time than now?" she returned, her words a light challenge.

"Quite," he returned dryly. She was too precocious.

"Might I ask you a question?"

"Ask away. This night I am completely at your service."

"You speak of the Tantra. What is it?"

"You do not know?"

"No."

"Surely your father . . . He was well versed on the subject."

"Truly?"

"I suppose it is understandable you did not know. Your father was a proper Victorian gentleman in all ways."

"He did keep some of his books locked away. I believed them to be valuable, but perhaps he knew I would read them. Now, I realize, he did not deem them fit for young female consumption."

Dunraven smiled to himself, remembering his old mentor.

"The Tantra would probably bore most young females. It is a series of esoteric Hindu books that describe—ah—certain sexual rituals, disciplines, and meditations. These ancient Indian books are over two thousand years old. The books were written in the form of a dialogue between the Hindu god, Shiva, who is the penetrating power of focused energy, and his consort, Shakti, who represents the female creative force. Tantra is a spiritual system in which sexual love is a sacrament."

"A sacrament—I am intrigued," she confessed softly.

She would be, thought Dunraven on the aside. He cleared his throat circumspectly. "Being avowed to celibacy these past years, some aspects of my Tantra are a bit rusty."

"What better time to oil the hinges than now?"

The woman was incorrigible. He felt the shy press of her small hand upon his knee. Undeniably, her touch stirred him.

"Come, get more comfortable." She moved away from him and into the dark cavern of the bed. He felt her hand on his shoulder. "Move, here, beside me." She patted the pillow bolsters and shifted herself against the headboard.

He lifted his legs upon the bed and relaxed back.

"Your boots, let me help you remove your boots."

Her offer took him unawares. "No—I—"

"No, you must let me."

After some effort on his part, and a near tumble off the bed on hers, a boot slipped off.

"Heave ho!" She gave a shout and broke into laughter with the yank of his other boot.

He liked her laughter, it was familiar. In the darkness, he began sensing things about her. She seemed buoyant, energetic, yet refined. Obviously she was a serious thinker, most likely an inherited trait from her brilliant father. He liked her combativeness even from the beginning, when she had been presumptuous enough to speak up upon the intimate matters of their marital arrangements.

"Now"—she was back beside him, her hips sidling beside his own—"now, you must instruct me further in the Tantra."

"I must, must I. Your father always said you were curious to a fault."

"Did he talk of me often?"

"Yes, he did." Upon retrospect, Dunraven remembered Andrew speaking of his daughter with immense pride and a touch of pity. He mourned that she would never experience life to the fullest because of her disfigurement.

"That pleases me to know it. But we are not here to reminisce about my father. Are you forestalling my education, Adam Dunraven? Do you hope I will tire and fall asleep, thereby releasing you from the obligation of making love to me?"

He chuckled. "It did cross my mind."

"You do not have to make love to me, you know."

"I don't?" he tried to disguise the creeping relief in his voice.

"No, you don't. If you wish, I will make love to you. But you must instruct me, step by step."

The woman was absurdly charming and flagrantly attempting seduction. Under other circumstances, he would find her company diverting, even companionable.

"From this instant on, I am at *your* service, Adam

Dunraven. If you are not pleased with the outcome of our lovemaking, it will merely reflect on your ability as a Tantric tutor."

He nearly guffawed in her face—if he could but see it. There was no denying it now, the woman was a Bluestocking if ever he'd met one. Her polite taunting of his virility riled him. Hell or high water, this night he would rise to the occasion.

"Let us hope you are an apt pupil, madam."

"I am more than apt, Dunraven—" her voice lowered to a confiding whisper—"I am wanton."

He could have laughed, but he did not. He did not laugh for the reason that he heard such a despairing in her tone, a longing for something more. . . . Too well, he knew that longing and now he recognized it in the heart of another.

In a spontaneous act, he sought her hand and took it in his own. He lifted it to his lips and brushed a light kiss across her slim fingers. "By all means, let us begin," he said.

"I am all ears," she replied, her fingers circling his own.

"The Tantra, dear lady, is the art of conscious loving. Its goal is ecstasy with one's beloved."

"And who is your beloved, Adam Dunraven?"

Her question took him off guard and gave the final charge to the tension snapping in the atmosphere. He turned her hand over consideringly and touched his lips to the warm, soft flesh of her palm.

"Tonight, it shall be you."

The ardency with which he reached for her surprised even himself. His hands caught the delicate narrowness of her shoulders and he drew her across his lap, cradling her in his arms. The swell of emotion he experienced as he caressed her left him shaken. It was as if Lily were in his arms—how could it be?

The bed?

The legend could be true; perhaps the bed was enchanted. The way she fit in his arms, the thick mass of hair, her scent. Good God! He prayed the illusion would hold until he'd given Lilith Cardew her night of love.

As their mouths searched for and found each other, he surrendered fully to the magic. He kissed her, lovingly and long, with the passion of unpretense. She returned his ardor, giving herself deeply, twining closer, her mouth spread wide to his, open to the sensual stroke of his tongue.

He licked the pliant silk of her mouth, traced the soft inner lip with the familiar expertise of a longtime lover.

He begged exchange. "Give me your tongue."

Compliantly, though somewhat timidly, her tongue slipped between his lips. He sucked her into himself. She tasted deliciously familiar and, yes, wanton.

His hand moved to unfasten the sash at her waist and her robe gaped open. Her skin felt warm as gold, smooth, satiny, and vibrant. She wore nothing beneath her wrapper and soon it pooled around her hips. He found himself lowering his kisses to the hollow of her throat, then to the intimate furrow of her bosom. His tongue tip laved the piquant bud of her breast, and he heard a breathy moan issue from her lips.

The life force was awakening in her. In a slow dive, his hand caressed downward to cup the soft mound of her womanhood. The connection sparked his own desire and he felt his manhood swelling with the creative drive.

"Now, Lilith," he whispered to her ear. "You must undress me." He drew his hands away from her.

"I am inexperienced at such a task. You must be patient for it is very dark," she said, moving to straddle him.

"I could light a candle—," he offered.

"No! No, I will manage."

"I want to see your eyes. I know it is common in more repressed societies to make love in the dark, but I believe it eliminates the potential for a deeper bonding experience."

"I am sorry, but no."

He knew he must honor her wish, but he felt sorry that she must live her life hiding her face from all. "What color are your eyes, Lilith?"

"My eyes are . . . What color are the eyes of the woman you gave up celibacy for?"

"How did you know it was a woman which brought about my change of heart?"

"Call it intuition."

"Her eyes are black like midnight pearls."

"Then tonight, Dunraven, my eyes are black."

He felt the brush of her nails as she began unbuttoning his shirt. His own hands reached to gently knead her shoulders while he kept the pleasuring connection with her skin.

She helped him shrug out of his shirt and, in a spontaneous gesture, she raked her nails lightly across his chest and played the nubs of his nipples with the balls of her thumbs.

He arched to her stroking.

He felt her lips at his throat and, in a reflection of his earlier example, her richly moist tongue tip snaked down, circled the hard muscled mound of his chest and captured a taut nipple.

A groan escaped his lips; she was more than apt.

Her nimble fingers began an adept attack on the top fastenings of his breeches. He was fully aroused and he ached to break free of the confines. She wasted little time removing his clothes.

"I have always wanted to kiss every inch of a man's body. Tonight I intend it to be yours, Adam Dunraven," she confessed in a molten silk voice.

This promise fired his imagination and he was beginning to wonder who was the tutor here.

Good to her word, her lips explored lower, to the concave of his navel. Starting at center point, she showered kisses over his stomach.

The anticipation of what she might do next fairly paralyzed him with desire, but he realized the night's purpose was not for his sole pleasure.

Sitting up, he drew her around so she lay on her back beside him. Bending over, he kissed her deeply, his hands sweeping over her shoulders, to the plushy swells of her breasts, then down to her belly until he settled on the furred nest of her woman's mound. She felt beautiful to him and he wanted to tell her in a way she would believe him.

"Lilith, your skin is satin to my touch. Your breasts fill my hands with joy. Never has a woman surrendered herself to me so readily." And then he found himself saying, "You are beautiful, Lilith." And he believed it as well.

Her arms circled his neck, and in an emotion-choked voice, she breathed, "Thank you, Dunraven, thank you for saying it."

He pressed his cheek to her own. He felt the wet heat of tears and a part of him wanted to stay with her through the night and love her in totality.

His lips touched her forehead, awakening the crown

of love, then to her throat, heart, and navel. Opening the jeweled petals with the lightest pressure of his fingertips, he began a careful awakening of her sacred spot as he kissed her mouth.

She arched to his touch and hummed a deep-throated sigh. Her hands gripped his shoulders and she pulled him to her. "I want you, now, inside me. Please. . . ."

He was hesitant to enter her so soon, but if he was careful, her need would overshadow the instance of virginal pain. He moved over her and rose up on his knees.

Her fingers splayed and clutched his thighs while she gave an intense plea of her desire for him by winging wide her slim legs. He parted the delicate flesh and guided himself into her. Amid the exquisite pleasure of his entry came the vague awareness that Lilith Cardew was no virgin. But the facility of his entrance was soon overshadowed by a strange, wild sensation of spinning.

Drifting from somewhere came the tinkle of shell chimes and the smell of the sea. . . .

Dunraven cracked open one eye and saw not the black chasm of the canopy bed, but a starry night sky, the night sky of Reva Ra. Lily was in his arms and they lay together naked on the coral sand beach. A part of him knew it was illusion, but he felt the grate of sand on his bare back, the press of Lily's plush breasts against his chest, and the fall of her dense spill of hair upon his arms.

She rode him in slow undulations, the tide lapping foot and thigh. He would flow with the moment, cherish it, savor it, and hope it would last indefinitely. He gathered her body close, splaying his hands over the full rounds of her hips possessively. "Lily, beloved Lily," he whispered into her hair.

She answered with a deep-felt sigh, and nuzzled his lips in a soft demand for more kisses. "I love thee, Tahua Tane. I love thee."

His blood was coursing through his veins and his nerves were burning bright flares of sensation. He could see the twin stars of her eyes now and it was as if he beheld her soul. The sight of her was the ultimate healing and nourishing. She began scattering hot, grasping kisses over his forehead, his cheeks, his throat. And then, soft winds of breath escaped her lips as she began to arch and bloom with the thousand-petaled lotus of feminine life force.

He remained still, breathing slowly and deeply, allowing her the full measure of her ecstasy. His shaft sheathed in the intimate depths of her womb, he felt her resonating energies of creation pulse in waves of pure satisfaction. Over the years in Lasli, he had disciplined himself to master his sexual energy and now, purposefully, he did not take release himself. This night of lovemaking was only for her. He wanted nothing for himself but the gift of pleasuring her.

And then—

He found himself back in the bed of scarlet, locked in an embrace with the woman Lilith Cardew.

A woman can only dream of a night of such loving. When Rupee came into Lilith's room in midmorning, she opened the window curtains and the silver slash of daylight radiated into the room. Lilith stretched like an awakening feline while a slow smile of satisfaction spread over her lips.

The household was astir with morning, but she, she

was astir with love. A rare white orchid rested against her cheek. She blinked with surprise wondering how such an exotic flower could just appear. She slipped it behind her ear and felt like jumping as high as heaven. She wanted to dance through the household, scattering flower petals and laughter, but of course she could not, for Dunraven still did not know who she really was.

"The master Dunraven requests that you take breakfast with him in the court, mistress." Rupee's voice filtered through the bed-curtains.

Lilith's eyes snapped open. "He invites me to share his breakfast?" *He loves me,* she thought. *He loves me, Lilith Cardew, and he will not want the annulment. I will tell him the truth.*

"Yes, mistress."

She was up and leaping from her bed before she remembered that Rupee must not see her without her veil.

"Rupee, leave me. I will tend to myself. Tell Dunraven I will be there shortly."

Some minutes later, Lilith appeared in the court colonnade. Neatly dressed, she smoothed her veil and anticipated that it might be the last occasion she need wear it.

A table set for two with silver and white china graced the center court while, beside it, stood Dunraven. To Lilith's eyes, he looked magnificent— the play of daylight on his skin and hair, the lithe and unself-conscious movements of a lean body clothed in impeccable style.

Still vivid in Lilith's mind was their night of loving. It was all she could do not to run forward and throw her arms around him. Instead, she approached with a sweetly hailed, "Good morning, Adam Dunraven."

"I would agree," he returned, his face softening. With fluid ease, he stepped around and held her chair and then sat himself. Narota offered a tray spread with a variety of delicacies.

"What is your preference?" asked Dunraven.

After days of emotional disquiet and picking at her food, Lilith felt hungry. "I will begin with the Spanish oranges and sugared violets. I am fairly famished," she declared.

He quirked a brow, "I will not ask what induced your appetite."

"Nor should you, when you already know."

He chuckled then, motioning to Narota to pour the tea. "You spent a pleasant night, then?"

"Is it always your habit to ask questions to which you already know the answer?"

"In this case, yes. I am wondering if you might like to attend a social gala? Lord and Lady Wimberly have invited us to their annual spring costume ball."

"A costume ball?"

"Yes, have you never been to a costume ball?"

"Never!"

"Then I shall accept for both of us."

Lilith's mind was churning. "Oh, indeed yes! It would be the perfect—" she caught herself.

"The perfect what?" He prompted her to finish.

"Ah—the perfect thing to do."

"Excellent," he said succinctly.

She looked over at him. "You are not eating. The oranges are delicious. Don't you wish something more than tea?"

"No, I am fine. I've already eaten. I was up earlier preparing some paper work."

"Paper work," she echoed, sipping her own tea.

He cleared his throat. "Yes, I want to be sure . . ." he paused.

Lilith had known him long enough to realize when he cleared his throat and paused, he was skirting.

Actually, his intent hit her on the fourth bite of orange and the second taste of sugared violets. He was not hosting breakfast for her because he wanted to continue their newfound intimacy. He was hosting breakfast for her because he wanted to be sure she would give him the annulment he sought.

The devil! The orange immediately puckered her tongue as her appetite evaporated.

She decided upon direct attack and, in a cool voice, asked, "Might I finish my breakfast before I sign the annulment agreement, or is it hidden somewhere between the sweet buns and cream?"

It was an off-key note to have struck at so pleasant a time and place, but she felt spurned. No matter that she had agreed to it.

"Goad me if it suits your mood," he said levelly. "Believe it or not, that particular agreement has not as yet been drawn up."

"What are you waiting for?"

Had Dunraven been able to see beneath her veil, he would have seen black eyes tormented with emotion.

"I am waiting for the time when it would not cause undo offense."

Lilith put down her teacup. She took her napkin off her lap and dropped it on to the center of her plate. "I am afraid that time will never come, Adam Dunraven."

Chapter

13

"Mistress, I was sent to tell you that Charles Vivian has arrived and the carriage waits," announced Rupee through the door. "Can I help you with anything?"

"Come in," invited Lilith.

The door latch lifted and the slipper-footed Rupee stepped inside.

"Do you wish to see my costume?" asked Lilith, her back to Rupee. "I must show someone."

"Oh, yes—" she said, her voice fully curious.

Lilith turned around, her hair loose over bare shoulders.

"Mistress—" gasped Rupee, her hand lifted over her mouth.

"Do you like my *pareo?* The women in the islands wear such a dress. Do you think it is too daring?"

Rupee did not answer, but openly stared at Lilith, her eyes wide with surprise.

"Is something wrong?"

"Mistress, your face, what has happened? You are beautiful!"

"It is a long story, Rupee, with not enough time to tell. But after tonight, everyone shall know." She reached for her cloak and veil. "I will never have to wear this veil again. Never, Rupee, never!"

"Oh, mistress. I am so happy for you."

"Please, do not tell anyone yet. It shall be a secret still—until after the ball. No one must know, not my mother, Dunraven, or Charles Vivian."

"No, no, I will not tell."

Lilith swirled her cape to her shoulders, adjusted the veil over her face, and moved through the doorway. Rupee did not follow, but stood watching, her brown face alight with wonderment.

The birds in the garden court flitted through the palm foliage as Lilith passed down the colonnade. She could hear the low flow of masculine voices as she approached the entry.

Dunraven turned. He looked ravishingly handsome in a loose lawn shirt and tight black breeches.

"Ah, here you are," said Charles welcomingly.

Lilith began to laugh upon seeing Charles. "Charles, whatever are you?"

He was wearing a ceremonial headdress with long, beautifully woven ribbons of cotton, ending in tassels of human hair. The remainder of his outfit consisted of a white-beaded choker, a hip wrapper adorned with feathers and monkey's teeth, and clay body paint.

"I am very authentic. I am a Jivaro witch doctor."

"I suppose you will shake your rattle at any contriving mama who sends her marriageable daughter in your direction."

"Thank you for the idea," Charles laughed.

Her head tilted. "And you, Adam Dunraven, who are you?"

"I go as myself, madam."

"In truth, he needs no costume; his reputation alone precedes him," added Charles.

"And you, madam?" Dunraven's gray eyes fixed upon her. "Are we again to see only the black of your veil? Pray, could you not at least change the monotony of color? . . ."

Charles cleared his throat, unsettled by the insult of Dunraven's tone.

Lilith suspected what was grating him. Since the morning of their breakfast together, they had not conversed. She had avoided him.

She boldly challenged, "Pray tell, Adam Dunraven, who would you have me be?"

He said nothing, but his silence said everything. His eyes darkened with a flintlike intensity.

"She does lend herself to the mysterious, I daresay," smoothed Charles.

"Yes," returned Dunraven finally, his tone icy. "She is that—if one has something to hide."

His eyes did not leave her. His gaze seemed to penetrate through her veil. Had he guessed?

"Well, let us be off," she urged, attempting to cover her nervousness with chatter. "I have never attended a ball and I do not wish to miss a single moment."

Charles offered her his arm, which she took. Narota opened the door, offering his hope that the evening would be pleasant. With Dunraven following, the three proceeded outside to the waiting hansom.

The spring night air filled Lilith with pungent expectancy. She breathed deeply, but let loose only a shallow sigh. Soon her masquerade would be over.

Charles assisted her into the dark confines of the cab and came to seat himself beside her. Dunraven sat directly across, his legs pressing hers into the intimate V of his own.

Neither Lilith nor Charles was immune to Dunraven's testy mood that pervaded the inner atmosphere of the carriage. Both were content to allow the clack-clop of the horses hooves and the outer street noise to substitute for conversation.

At last, Charles rallied and spoke. "I am obliged to you, Adam. I become quite queasy if I am set to ride backward."

Lilith jumped in. "Then I would advise you never embark upon a sea voyage. The roll of a ship would send you into fits."

"Has this been your experience, *madam?"* quizzed Dunraven.

"No—I—"

"You sound as if you speak from experience."

"Oh—I—" Lilith faltered. "Why no, I have only read this. . . ."

"I dare not even imagine a sea voyage," mused Charles. "I fear I shall ever be an armchair traveler." He affectionately took Lilith's hand that rested near his own. "Lady Dunraven and I are like-minded in this regard. While the 'derrings-do' explore the world, we shall find amiable company beside the home fires."

"Your own or mine?" ripped the cool blade of Dunraven's voice. "I prefer not to be cuckolded before my own hearth."

"The devil," sputtered Charles, releasing Lilith's hand. "I have no intention of . . ."

The carriage abruptly halted.

"Ah—we are here." Dunraven ignored Charles' mumbled apologies and moved out the door.

Lilith was growing a wee bit angry herself. She touched Charles' arm and said, "It is quite all right, Charles. You have said nothing wrong. He is in a foul mood this evening, but I soon will have him at rights. You wait and see."

She was flanked on either side by Dunraven and Charles as she stepped from the carriage. Dunraven did not offer his arm to her so she relied on the good grace of Charles. Her knees were shaking as she moved up the stone steps and entered the decorous mansion of Lord and Lady Wimberly. Lilith could hear the vibrant strains of a waltz while her eyes devoured the glittering gala of costumes assembling into the great hall.

A white-wigged servant approached to take their cloaks. Dunraven had not worn one, but Charles was not so Spartan.

Now was the time.

"Adam, would you assist me with my cape?" she asked sweetly.

Saying nothing, he stepped behind her and she felt his hands remove it from her shoulders. Her own fingers simultaneously lifted off her veil and she turned fullface to him.

She smiled at him with all the love in her heart.

His head jerked back and he drew up to the stance of a man unabashedly stunned. Frozen in motion, the only thing that moved were the pinwheels of confusion swirling in his hematite eyes. She saw the flash of recognition alight on shocked features.

"Lil—"

She prepared to rush into his arms, but before she could move, his expression shifted from awe to a cutting, inbred reserve.

He stepped back and tilted his head with wary calculation.

Looking perfectly composed, he said, "Madam, we are leaving."

"Leaving?" echoed Lilith, all joy collapsing. "We have just arrived. I am—"

"Leaving!" The finality of his tone held a warning she dared not ignore.

The poor servant stood mouth agape, looking one to the other, his hand reaching for the cape which Dunraven still grasped.

Like an errant schoolgirl, Lilith caught her lip between her teeth. Her eyes dipped downward and then stole sidelong to Charles. He looked at her like he would a stranger—a mortifying stranger at that.

She swallowed and gave Dunraven a pathetic smile. Then she stooped for her veil that had fallen to the marble floor.

"Good God! Leave it!" he flared as he whirled the cape about her shoulders.

His fingers clutched her and he propelled her forward as if she were a croquet ball and the door a wicket.

"Charles, I trust you to your own devices. Good night," he clipped.

By the time he shuffled her into a waiting hansom, Lilith was tear blind and in the beginnings of an acute hiccup attack. Each time her breast jumped like a cricket on May Day, Dunraven favored her with a lethal glare. She shrunk back as best she could into the shadows.

More than anything she wanted him to hold her in his arms and shower her with sweet words of reunion, but all the while he remained vindictively silent. He sat across from her, not beside her, just staring at her. His eyes pinned her like a pair of insect mounting needles. She withered and wished for the protective anonymity of her veil. The ride back to Eden Court had become the longest of her life, clearly the most dismal and, unforgettably, the most heart shattering.

He would hate her forever.

Narota opened the door and his usually bland face registered a slight expression of surprise when he saw Lilith. Too well schooled to question, he went through the motions of taking Lilith's cape and, yes, veil that she clutched to her breast like a mourner's handkerchief.

"I shall be in the library. Under no circumstances am I to be disturbed."

Lilith wondered if this meant her as well. Or was she to go straight to her room and be rationed on bread and water for a week? She decided to test it and continued on down the hall.

However, his hand caught her forearm like a vice and stopped her dead on the spot. Resigned, she avoided looking at him, but obeyed the firm guidance of his hand upon her arm as he escorted her into the library.

It was as though it were that first interview again. Ever intimidating, he stood before her in masterly stance—always the astute, collected, maddeningly handsome male.

She felt like lowering her eyes and bowing on bent knee as Heikua had done to Tiaro the night of the fire walk. But that was when she was Lily, and she was no longer Lily.

Her lips were dry. She thought of asking him for something to drink to stop the hiccups. But instead she licked her lips and said softly, "Do you wish me to throw myself at your feet, *hiccup* and beg for mercy in *hiccup* melodramatic fashion?"

"I only wish to hear the truth."

Will he love me less or more for it? she agonized internally.

"And where shall I begin?"

"At the beginning."

Could she really begin at the beginning? Could she tell him the beginning was when she was thirteen years old? When first her father wrote to her of him and how she fell in love as only a thirteen-year-old girl could—obsessively and unconditionally. No, she would not tell him this. *But you must,* prompted a voice. *You must be truthful now or lose him.*

"I have loved you shamelessly since I was thirteen years old," she disclosed with a sigh.

"What? How could you? I had never met you."

"In my father's letters, he wrote of you. You were everything I was not. It was pure idolatry at first. Over the years, it became more than that as I learned more about you. My father loved you as a son and spoke of your generous nature, your insights and philosophies. I loved you from a distance and that was enough— until that day we met and married. I could not keep my love in an ethereal form any longer. The dream stood before me alive, vibrant, and virile. I wanted a life with you. I wanted to be with you. I had always wanted to travel and I saw I could—I could travel to be with you." She clutched her breast in a vain effort to will away her hiccups. "Your generous stipend to myself and my mother enabled it. Charles had mentioned *hiccup* you were traveling to the South Pacific and I—*hiccup*—I thought it a good place to begin my own travels. You—*hiccup*—you would be there, and I planned on meeting up with you and offering my services as secretary."

"You are too simplistic. Did you not calculate the dangers of a woman traveling alone?" He sat back in the chair opposite her.

She leaned slightly forward, an earnest edge touched her voice. "There is no danger as leveling as spinsterhood."

"But you were married. I had given you my name and protection."

But not your love. . . . She shifted back and pulled her legs up beneath her. "I wanted *hiccup* more. I wanted to experience adventure, see life for myself. Charles is wrong in believing we are alike in being armchair explorers. Were I a man—*hiccup.* . . ."

"Thank god, you are not," he muttered under his breath.

She looked up, almost hopefully. All was not lost.

"Were I a man, I would have gone with my father. Nothing would have held me back."

"So you found your avenue through me?"

"Yes and no. When I arrived in Tahiti, you had gone. I took a cargo vessel and during a storm, ended up castaway in a dinghy. I would have died, except for the Rangahua. It saved my life and brought Tiaro and his people to me. Oddly, *hiccup* because of a scrimshaw brooch I was wearing, they believed I was the long-lost Atua Tamahine. Perhaps I was." She stared into the fire, reflecting.

"But what of your disfigurement?" His voice held a touch of impatience. "I was under the belief you had been burned in a childhood fire."

"I had," her eyes snapped back to his defensively. "In the beginning, Heikua took me to the heights of

Reva Ra and showed me a rare plant which grew near the volcano's mouth which could cure scarring. I did not believe her at first, but soon, miraculously, her claim proved true. By the time you arrived, my scars were gone and I had all but forgotten Lilith Cardew. You see, I was no longer the woman who had left England many months before." She said all this in breathless haste, without one single hiccup interruption.

He ran a thoughtful hand over his chin. "This is all beyond belief. Had I not seen you there, and were I not seeing you now, I would never believe such a tale."

"Believe it, Adam Dunraven, *hiccup* believe it."

"But why didn't you tell me when I first came?"

"Would you have believed me?"

"I don't know what I would have believed. Of course, I would have questioned you."

"Then, you would have sent me back to England. That is what I feared, you know. I did not want to return."

"Then why did you return?"

"Because—*hiccup*—" she lowered her eyes as the hiccups and emotion clogged her voice—"because I loved you. I love you still. I was afraid you would not return to Reva Ra."

"I gave you my word," he said sharply.

She did not look at him, but she knew he had come to his feet. He walked to the hearth and rested both hands on the mantel, and with his back to her, he stared into the fire.

"I knew you were full of wanderlust—just like my father. So—*hiccup*—I followed you back," she explained weakly.

"Back to deceive me! Good Lord, *Lily,*" he swung

around. "Do you realize what you've put me through? I thought I'd found paradise."

"You did. We did." The tears were streaming down her face now.

"But you are not Lily—really. You are Lilith Cardew."

"And what is wrong with Lilith Cardew? What?" she cried out.

"You are a gently bred Englishwoman, not a—a—"

"A sea nymph!" It was becoming too clear now. "I can think for myself, I can talk back, I am educated. Am I too civilized for you, Adam Dunraven? *Hiccup* Is that it?"

She had raised up on her knees in challenge. He crossed over to her and took her shoulders in his hands and put his face within inches of her own.

"You have put me through hell, woman. I have broken and betrayed vows. You have beguiled and deceived me. I have lain awake nights, my loins aching for you, and you . . . Damn you! You were in the same house!" His hands gripped her unrelentingly.

She began crying fragile tears. "You aren't the only one betrayed." She sniffled out. "Who came to me three nights ago?"

"You provoked it."

"I provoked it?" In that instant, her wet cheeks flushed and her hiccups abruptly abated, being replaced by the more consuming malady, anger.

"Indeed! You would not give me the annulment unless I gave you your night of love. Hah! Now I know why you were no virgin!"

"Of course, I wasn't!" she flared back. "You had seduced me months before on an island thousands of miles from here."

"I did not seduce you!" he bellowed righteously. "It was more the other way around. After all, you became my bride."

"And what of Lilith Cardew, your other bride? You married me in Reva Ra, all the while knowing you had a wife in England." She came close to sneering. "Where was your honor then?"

In a deadly voice, he answered. "My honor, dear lady, was sniffing the night, hunting for you, for your hot heart like a hungry leopard stalks the fleshy barrens of a watering hole."

Their eyes held. She saw ferocity—his lips were so close, his breath fiery—If he kissed her now . . .

He did not kiss her.

He released her. Running a distracted hand through the golden strands, he fairly clicked with anger. He turned his broad back to her.

"Leave, now, before I take you in a most barbaric and regrettable fashion."

The drumming began before she even crossed the colonnade court to her room.

He had rejected her.

Dunraven sat on the front pew of the Royal Geographic assembly hall. He'd never seen the hall filled to such a capacity. But, of course, nearly all of London would attend to hear the renowned Lyman Brazen. His mind was hardly upon exploring. His mind was on the woman. She had brought him to the nadir of his integrity and honor. Whatever their soul connection, he could not forgive her deception, her hold over his heart, her interference in his life.

After a night of sleeplessness, he had come to a decision—a decision he would keep to.

Beside him, Charles snapped open his pocket watch. "They're running a bit late."

The chairman rose to the podium, mumbled inaudibly, and then turned back to confer with his colleagues. He cleared his throat surreptitiously. "As of yet, I am afraid our esteemed speaker has not arrived."

Suddenly a woman's voice sounded loudly from the back of the hall. "Indeed, sir. He has arrived and I am she."

"What? . . . ." The chairman's mouth dropped open and his jowls puffed with confusion.

Charles, along with everyone else, craned his neck in a wide scan of the back of the hall.

However, Dunraven fully recognized that voice. He lifted his eyes heavenward and swore discreetly under his breath. It all became unwittingly clear. Of course, she was also Lyman Brazen. Lightly disguised, many of the instances and adventures in *An Explorer's Handbook Out* were extremely familiar. Change a destination or two, and he knew she'd compiled the book from her father's writings and memoirs—and without a single error, he added mentally.

Her duplicity and the lengths she would go no longer astounded him. Assuredly, she belonged in an asylum or the out, out back. When she approached doddering dowagerhood, he might appear personally to escort her to that end.

He felt the room vibrate with masculine affront as she came forward. On the one hand, Dunraven applauded her courage; on the other, he wanted to stand before all and throttle her. He sat wrestling with the duality of his thoughts, not sure how he would respond in the end.

Disapproving coughs sprinkled the silence. Some got up and left, but most remained, captured by the spectacle.

"I say, madam, this is highly irregular," announced the befuddled chairman.

"I am no impostor, Sir Gathree, I am the daughter of your learned, but deceased colleague, Andrew Cardew."

The room rumbled with comment. She had lifted her veil and her face looked quite pale to Dunraven. She is not so *brazen* as she pretends, he thought wryly.

After a conference with his colleagues, the chairman allowed Lilith to take position at the podium. Then, gnashing his teeth, he reluctantly took a seat.

As an introductory rule, the Society as a whole stood for its speakers as an expression of courtesy. As of yet, no one had stood. Dunraven watched her gather herself. Her shaking fingers arranged her notes. She nervously cleared her throat and began. "Gentlemen," she said, casting a fiery-eyed challenge directly at him. "If you cannot stand for me, at least stand in respect for my father."

Dunraven looked about. No one stood.

Even though she had falsely represented herself, he realized in her position, she had no other choice. He could forgive her for being Lyman Brazen, he could not forgive her for her deception in their relationship. With a sigh of forbearance, he came to his feet and bowed to Lilith. Her eyes graced his, but only for a fleeting glance of straightforward gratitude. He was warned, however, one smile would not his forgiveness win.

The pews creaked and others followed his lead.

Soon, nearly everyone had stood, but a handful of the diehards who remained rooted in collective insult.

Lilith smiled demurely. "Thank you. Please take your seats once again. I will proceed to discuss the magnitude of my father's contribution to this illustrious, yet unfortunately *all male,* association." Her comment brought a titter of amusement from the scattering of females in the audience.

Her voice stronger, she continued: *"An Explorer's Handbook Out* is distilled from Andrew Cardew's life's work. Unbeknownst to him, I began writing it years ago. It is my tribute to him, and if you are canny enough, you will see it is dedicated to AC on the frontispiece. I regret he did not live to see its publication."

Initially, she spoke of her father's exploits and then digressed into her own. Dunraven was very much interested in her own, for it filled in many of the missing pieces. She related the event of her shipwreck and told about being mistaken for a chief's long-lost daughter. Most shocking to her listeners came her confession that she lived as a native, dressed as a native, and married a man in tribal tradition like a native.

"You married a heathen?" came a strident query from the second row.

Dunraven straightened with ill ease.

"I wouldn't exactly say heathen. I will use the term "uncivilized man." Indeed, I prefer the uncivilized man. In my experience, he is heedless of the false trappings of civilization, he is secure in his manhood. His mating dance is not a sham of false pretenses, but one of full-bodied passion."

The room fomented with low comment and innuendo. Her eyes briefly pinioned Dunraven.

"Good God!" he muttered under his breath. *How dare she!* Not only did she indirectly insult every civilized man in the audience, she was chiding him, throwing his own regrettable philosophies in his face. Damn her!

The air clicked with attention to what she might reveal next. She turned notes and continued, "The most notable and dangerous of my experiences was fire walking. Might I declare, the phenomenon of fire walking entails mind over matter."

A skinny, termite of a man rose suddenly in the middle of the assembly. "I do not believe you, a woman, could have walked upon fire and not been burned. I call you a prevaricating fraud."

Still muttering, Dunraven, in an inordinately compassionate act, rose and faced the assembly. "If you necessitate a verification of her claim of walking upon molten lava, I am here to provide it. I was there, and might I add, I have never witnessed in my life so complete an act of courage!" *And done out of love for myself,* he internally remembered, with bittersweet chagrin.

He sat down, all the while seeing that Lilith was so visibly moved by his testament that she had to compose herself before she could further speak.

She continued with a well-delivered commentary that proved provocative, scholarly, and entertaining, but he heard little of it. He was in turmoil. The woman had sacrificed herself for him, true. But she had also lied, entrapped, and broken trust with him. The damage between them was irreparable.

At the conclusion, she received enthusiastic applause, but not from him. He realized if he was to approach her it must be now before the crush.

Standing, he walked up to her. "My compliments. You are your father's daughter in every way."

She smiled up at him, a smile he would ever hold in

his heart. "You cannot know how happy you have made me in saying so, Adam Dunraven. I thank you for standing on my behalf."

"It was my duty and—" he bowed—"my pleasure. Now I must leave you to your admirers. Good day to you, dear lady—and good-bye."

Dunraven left Lilith's side, pushing his way through the crowd. The tone of his good-bye sounded threateningly final. A little bell of panic rang inside her head. She continued shaking hands but followed him with her eyes.

"Where is he going?" she asked aside to Charles.

"Away."

"Away?" she returned.

"Away," affirmed Charles.

"From London?"

"Yes."

"Where, Charles?" her voice was anxious.

"Tibet. He is returning to Lasli."

"Oh no," she turned to Charles, shock wrenching her face. "Not to stay. Please Charles not to stay."

"Yes, Lilith. . . . To stay."

Chapter

14

The din of sacred chanting surrounded Dunraven. He moved through the labyrinth of monastery passageways, where incense lingered thick in the air. Six months, and he had found no contentment here. At night, the Rangahua appeared in his dreams and visions, leaving him unsettled, disconsolate, searching. . . .

His naked feet padded along cold, stamped-mud floors, carrying him past teakwood doors and crumbling whitewashed plaster walls.

Always the woman—she possessed him like a lingering sickness. He'd leaned out; the food was poor, subsistent. Before on this diet he had flourished, but now. . . .

He stepped inside a small vestibule ornamented with filigreed Tibetan dragons, garlands, brass censers, and wax-dripped candelabras. He heard whispering and a young, black-haired boy appeared beneath an adjoining archway, his dark doe eyes lambent and wide. Her eyes. She haunted him.

He beckoned him through a beaded curtain into the presence of the Lama. He was drinking tea and looked up, a welcome on his gleaming and furrowed face. He set down his cup and the boy took it away.

The Lama rose and folded a white muslin scarf around Dunraven's neck, a ritual of greeting. "I knew you would come this morning."

Dunraven had not known himself.

The Lama's expression serene, Dunraven felt his steady eyes. He gathered himself, his own eyes scanning the worn silk weavings hanging on the walls.

"You know why I come." His voice was reverent.

"I do."

"I am here because of a woman."

The Lama chuckled. "We are all here because of a woman."

Dunraven allowed himself to smile and continued, "I believe she is my twin soul."

The Lama grimaced. "If you only believe she is your twin soul, then she is not. My friend, when did you last look into the mirror of self-honesty?"

Dunraven pursed his lips and briefly averted his gaze from the Lama, thinking that is what he had been attempting to do for the last six months. Yet, he had failed miserably.

The Lama reached over and pinched Dunraven's little toe as if he were a small child who wasn't paying attention. Then just as quickly, he released it.

"That is your wake-up call!" announced the Lama. "The woman is your wake-up call. How is your soul to find liberation if you ignore the call? If she is your twin soul, she will be the mirror of all which is in disharmony within you, as well as all that is in harmony."

His words resonated with Dunraven. Yes, the Lama spoke the truth, she did bring out the worst and the best in him.

The Lama relaxed back with the content look of a man without a single sin upon his conscience and said kindly, "Know that during the weary search for one's twin soul, there will be many side paths, many meetings that first appear to be genuine, then fade. Even when the twin soul is at last discovered, there are many testings of worthiness which cause much pain. Sometimes, it seems that the problems of two people who love each other are hopeless; the wall that separates them too high to ever surmount. I ask you, do you love her enough to surmount all barriers?"

"I think I do."

The Lama rolled his eyes and gave him a tolerant smile. "If you only think you love, you do not love. To love, you must feel."

Dunraven *did* feel—he felt foolish. "I do feel. I feel as I have never felt before. But, by choice, I would not love her."

The Lama laughed. "The reason for life is to love, Dunraven. If you do not know this, all your meditations are empty. You English! You come a pilgrim in search of truth. To see truth, see yourself! Each one must choose who or what is loved, but in the end it is always love's longing for itself. At this time, truth takes for you the form of a woman who may or may not be your twin soul. No matter, in loving the woman you will find truth."

Pondering these words, Dunraven held the Lama's fathoming gaze. An unspoken exchange flowed between them while deep in the monastery's heart, drumming erupted beside low guttural chanting.

In lyrical tones of a mystic, the Lama spoke once more. "If your love is only a will to possess this woman, it is not love. If you know only your needs and ignore the needs of the woman, you do not love. You may destroy the woman you are trying to love. Do you wish to destroy this woman?"

"No."

"Do you wish only to possess this woman?"

"I did possess her. It near destroyed us both."

"Do you want to make this woman suffer?"

He hesitated before he answered. She had deceived him, yet, he was past requiring retribution.

"Not by any means."

"Ahh—," grinned the Lama. "You have learned."

"I have learned . . ." Bitterness touched his words. "And I will learn more, but not in the way I had planned."

The Lama touched his shoulder, gently. "It is always so. The universe sends us what we need, not what we want. True love needs understanding. You cannot resist loving this woman when you really understand her. The virtue of love is that you can only do it by doing it. Have you the courage to open your heart to love?"

Dunraven did not answer. He closed his eyes and breathed with awareness. He had never lacked for courage and, yes, he had opened his heart to love and had been deceived. His heart was open to love; he still loved her, but could he trust again? Could he risk?

The drumming merged into the liquid flowing chant of a single voice, a woman's voice, Lily's voice. Her singing shocked through his mind and senses, holding him in a chaotic moment of introspection. Then the chant faded and again silence reigned through the monastery's maze of rooms and corridors.

Dunraven returned to himself.

He opened his eyes and he knew with assurance that he no longer belonged in the monastery. But where?

He lifted his gaze to the Lama.

The Lama had disappeared.

Chapter

15

Lilith's penance was a return to paradise.

But can one return to paradise?

Whisper upon whisper, the loss of Dunraven was always there, that cavernous hole in her heart that could only be filled by love, his missing love.

With each morning's sunrise, when sea and land awoke, she began wandering from one end of Tiaretapu to the other. Sometimes, she spent hours crossing over the acres of sand hills following turtle tracks like an expert sleuth. Later, she would search for *wongai* fruit or fallen coconuts. Dunraven was the one who had mastered the art of tree climbing; she had not. It had never ceased to fascinate her the way he, with agility and strength, shimmied up the coarse trunk of a lofty palm. He would drop the nuts down and it was her duty to peel off the outer husk and pierce a hole in the drinking eye.

She missed Dunraven from her extremities to the very core of her soul. Always underlying her excursions over the island was his phantom presence. Here by the tea tree, he had kissed her. There, beyond the sandspit, he had spearfished. Wherever she turned, on and on crashed the memories like endless waves.

In the dark body of the night—the worst time for her—she lay awake watching the stars until longing drove her down to the moon-spun waters of the lagoon. Feeling like the lone inhabitant of Earth, every part of her being chanted a call to Dunraven. When her voice fell hoarse, she folded her arms across her breasts. Disconsolate, she crouched, rocking back and forth on her heels. Her cheek rested on her knees and she wept.

Months passed.

The endless flood of sea lolled beyond the protective circle of the reef while she continued to weakly pine and search the horizon. Day in and day out, she skirted the hissing foam petticoat of the sea, tossing garlands of flowers upon the tides. Inland, sun-bleached vegetation rustled like spirits in the breeze, the earth was dry, thirsting for the monsoon season. She thirsted as well. The vines of passion fruit blossomed and ripened, but they did not taste so sweet as she remembered.

When she could bear it no longer, she made a pilgrimage into the hidden heart of Tiaretapu to the ancient shell temple. She lay down on the cool floor, staying still, just remembering and dreaming. Her body filled with a sensual ache while seductive sunbeams danced over her naked breasts and bronzed belly like consenting lovers. But sunbeams were no substitute for Adam Dunraven. All she had done over the months was to dream him. She was worn out from dreaming. She did not want to be a dreamer dreaming dreams of him any longer. She wanted to awaken to him. Her heart leaden, she left the temple and realized she could never go back—alone.

The islanders were preparing for the full-moon celebration. Lilith could not believe that one year had passed since she had gone through her ordeal of fire and wedded Dunraven. The remembering sent her into melancholy. On the afternoon of the celebration, Tiaro paddled his canoe over to Tiaretapu. She greeted him on the shore and happily received his full-arm embrace.

"You must come to the celebration, Atua Tamahine. I know your heart is heavy, but you are young and there are many fish in the sea."

Lilith smiled tolerantly. She had heard this bit of folk wisdom once too often. "I am not fishing today, Tiaro."

Though his thick eyebrows gave him a slightly fierce look, Tiaro's eyes radiated benign understanding as he said, "Come dance and sing with us. You cannot stop life."

"Soon, I will come back and live with you on Reva Ra, but still I must be alone."

Reluctantly, he left. Lilith watched his *va'a* glide across the lagoon. More than anyone else, she wished she could forget Dunraven. But forgetting him would be like forgetting herself. Later, when the tide was in and the sun lowering in the sky, Lilith went down to the water to bathe. She eased herself into the turquoise depths of the shallows and surrendered to the warm, soothing lap of the sea. She lazed luxuriously, gilded in sunlight and ripples. She gave herself to the sea and floated and undulated like a mermaid on respite from the deep.

Drifting, she moved farther out into the water and

began feeling suspended between one world and another. Suddenly, she heard the familiar echo-wafting clicks of the Rangahua, and then came a barrage of return calls. She winged her arms and lifted her head from the water. Her eyes scanned the lagoon and spied not one, but two dolphins leaping above the surface.

The appearance of two dolphins caught her off guard. Then the pair swept past, off-balancing her in the wash of their current. She began laughing and spun herself in the water to better glimpse the new one.

Had the Rangahua found a mate?

Then alone, like a sleek and silvery apparition, the new dolphin came up behind her. She sensed it before she saw it. With a bare hint of movement in its tail, it floated beside her in the water. Slowly, she turned about. Its sapient eye was only inches from her own, staring. She stared back, feeling an immediate kinship. It released a rush of air from the top of its domed head and inhaled exuberantly. It circled her, moving around her body, emitting an array of skin-prickling clicks. She began to tingle from the vibration of its oceanic voice and warmed from the seductive potency of its bemused smile. Male or female, she wondered? Male, she sensed. It was not the other Rangahua's mate.

"Ia ora na," she spluttered through the water.

The dolphin whistled, making a rusty hinge sound and drew closer, gently nudging her cheek. Wholly endeared, the greeting seemed a sweet reunion and Lilith felt she knew this Rangahua already.

She reached out to stroke its smooth, chamoislike skin and soon found herself enmeshed in a playful dance in the sea. It sidled its bottle nose between her legs, slipping up beneath her, lifting her from the water upon its back with the carefulness of a lover.

It sculled and skimmered until Lilith felt its muscles tense and its backbone bend as it gathered to leap. She sucked in air, caught a handhold on the dorsal fin, and prepared to soar. A mighty thrust of tail fin and the dolphin rose . . . exploding in a rainbow arch above the mirroring surface. The wind and spray luffed across her face. Lilith grinned with the sheer joy of sailing free.

Then down, down it plummeted. Immersing, Lilith bit the crash of liquid glass and felt her breath knocked deep into her lungs. She lost her grip and fell forward, rolling and tumbling in the cushion of quavering current. Her tangle of hair blinded her, yet she relaxed, surrendering to natural buoyancy to carry her to the ceiling of the sea. Vibrancy bubbled in her veins like ecstasy as her head broke the surface. She gasped and revived, ready for another bout with her new-found companion.

The dolphin circled her, slapping its tail in a teasing splash. In a show-off leap it disappeared in a puff of spray and reappeared, and then plunged again, lost to view.

She waited, excitedly attempting to guess how close to her and where the dark fin would emerge next. The emptiness she'd experienced for so long seemed to ease.

The minutes passed. She could only spy one Rangahua. Where had the new one gone?

The colors of the sun were bleeding to crimson. Her eyes moved over the lagoon, and paused momentarily at a figure standing on the beach. At first she blinked, not believing what she saw. She winged through the water, swimming toward the shore. Every so often, she slowed and surveyed the shore to assure herself she wasn't seeing things.

What her eyes saw, her mind refused to believe. Dunraven, naked, tall, with no spare flesh, sauntered along the beach of Tiaretapu.

Her heartbeat quickened. Maybe it was the light play of sunset, or just another figment of her endless dreaming—or maybe it was a mirage.

When she found foothold, she dragged herself through the surf. Out of breath, she still ran up the beach, but he had disappeared. Looking about, she stood still while her breast rose and fell from the exertion of running. Somewhere in the sinking pit that had become her stomach, she knew it had been only her imagination.

Then she looked down and saw the footprints in the sand. His footprints.

She swallowed hard. Her lips kneaded together with anticipation.

A jubilant call from the lagoon took her attention. She looked and saw the Rangahua surging upward from the water, tail walking and ratcheting enthusiastically.

The full magical picture began to fall in place. Yes, Dunraven was on the island. How, she could only speculate. He was here!

She began to follow the footprints that led up into the palms. She wove slowly through the labyrinth of bushes and trees until the sand thinned and she lost his track. Her ears perked to a rustle of leaves.

Then, from across the lagoon, she heard the celebration drums awaken in a resounding throb. A wild, reveling call jolted through the jungle air around her—was it from behind or in front? She could not tell. She had heard it before and the message was intensely primal.

An impetuous flame ignited in her body and a consenting grin spread over her lips. The chase was on, though she wasn't sure if she was chasing or being chased.

Creeping forward noiselessly, she advanced as stealthily as a goanna. She made out a silhouette in the darkening shadows. She drew closer. Quickly, the shadow shifted and dissolved into the vegetation.

Instinctively, she followed. She snaked into the prolific fern and dense net of foliage toward the island's heart. As the darkness closed in, she realized she held the advantage of knowing the island better than he. Yet, even as the moon would soon rise, she knew where the pursuit would end.

Wild impatience to see him again drove her recklessly forward. Her feet hardly touched the earth as she set off on the shortest route to the shell temple.

When she stepped through the archway, she waited for her eyes to adjust before she continued. Along the walls she noticed a circle of oil shell lamps whose flames were reflected on the pearl shimmering walls.

Then she saw *him*.

He stood in the center, his back straight and his arms relaxed at his sides. His damp hair was longer than she remembered, draping in a loose swag over the prominent ridge of his shoulders. The shadow play of light on his face accented the gaunt sensuality of his cheekbones. His smoke-colored eyes pinioned her own. Her breath stopped. She had forgotten what he looked like. The sight of him became a resounding shock of pure joy. His eyes blazed with greeting and such radiance in his composed features, such directness, even humility of manner—

Suddenly, he was there. His flesh pressed to hers—his lips on hers and the taste of him on her tongue. Too long she had waited. Her hands caught in his hair and she surrendered herself to his kisses that rushed upon her like the sea.

"I did not think I would ever see you again," she breathed between the waves. Tears glistened on her cheeks.

He nuzzled her hair and said softly to her ear. "Are you not the Woman Who Swims With the Rangahua? When you called me, I came."

"You heard my call?"

"Yes, I heard your call. Not only in my heart, but my dreams, and then finally one day in the monastery, I heard you singing."

"You did?"

"I did. I have learned never to underestimate the power of love." The curve of his smile brushed against her cheek. "I have also learned I must trust."

"But I am the one who broke the trust. Oh, Dunraven, forgive me," she pled gently.

"Lilith, I must forgive and be forgiven."

"Of course, I forgive you a hundred times over. I am ashamed of my deception."

"What you did was out of love and an honest fear of speaking your truth. You did it because you did not know what else to do. I was the fool to leave you. But now we are together," he murmured, touching a kiss to her hair. "I swear I'll never leave you again! You are my Eden, Lilith. And I am the serpent beguiled."

"You are that and more," she whispered and tenderly kissed the tattoo upon his cheek.

Melting into his embrace, she trusted him and immersed herself into the ecstasy of his being. His all-encompassing arms cradled her and with his full intent, he began love's ancient ritual of honoring body and spirit. In the flickering light, their shadows flowed together, casting an erotic tableau of love on the temple walls—ever dancing, two souls connected, without ending.

Author's Note

I would like to credit Heathcote Williams'
book, *Falling For a Dolphin,* as a research
source. I highly recommend it to anyone who
fancies herself/himself A Swimmer With Dolphins. I like to hear from my readers. Write:

PO Box 118,
Centerville, Utah 84014.

Printed in the United States
By Bookmasters